"I need your help, Nina," Rossi said quietly, his eyes boring into hers and giving her butterflies. "Something's going on beneath the surface here, something on *The Turning Seasons* set itself." He attended to his food again, letting his words sink in, then continued. "What I need is a pair of ears in the studio, someone to nose around, to report on any oddball things that might be taking place. Someone who—"

"Me?" Nina interrupted, her pulse racing.

His voice was patient. "*Someone*," he said, "who has a nose for detective work. And you, Nina, *do* possess that rare quality." He paused. "What do you say?"

Confusion warred with elation on her exquisite face. "You mean you want me to rat on my friends? Oh, no, Dino—Lieutenant Rossi— I couldn't do a thing like that!"

"Friends?" Dino echoed. "Do friends poison each other, push each other off cliffs? Look at it this way, Nina. A murder—two murders— have been committed. Two people closely connected with *The Turning Seasons* are dead. Don't you want to help catch whoever's responsible?" A meltingly earnest expression shone in his eyes and Nina was helpless to refuse.

Also by Eileen Fulton

HOW MY WORLD TURNS

# Eileen Fulton's
# Take One for Murder

IVY BOOKS • NEW YORK

Grateful acknowledgment is made
to Mr. Thomas P. Ramirez
for his editorial advice and counsel.

Ivy Books
Published by Ballantine Books
Copyright © 1988 by Butterfield Press, Inc. & Eileen Fulton

Produced by Butterfield Press, Inc.
133 Fifth Avenue
New York, New York 10003

Back cover photograph by Tom Gates

Library of Congress Catalog Card Number: 87-91006

ISBN 0-8041-0194-9

Manufactured in the United States of America

First Edition: April 1988

To Merrill Lemmon,
who made this book possible
just by being himself.

# Chapter One

Looking down from the flagstone walkway skirting the edge of Mortimer Meyer's estate and seeing the rushing waters of the Hudson far below, Nina McFall couldn't help shuddering. Heights always affected her that way. It was at least an eighty-foot drop to the narrow, rock-rimmed beach; the mere act of looking at the rick-rack of wooden steps leading down to the Meyers' boathouse made her queasy. Though it was a fairly balmy evening in mid-June and she wore a long-sleeved faille jacket over her white chiffon gown, still she shivered.

Her friend Robin Tally, also dressed in gala finery, noticed. She touched Nina's hand questioningly. "Something wrong, Nina?"

"No, not really," Nina responded with a smile. "I felt a chill for a moment there. Someone's walking on my grave—isn't that how the expression goes?"

Robin arched one brow. "Are you sure that's all it is? You're not coming down with the flu or anything, are you?"

Nina laughed. "Hardly. I'm healthy as the proverbial horse. Just a case of the shivers. Let's change the subject, shall we?"

1

Robin leaned forward, bracing herself against the steel guard rail, her long black hair and the full skirt of her red dress blowing in the breeze.

"What a layout . . . what a view! And what a shame it has to be wasted on creeps like Helen and Mortimer Meyer."

"Easy now. You're talking about the lord and lady of the manor, you know," Nina quipped. Lowering her voice conspiratorially, she added, "I wouldn't put it past them to have the entire place bugged. Cover all bases, that's the Meyer style."

"Sorry. I do run on, don't I? I should be used to it by now. When I think of all the months I spent out here, cooped up in that so-called writers' studio with Morty breathing down my neck every minute . . . ! God, how did I ever stand being around that animal as long as I did? Talk about obsessive-compulsive! He was after me every time the Dragon Lady was out of sight. And he's an *international* letch, to boot." She giggled. "Roman hands and Russian fingers! Nina, you won't let me out of your sight tonight, will you? I'm afraid if he catches me alone . . ."

"Promise," Nina assured her. She had heard the story before. There were no secrets between her and Robin. They had been close friends and confidantes since Robin's first day on the set of *The Turning Seasons*. Their friendship was built on implicit trust and loyalty, even though at thirty-four, Nina was eight years Robin's senior. "This could be such a wonderful party, if it wasn't for our charming host and hostess. All my favorite people, this gorgeous setting, haute cuisine, fine wines . . ."

Another raised brow. "All your favorite people? What about dear Bellamy? And super-bitch Angela Dolan?'

Nina arched her lovely neck, the triple-strand pearl choker at its base enhancing her creamy, clear skin. She narrowed dazzling jade-green eyes. "What is life without challenges?" she said airily.

"Tranquil and serene, dearie," Robin retorted.

"When you used to work out here it must have gotten kind of thick at times."

"Tell me about it!" Robin sighed. "Almost incestuous. Just one big miserable family. Morty even had a live-in personal secretary—Miss Gladys Parr with the moon-calf eyes. I have some private thoughts about *that* arrangement, too. Talk about your office wives! Gladys worked that one into the ground, all right. She even had her own cottage behind the main house." She sniffed. "Probably still does. Convenient for taking dictation after hours."

Once upon a time, the Meyer property had been a thriving dairy farm, the edge of the bluff ringed with barbed wire to keep the cows from falling into the Hudson. In one corner of the ninety-acre estate had stood a decrepit, falling-down barn and silo, abandoned since the early 1900s. What remained of the barn's lower floor was now filled in with debris, and most of the beams had collapsed until it actually became an enclosed cave, moldy and dank. The combination crypt/tower created a natural sanctuary that attracted every stray bat in Westchester County. They now numbered in the hundreds, and on summer evenings at dusk one could watch the cloud of bats explode from the ramshackle tower, separate, and stream across the countryside in search of prey. The *whoosh* of their mass exodus from their daytime lair could be heard a quarter of a mile away.

Hundreds of outrageous tales had been fabricated over the past eighty years about the evil deeds committed by the original property owners. Eventually the farm came to be dubbed "Batwing," and the spook stories continued to proliferate.

Mortimer and Helen Meyer had done their best to expunge that ominous reputation since acquiring the property in 1974. Still, Helen found the name not without a certain peculiar charm. Thus she and Morty had attempted to retain a small hint of mystery, bowing to local tradition by rechristening the place without totally destroying its character.

"Leatherwing," the black wrought-iron grillwork over the massive stone gateway to the property announced. Driving up from the city in her racy metallic blue Mazda RX-7, Nina had been amused by its Grade-B horror movie connotation. It was her first visit to the Meyer domain, and she'd also been duly impressed with the handsome pile of rock itself. The estate and the rambling fieldstone mansion the Meyers had built had been featured frequently in New York newspapers, in *House and Garden,* and in many other publications devoted to ultra-expensive real estate and interior decoration. It was a showplace, to be sure. But behind Morty's and Helen's backs it was snickeringly referred to as "The House That Soaps Built."

Which was the whole truth and nothing but. For this was the same Mortimer Meyer who had founded the fabulously successful Meyer Productions in 1965. Said Meyer Productions also owned the sprawling, state-of-the-art West Side Studios on West Sixty-sixth street in New York City, home to *The Turning Seasons,* the most popular daytime television series in soap opera history. Unfortunately, television professionals had a lower opinion of the ruthless ambition and brutal tactics of its owners. As with Leatherwing, stories proliferated. But in the case of the Meyers, the stories were all true.

4

It was to this vast fiefdom that the show's entire cast of twenty-five, plus three of the main writers and a sprinkling of administrative bigwigs, had been summoned this Saturday evening, ostensibly to celebrate the Meyers' fifteenth wedding anniversary. Dim-view specialists all, the guests suspected that an ulterior motive lay behind the ornately engraved invitations each had received. Perhaps lawn-bowling after dinner? With human heads?

It was 7:30 P.M., with sunset waiting in the wings. Holding her birdbath-sized Margarita glass in one hand, abstractedly poking a dainty pink tongue at the salt-frosted rim, Nina McFall fought to shake off the sudden and unexplainable darkness of her mood. She stared down at the Hudson, watching a solitary cruiser slice a silvery trough in the water, admiring the fiery, dazzling crown bestowed by the sunset where the wake spread.

She glanced over at Robin, took in the ruddy luster the dying sun imparted to her otherwise pale face, the muted sadness in her eyes as the younger woman leaned against the railing, lost in thought. But Nina wasn't overly concerned. That was just the way Robin was. Mooning over another tiff with Rafe, no doubt. It was a way of life with them. At least Robin had someone to fight with. Whereas Nina herself . . .

The woman in the uncharacteristically self-pitying mood was single, strikingly beautiful, and possessed of a delectable peaches-and-cream complexion. She was on the tall side—five-eight in her pantyhose, shoe size 7B, weight a constant 128, and looked smashing in whatever she chose to wear, whether it was tonight's white chiffon and pearls or casual sweats.

Aside from the tigress-sexy image Nina tended to

project at times, and the startling jade-green eyes, her other most striking feature was her glorious red hair. It wasn't simply auburn, or chestnut, or carrot, but had a subtle rose-gold cast that in certain lights seemed a hazy nimbus around Nina's lovely face. The angelic effect was offset, however, by a faint sprinkling of freckles across her small, pert nose that endowed her at times with a mischievous gamine quality. White, perfect teeth (no caps, thank you— all natural) could flash in a smile, warm and open and yet somehow mysterious, that drove men crazy. Her soft, full lips were a temptation few of them could resist. A slender yet voluptuous figure, long slim legs, and the effortless grace of an athlete or dancer made her look much younger than her actual age.

Then why, Nina wondered now, was there no Mr. Wonderful on her immediate horizon?

Abruptly, she told herself to stop complaining, to concentrate on the positive aspects of her life—count her blessings, as her grandmother would have said. Here she was, one of the stars of the nation's most successful soaps, drawing a fabulous salary, on top of the pile and loving every minute of it—well, almost every minute. Granted, her role as Melanie Prescott, hard-driving career woman and man-eater, wasn't the most sympathetic on the show, but Nina's talent had invested Melanie with a life of her own, and whether they liked Melanie or not, the viewers truly adored Nina McFall, as her fan mail proved every day.

She smiled, squared her shoulders, took a sip of her Margarita, and gave herself a mental shake. There was absolutely nothing wrong, nothing at all, except the absence of a man in her life. And that could be remedied at a moment's notice if she chose.

6

There were certainly applicants aplenty, but none of them aroused the faintest flicker of interest. Maybe I'm just getting too old for romance, she thought a little sadly, then banished the idea immediately. Thirty-four was hardly over the hill. Perhaps she was just too choosy, too well aware of exactly the sort of man she was looking for to be satisfied with a stand-in.

She glanced back at the house, conscious once more of the buzz of conversation, the random lilt of laughter, music, the clink of glassware coming from the spacious patio. The cocktail hour had entered its final stages; soon dinner would be announced. Nina wanted to join the others, and yet she didn't. Still, another Margarita—a small one this time—might help insulate her against whatever dimwitted dinner partners fate and Helen Meyer might shortly deal her. Helen was compulsive about "mixing" the crowds at her parties. Nina had seen samples of her eccentric groupings at various luncheons and dinners Helen had given in Manhattan.

"What do you say, Robin?" she said to the silent young woman at her side. "Think we should get back to the madding crowd?"

"I suppose." There was no enthusiasm in Robin's voice.

Nina sighed. "Do you want to talk about whatever's bothering you? I can only assume it's the dashing Rafe Fallone again. What's he done this time?"

Robin seemed to shrink slightly, hunching her shoulders as if she were chilly. "Nothing."

"If it's not Rafe, then what *is* it, darling? You hardly said a word on the drive out here, and that definitely isn't the Robin I know and love. No way. At the risk of seeming insufferably nosy, I really want to know what's wrong."

"It *is* Rafe," Robin told her. "And it's nothing he's done. It's what he *doesn't* do."

"Bellamy again?" Nina was referring to Bellamy Carter, the assistant director of *The Turning Seasons*, a prissy, pompous martinet who gloried in throwing his weight around. And with Spence Sprague, the director, off for a few days, Bellamy had been in rare form this past week. "He got a bit pushy yesterday afternoon, that's for sure."

"It wasn't just yesterday," Robin said, her brow furrowing. "It's every day. And everybody. Rafe can be stubborn as a mule with me, but when it comes to standing up to anyone else—one of the directors, another cast member, even the makeup crew—he just lets them walk all over him. Even Morty's been abusing him lately," Robin continued, "humiliating him something awful in front of everybody. You must have noticed. It's as though he had a 'Kick Me' sign hanging on his back!" Her voice became slightly quavery. "Oh, what's the use? He's a fine actor, but he just doesn't have enough confidence in himself."

"Maybe Rafe should sign up for one of those assertiveness classes," Nina suggested, only half joking. "Seriously, Robin, are you sure you aren't blowing this up out of all proportion? Bellamy gets on everyone's case whenever he gets the chance, and as for Morty—well, we all know how much he likes keeping the serfs in line. Yesterday just happened to be Rafe's turn, that's all. Rafe's a big boy. I wouldn't worry about him so much if I were you."

"That's because you aren't hung up on him. You don't see him in action every day of your life, eat with him, sleep with him . . ."

Nina laughed. "I never dreamed I had a chance," she teased, "because *he's* so hung up on *you*. Now if Rafe were about ten years older and you weren't my good friend, I might give you a run for your money, but as it is . . ."

"Oh, Nina! Can't you ever be serious?" Robin pouted.

"Only on every third Tuesday when the moon is full, in leap year."

She took Robin gently by the elbow and began moving her toward the wide stone staircase. "Robin, dear, let's try to remember that this is supposed to be a party. Parties are supposed to be *fun*. You go find Rafe, pretend everything's fine. Kiss and make up. It must be hell for a man to have his beloved think he's a wimp. Give it a rest for tonight, okay?"

As it turned out, Rafe Fallone—who incidentally did a knockout job of playing the show's most obnoxious heavy—had seen them heading for the patio and was coming down the steps toward them as the two women started up.

"Baby," he said, his dark eyes brightening. "I've been looking all over for you. I thought maybe you'd fallen into the river."

Robin didn't say a word, just kissed him full on the mouth, much to Rafe's pleased surprise. Giving Nina a wink over her shoulder, she tucked her arm in his and a moment later they were swallowed up by the crowd.

Feeling a momentary stab of loneliness, Nina stood on the edge of the patio, looking around for one of the tray-bearing waiters. Seeing none, she began threading her way to the temporary bar that had been set up under an awning in a sheltered corner close to the house.

"Hey, Nina!" said a voice in her ear, as a hand, appearing apparently from nowhere, snatched her empty glass. "Let me take care of that. Margarita, right?"

"Oh, thank you," Nina said, fighting to control her distaste. "How kind of you, Byron. On the light side, please. I don't want to fall asleep in the soup."

Byron Meyer, thirty-one and handsome enough in a slightly oily way, was the lone issue of the soap opera tycoon's first marriage. Since Mortimer and Helen had no children of their own, Byron would one day inherit the vast Meyer fortune. Nina seemed to see "Handle with care" written all over him in letters six inches high. Vapid and sappy though he was, with brains that would fit into a thimble with room to spare, he was nevertheless given preferential treatment whenever he entered the studio—like father, like son. Sometimes Nina found the deference difficult to summon up. As one of the cast's most beautiful and available females, she had had her innings with "Super-Brat," as Byron was secretly called. He considered himself God's gift to women, and Nina felt that if he was, God had a rather perverted sense of humor.

Byron was around five-ten, wore his hair long at the back and sides, and cultivated the same walruslike mustache his father wore. He could have dropped ten pounds to good advantage, though his expensive custom-tailored suits did a fairly good job of camouflaging his excess weight. His small, apologetic smile gave him a deceptive aura of harmless, puppy-dog charm, but when push came to shove, there was nothing at all bashful about Byron Meyer, especially where women were concerned.

Mortimer Meyer had squelched his feckless son all his life, preventing him from asserting any real authority at all. Byron held a token administrative position in the firm's publicity department, a paper-shuffler job any moron could have handled. Even so, there were times when Number One Son was hard put to keep up with his duties. It was tacitly understood that you didn't drop anything requiring judgment or hard, decisive response on little Byron's desk.

Now he was back at Nina's side, smiling ingratiatingly, a fresh overbrimming goblet in one hand. "Here we go," he said, his words slightly slurred. "One Margarita for the beautiful lady."

Nina took the drink cautiously, then sipped off the overflow to prevent its spilling on her gown. "Thank you, Byron. I'm sure glad I didn't ask for a double."

He pumped even more wattage into his grin. "Long time no see," he said. "Here's looking at you, kid."

Original line, Nina thought. He must have seen *Casablanca* last night.

"How've you been?" she asked politely, for lack of anything better to say.

"Lonesome, Nina. I don't see nearly enough of you." The way his bloodshot eyes scanned her body made it clear exactly what he meant.

"Just flip on your TV at two o'clock every afternoon, Channel Eight. I'm always there."

"You know what I mean, sweetheart. We've got to have dinner together one of these nights."

"We *had* dinner," she reminded him coldly.

"So? The man doesn't deserve a second chance?"

Remembering that unpleasant occasion, Nina retorted. "Man? I thought I was out with an octopus."

"Nina," he said soothingly, moving even closer, "don't be that way. Don't be bitter—reconsider. You can't blame a guy for trying, can you? You're so damn beautiful. That face, that bod, those lovely, long legs. that sexy voice of yours. What man in his right mind could restrain himself with something like that around?"

"Byron, you silver-tongued devil," Nina purred, taking another sip of her drink and wishing desperately that someone, anyone, would come by and rescue her from this leering, heavy-breathing young bore.

"So I had a little too much to drink that night. So what? I promise to behave the next time."

"Thanks, Byron," she said sweetly. "but I'm afraid not. My doctor says I should stay out of dark, damp places." Like under rocks where slugs like you hang out, she wanted to add but didn't.

"What's that supposed to mean?" Byron scowled blearily at her.

Nina patted his arm. "Think about it for a while. I'm sure you'll be able to figure it out."

"Careful, Nina," Byron said, squinting slightly as he struggled to keep her in focus. "Maybe you're forgetting just who you're talking to. You aren't completely indispensable, y'know."

"Aren't I?" Her tone was mildly surprised. "I've got a contract that says I am. I can't believe you're unfamiliar with the terms of that contract. If you are, I suggest you have someone read you the fine print."

Byron flushed and slurped irritably at his martini, avoiding her eyes. He wasn't too dumb or too drunk to know when he'd been put down.

"Well!" Feeling a little ashamed of herself for baiting such an unworthy opponent, Nina pasted on her second-best smile and asked, "Anything interesting happening in your exciting, glamorous life?"

"Nothing much. I hit the big Genesis concert last week, and I'll be driving up to Connecticut for a rock festival next weekend. Want to come along?"

He was leering again, animosity forgotten for the moment.

She waved her fingers at him vaguely. "Busy, busy . . . you know how it is. I'm sure you'll be able to find someone among all your girlfriends who'd just love to keep you company. Who's the lucky lady these days?"

Byron shrugged, spilling some of his drink on his immaculate white dinner jacket. "No lady. Nobody special, anyway." His expression turned calculating. "You have somebody in mind? What about your friend Robin? Think you could fix me up? Now *there* is one sexy bimbo. I kind of think she has the hots for me."

Nina couldn't believe her ears. Just how crass could this man get?

"Byron, please. I may be ill. She *is* my best friend, after all. I'm afraid I can't 'fix you up' with Robin. I don't think somehow that Rafe would approve. But I'm sure that, with all your inexhaustible social finesse and that super line of yours you should have no trouble connecting with some other available *bimbo*."

Byron glowered. "Spare me the sarcasm," he said. "Sorry I troubled you. Try to be nice, and that's what you get." He turned and moved unsteadily away, calling over his shoulder. "Catch you later, sweetheart, a couple of years down the road maybe. You won't be so high and mighty when you're pushing forty. That bod won't last forever, y'know."

Nina resisted an almost overpowering urge to throw her glass at his retreating back. What a slimy character! She could almost feel sorry for Mortimer Meyer, having a son like Byron. But on second thought, Morty deserved just what he got. Like father, like son indeed!

As Nina turned to exchange pleasantries with some of her fellow cast members, a rotund black man wearing a powdered wig and ridiculously elaborate livery of baby blue satin trimmed with gold braid appeared in the open doorway.

"Ladies and gentlemen," he intoned as he hit a small brass gong with a padded mallet, "Dinner is served."

# Chapter Two

Nina was seated between Noel Winston and Larry Spangler, and she was genuinely grateful to be assigned to the ''duffers'' section. Helen Meyer had more than likely arranged the seating with malice aforethought, but after her just-concluded run-in with Byron Meyer, the unthreatening company was most welcome. She was certainly in no mood for more hasslings from hormone-rampant types like Super-Brat. Noel and Larry's safe, plodding ramblings would suit her just fine, thank you.

Noel she especially cherished. In his early sixties, a widower with a shock of wavy, white hair that Nina found completely enchanting, he was absolutely gaga over the twin granddaughters his oldest daughter had recently seen fit to bestow upon him. Behind his carefree facade he still grieved over the passing of his wife, Betty, who'd died two years ago, and he was an extremely lonely man. Nina was happy—even eager—to grant whatever small conversational comfort and friendship she could.

On *The Turning Seasons* Noel played the role of a tyrannical father who interfered with his daughter's life (Robin Tally) at every turn. Actually he would have much preferred a more sympathetic part. "I don't know what Kerry and Krista would think," he often remarked, referring to the twins, "if they ever saw Bom-pa carrying on so outrageously. They'd burst into tears, run screaming, I suppose." And after a pause, he whispered to Nina, "God forbid that they should *ever* see such tripe!"

Larry Spangler was fifty-four, partially bald and portly. He played a conniving attorney in *The Turning Seasons,* and loved inserting even darker nuances to his characterization than the writers intended. Divorced, he had quickly found himself a gentle and supportive live-in, and was a most happy man.

Directly opposite Nina sat Angela Dolan. The show's self-appointed doyenne, she admitted to forty-two years, and was pure trouble, on camera and off. Rumor had it that Dolan was actually fifty-two, but she was careful about her weight, dressed fabulously, had great legs, and always had her silver-blond hair done in the latest trendy fashion. Who was counting?

Actually she was an attractive enough woman, if only she'd lighten up a little, Nina thought, and quit pretending she was queen of the American theater. Her airs were insufferable.

Yet there she sat, between Rick Busacca and Bob Valentine, who had to be the youngest male cast members. Cosmic joke? More than coincidence? Neither of the men could be particularly overjoyed about the arrangement, but Angela looked delighted.

Out of idle curiosity, Nina let her eyes sweep the length of the long table to see where Byron had landed, and found him seated between Robin Tally and Valerie Vincent, two of the youngest and prettiest ingenues in the soap opera's cast. *Droit du seig-*

*neur* with a vengeance. Nina bet he'd had a hand in that seating arrangement.

"Quite a spread, huh?" Noel Winston said, drawing her back from her momentary driftaway. "Wonder what all this lobster set old Morty back? And the wine—Chateau Mercein '71. He's spilling it like it was Mogen David. Trying to dazzle the serfs, wouldn't you say?"

"Enjoy," Nina replied, smiling. "It's as close to the vault as any of us will ever get. Would it be gauche to ask for a doggy bag? I've got lobster enough for three meals here."

"Shovel it my way if you can't finish," Larry Spangler interjected. "Me and lobster. Never get my fill of that gorgeous stuff. Just give me a whistle, I'll engineer the whole thing without embarrassing anybody."

Nina McFall *was* impressed, though she hated to admit it. Looking down the damask-covered table, taking in the crystal, the silver service, the heavy antique candelabra placed every few feet, she sank into what was almost a trance, enthralled by the atmosphere. The overhead chandeliers were turned low, and the room—a pseudo-baronial hall, with huge wooden beams, plaques, shields, and weapons on the walls lit mainly by the candles on the table—was cast into deep, yet warm and somehow comforting shadow. Nina wondered how the serving personnel were managing to find their way from guest to guest in the gloom.

The candlelight did marvelous things for the women's faces and made the men look more handsome than they were as it danced on silk and satin formal gowns and white dinner jackets. It glittered on diamond and rhinestone earrings, necklaces, and chokers, even a tiara. The contrast between the highlighted faces and the surrounding dimness gave the scene almost a medieval feel, and Nina was momentarily transported back in time. She could imagine ladies in tall, pointed headdresses and lowcut gowns, men with shoulder-length hair, jeweled velvet toques upon their heads.

Then suddenly the magical moment was dispelled, and she was rudely returned to the twentieth century as she focused on scowling Angela Dolan across from her. Down the line, Byron Meyer was making his move, hanging all over simpering Valerie Vincent. Nina felt a momentary letdown.

She shook off the feeling as well as she could, wondering at her uncharacteristic turn of mood. Generally she was upbeat and positive, fun to be around. Everyone expected it of her. But not tonight. Why? She harked back to Robin's question. A premonition? Don't be ridiculous!

She pasted a smile on her face and turned back to Noel Winston. "How are those grandchildren, Noel? Kerry and Krista, isn't it? And your daughter Janice? She was having some back problems last I heard."

Winston chuckled. "Right, darling. How do you remember things like that? You've never even *met* Janice. Recalling the twins, okay. But that other stuff . . . Amazing."

"They've got an anniversary coming up. Eight months, isn't it?"

Winston's eyes widened. "Impossible," he said. "How do you *do* that?"

It was Spangler's turn. "That's nothing, Noel," he said, leaning across. "She sent Paula and me a card on the first anniversary of our living together. Now *that's* what I call a photographic memory."

Nina smiled. "Maybe I just care about you two lugs."

"C'mon, honey," Spangler challenged. "Only insurance salesmen remember stuff like that. Nobody's *that* nice."

"Maybe I'm just a Nosy Parker," Nina said thoughtfully. "I've got a curiosity quotient that won't quit—always minding everybody else's business. I hear something and into the computer it goes. My random access is crammed with the darnedest collection of trivia. My mom always told me I should be a librarian . . . all the crazy stuff I can dredge up out of this head of mine."

She slapped her forehead with her palm. "Oops! Mom's birthday is coming up next week." She kissed Noel playfully on the cheek. "Thanks for reminding me."

"My pleasure," he said, shaking his head in amusement.

There was time, as the meal progressed, for Nina to appraise the other guests and to study her host and hostess as they sank more deeply into their Lord and Lady act. Across and to Nina's right, she recognized David Gelber and Sally Burman, the show's main writers. (The freelancers and dialogue hacks hadn't been invited.) David and Sally seldom appeared on the set; Robin, who had once worked with them, had pointed them out to Nina. Their days and some of their nights were spent at Leatherwing, in the writing studio, under the close supervision of Helen Meyer, who fancied herself as an artistic driving force. Not only did they have to keep up with the murderous pace, the onerous task of keeping twenty-five main characters on line, but they also had to cope with Helen's tantrums. Small wonder they looked so harassed and weary.

Front-office people were also on deck. Nina smiled sympathetically at Horst Krueger and Ken Frost, both producers, who had Mortimer Meyer on their backs on a day-to-day basis, on top of an already man-killing work load. Obvious burnout registered in their glazed eyes.

To her far right, at the foot of the table, sat Helen Meyer herself. A well-preserved fifty-five, her frosted blond hair done in a severe upsweep, she was engaged in animated conversation with Rafe Fallone. Helen was firmly convinced that every handsome man on the set secretly lusted after her. There were times, when she drank too much, when things became decidedly sticky.

Tonight, thank goodness, she seemed to be in control. Nevertheless, Rafe, no novice in such matters, was keeping his distance, offering no encouragement. He *was* a handsome man, Nina thought, his face reflecting an angst that surpassed his thirty years. It was a philosophic, sad, world-battered look that many women found irresistible, Robin Tally being a prime case in point. Apparently those doleful eyes were working their magic tonight on Helen.

Helen wore dark blue, a dramatic creation with one shoulder bare. Cut low, it displayed her middling cleavage to unkind advantage, as well as her slightly wrinkled neck and mottled shoulders. Though the candlelight was kind to most of the women present, it was cruel to Helen, emphasizing the deep lines about her mouth and making intricate webs of the crow's-feet at her eyes. Her dangling diamond earrings and the overdone, fussy diamond necklace completed the picture of beauty somehow gone awry.

Be nice, Nina McFall scolded herself, cutting her caustic inventory short. She's your boss; she's done you no harm. She's tried, granted, but so far without success. Let her enjoy the moment. After all, fifteen years of trying to keep Morty in check is something to brag about, I guess.

Mortimer Meyer at that moment pulled himself to his feet and tapped his wineglass with a spoon for silence. A flamboyantly mustachioed, silver-haired buccaneer of sixty, he wore heavy, dark-rimmed glasses which gave him a definite Mafia godfather appearance. Standing six feet tall, muscular and ruggedly handsome despite his age, he was a commanding figure.

"Beloved guests," Morty, never given to understatement, began, "if I may propose a toast." There was a brief pause and a flurry as waiters hurried to refill glasses.

"Hear, hear," Bellamy Carter called from midtable. "A toast!" He was well on his way to being sloshed. Someone would have to impound his car keys when the party broke up, Nina thought.

"As you all are well aware," Meyer continued, "we are gathered here tonight for a most auspicious occasion. Helen and I are celebrating our fifteenth wedding anniversary, and we wanted to share our happiness with our dearest friends and associates."

"Darling," Helen murmured condescendingly from her end of the table, "no speeches. Short and sweet, please."

But Morty, well into his cups, ignored her. "I just want to say thank you to my beautiful and loyal wife, Helen. That's her down there. Ain't she a sweetheart?"

"Morty, you old fool," she said, but she looked distinctly pleased.

"Helen has stuck by me through thick and thin," he went on, "I want you all to know that. We had some bad times during those first few years. All my fault, I take total responsibility. But we came outta the storm okay, let me tell you." He paused, lifted his glass again.

"Friends, if you'll join me." He looked directly down the table, his eyes suddenly brimming with tears. Had all the guests not known Mortimer Meyer for the tireless womanizer he was, they certainly would have been touched. "To fifteen happy years. And to many, many more, as many as the good Lord sees fit to give us. I love ya, baby."

Everyone stood, drank dutifully. Loud applause filled the room. Cries of "Happy Anniversary" bounced off the walls. Congratulatory kisses and handshakes were exchanged at both ends of the table. Now Morty moved the length of the room to join his wife. More applause as they kissed over the huge, ornately decorated cake that had suddenly appeared as if by magic.

Nina McFall couldn't understand why, in the midst of so much gaiety and apparent good will, she felt so depressed again.

When the meal was finally over, all the guests adjourned to the vast living room, some occupying the various couches and overstuffed chairs, some standing, some sitting on the steps leading into a sunken area. Helen and Morty had just been presented with a fitting anniversary gift—a cash purse plus a matched set of luggage—which all present had reluctantly chipped in on.

"As you travel down life's highway," Helen read the presentation card aloud, "please remember that the journey, not the destination, is the prize. Enjoy every moment together, you lovebirds. Many happy returns. From *The Turning Seasons* family with love."

She looked up, smiling broadly. "Thank you,

everybody," she called. "What a wonderful gift! What wonderful sentiments! Thank you so much."

"Is somebody trying to tell us something?" Mortimer Meyer joshed from the high-backed chair in which he held court. "Sounds like you're trying to get rid of us." He cackled loudly at his joke. "Luggage, dough for tickets. Hit the road, Jack!" Another outburst of laughter. "Well, it ain't gonna happen, gang. We're gonna stay right here and keep an eye on you birds."

"Morty!" Helen protested roguishly. "You ungrateful creature. You must be taking your nasty pills again."

He opened his arms expansively. "Just kidding, Mommy. Would you rather I'd break down and bawl before God and everybody? Thanks, gang. I really appreciate everything. Thanks for coming, thanks for the gifts, for the kind words."

By then it was almost ten o'clock, and many of the weary guests were already making departure noises. Liveried waiters moved about the room, offering trays containing coffee, brandy, and liqueurs of various sorts. Mints, imported toffee, and chocolates were also available.

Nina was talking to Robin and Rafe, not far away from the chair in which Mortimer Meyer sat. Sitting next to Noel Winston, she let her gaze wander, and her eyes settled upon Morty from time to time. He was chatting with Horst Krueger, one of his closest friends and most trusted subordinates, who to Nina's mind was one of the few real gentlemen on Morty's team. Each was rolling Hennessey in his Bjornson snifter of smoke-toned glass in sleek Scandinavian design, sipping delicately, pausing to savor the bouquet.

Nina noticed that Morty had ice cubes in his

brandy. Typical, she thought. Trust good old Morty to ruin a perfectly good drink. The man simply had no couth.

There was no advance warning whatsoever that anything was wrong. In the general hubbub none but those closest to Morty would have noticed, anyway. Nina herself was concentrating on Robin and Rafe when it happened.

A quick movement registered in the corner of her eye, and Nina turned to see Morty suddenly lurch to his feet, the snifter flying. He groaned, the sound wrenched, gagging, from his throat. Both hands clutched at his collar. He staggered forward, made it almost to the middle of the room. There he spun as though someone had hit him from behind with a brick, the invisible impact driving him face down onto the richly patterned oriental carpet. He struggled to rise, then rolled onto his back, shuddered once, twice, three times. Then his body went dreadfully slack, seeming to melt into the substance of the rug as everyone stared, too shocked to move.

Across the room, Helen Meyer screamed.

# Chapter Three

For a moment the room was deathly still, everyone seemingly frozen in place in a heartbeat interval of utter silence. A game, their panicky, staring eyes said. Morty Meyer was playing one of his famous practical jokes. Any moment now he'd sit up, fix them with a wicked grin, laugh as if it were the biggest gag in the world.

But when Morty didn't sit up, grim reality sank in.

Helen Meyer took three tottering steps toward her husband and collapsed in a heap some ten feet short of the body. Angela Dolan and Martine Neilsen, an actress who played a minor role on *The Turning Seasons*, fell to their knees beside her, trying to revive her.

"Call a doctor," someone cried at last. "He's had a heart attack."

"Anybody here know CPR?" Larry Spangler called out.

"Christ," Bellamy Carter mumbled blearily, "somebody *do* something!"

Nina McFall was one of the first to reach Mortimer Meyer. Decisively she brushed Horst Krueger away as he prepared to administer cardiopulmonary resuscitation. She slid her hand along Morty's throat, pressing her fingers against his carotid artery, and felt for a pulse.

"A doctor won't help," she said quietly, somewhat surprised by the fact that she felt no emotion at all. "He's gone. Nothing's going to bring him back now."

"It won't hurt to try," Krueger insisted, elbowing her aside. He leaned over the body again and commenced CPR drills.

Byron Meyer approached, horror in his eyes, but hung back, as if he were afraid to get any closer to the body. "Dad, oh, Dad," he whispered huskily. He sank to his knees a few feet away and peered around Krueger's face. "Oh, God, Dad," he wailed. "You can't leave us now. What are we going to do without you?" His grief was terrible to see. Who would have thought that the self-centered creep cared so much for his loud, overbearing father?

Noel Winston squatted beside Byron, shook him lightly. "Who's Morty's doctor? We gotta call somebody fast. To establish the cause of death if nothing else."

"I don't know," Byron said faintly. "I never paid attention to things like that. He had a specialist in New York, but who he saw around here . . ." He scanned the room frantically, saw that his stepmother was still unconscious. "Ask Gladys Parr. She's Dad's personal secretary. She'll know."

"Hasn't she gone home for the night?"

"No, she lives on the grounds. She has her own apartment out in back. Dad set it up for her, so she could be on call day and night."

"Show me, son. I don't know my way around this place."

"Not now," Byron said impatiently. "Ask someone else. I can't go off and leave Dad like this."

"Come with me, Noel," Robin Tally offered. "I know where Mr. Meyer's office is. Miss Parr might be finishing up some work there. If not, we'll try her cottage."

The two hurried off.

"It's not good," Horst Krueger said, fear in his eyes. "He's not responding at all. We'll need outside help."

"When all else fails," Nina offered, wondering where this sudden take-charge talent had come from, "call the police. The paramedics at least. Give them a shot at Mr. Meyer. Perhaps they can apply one of those shock devices we're always seeing on TV, bring him back that way."

"Nothing's going to bring him back," Spangler said. He went to a nearby couch, removed a decorative afghan, then carefully draped it over the corpse.

When nobody made any further move, Nina looked around for a phone, finally found one on a far end table, and dialed zero. "We need help," she told the operator. "A man's just had a heart attack. Can you notify the police, have them send an ambulance? Oh, of course—Leatherwing, the Mortimer Meyer estate. You know where it is? Yes, I'm afraid Mr. Meyer's dead."

Putting down the receiver, she turned to find a somewhat recovered Helen Meyer at her husband's side, pulling back the improvised shroud. She half lifted his body, cradled his head in her lap, all the while wailing loudly. "Why, Morty?" she keened. "Oh, *why*? We were so happy, things were going so well for us. . . ."

Mary Kennerly, one of the "grandma" clones on

*The Turning Seasons*, attempted to draw her away. "Come on now, Helen. Poor Morty's at peace." Her own voice sounded ragged. "Come, lie down. Oh, Helen, please!"

The new widow stiffened, resisted. Staring up distractedly, as if importuning the heavens, she said, "He wasn't sick a day in his life. Someone did this to him. Someone was out to get him, I just know it!"

She became more agitated. "Please, won't somebody get a doctor? He'll tell us what killed my poor Morty. Darling, darling, I'll get the beast who did this! I'll avenge you, my love, just wait and see. A doctor, I said!" She collapsed on Meyer's inert form.

Nina intervened, helping Mary Kennerly separate Helen from the body. "We've already called, Helen. Help is on the way. Calm down now. Come over here and rest."

The two women managed to lead her to the nearest couch and persuaded her to lie down. Angela Dolan appeared with a blanket from one of the bedrooms, and together they wrapped Helen in it, holding her down until, little by little, sobbing one moment, vowing vengeance the next, she allowed herself to relax.

The other guests stood by in self-conscious helplessness, talking softly among themselves. As is usually the case in an emergency, they had no Miss Manners guidelines to go by. Krueger and Spangler sat on the ledge of the sunken living room with Byron, trying to provide what small comfort they could. Byron was sobbing loudly.

Nina asked one of the elaborately liveried waiters to wait at the end of the front walk for the police or paramedics when they arrived. As the man left, she discovered Bellamy Carter edging out the door.

"And just where do you think you're going?" she challenged, following him outside.

"There's no point in hanging around, is there?" he slurred, avoiding her eyes. "The poor man's dead. Nothing any of us can do will bring him back. I thought I'd clear out, give the police some elbow room. . . ."

"I don't think that's very wise, Bellamy," Nina told him. "I suggest that you go back in and wait for the police like the rest of us. They're going to want to question everyone. How will it look when you turn up missing?"

"Wait for the police?" he echoed.

Nina nodded.

The assistant director, grumbling under his breath, had no sooner reentered the house than a clatter of high heels sounded on the flagstones behind Nina. Robin, trailed closely by Noel, broke from the darkness. "Nina!" she gasped, her eyes resembling two holes burned in a sheet. "It's Miss Parr! We can't find her. Her cottage looks like a cyclone hit it, but she's not there, and she's not in Mr. Meyer's office either. There's no sign of her anywhere."

"Damned strange goings on if you ask me," Noel Winston added, frowning. "Someone really turned Parr's place upside down. If the police haven't already been called, I think it's about time. We're into some really rank stuff here."

Nina felt a sickening heaviness in her stomach. Could it be? Was there something in what Helen Meyer had been raving about? Was it possible that Morty hadn't died from a heart attack after all? "The police are on the way," she assured Noel. "How far did you look? Were there any signs of violence—to Miss Parr, I mean?"

"We couldn't go very far, not without a light,"

Noel answered. "We didn't go combing the bushes, if that's what you mean. And there was no blood or anything."

"Let's go inside," Nina said. "Just don't say anything about this to any of the others. Let the police handle everything."

She wheeled, almost colliding with Rick Busacca and actress Coletta Haney who, like Bellamy Carter, were trying to sneak off.

"Please," Nina said, "don't leave. I think it would be a big mistake." She forced a smile. "Just like in the Agatha Christie books—nobody leaves the scene of the crime."

"Crime?" Rick repeated, staring at her as if she'd suddenly gone crazy. "Since when is having a heart attack a crime?"

"Just a figure of speech," Nina said quickly, but she sidestepped, blocking his path. "Wait for the police. If they say we can go, then we'll *all* go. But for now . . ." She pointed toward the house.

"Hmmph!" Rick said. "Some people are sure as hell getting bossy all of a sudden. You been taking Magnum lessons, Nina?" He grabbed Coletta's arm. "Inside, honey." He added mockingly, "The lady says we stay, and she seems to be in charge."

Ten minutes later they heard the muffled wail of a siren in the distance and the follow-up *whoop-whoop-whoop* of the ambulance. Shortly two vehicles careened into the drive and sped up the long, winding approach to Leatherwing. Next came the staccato slam of car and van doors. A moment later the costumed butler led two paramedics, trailed by a young, uniformed officer and an older, overweight man in a baggy gray suit, into the living room.

The medics approached the afghan-draped body,

flung back the covering, and began thumping, listening, and examining. A scant sixty seconds later they redraped Morty Meyer's remains. "I'm sorry," the older medical technician said, "there's nothing to be done. There've been no vital signs for quite a while, it appears. This man is dead."

"All right," the rumpled man, obviously a police detective, said. "Who's in charge here? Who called the police?"

Nina McFall stepped forward. "I did."

"Please, officer," Horst Krueger interrupted, almost physically brushing Nina aside, "I am Mr. Meyer's producer. We are close associates. I think I can fill everything in for you."

The man ignored Krueger. "You, miss," he said to Nina in a flat, bored voice, "what's your name?"

"Nina McFall."

No reaction. Apparently he wasn't a *Turning Seasons* fan.

"You live here?"

"No. I'm a guest. We're all guests. We're here to help celebrate the Meyers' wedding anniversary. All of a sudden Mr. Meyer had what looked like a heart attack, and he just keeled over on the floor. We tried to help him, but we were too late. He must have died instantly."

"I see. And the immediate family?"

"That's Mrs. Meyer over there on the couch. As you can see, she's in no condition to talk." Nina sent a glance to Byron Meyer, who still sat on the low ledge, his eyes dull with shock. "That's Byron Meyer, the son. I don't think he's in very good shape either."

"How many people are here?"

"I don't really know. I didn't count. Forty or so. We're mostly all employees. Mr. Meyer produces a soap opera—*The Turning Seasons*. Maybe you've heard of it?''

Now the man's eyes brightened.

''Indeed I have, Miss McFall. From my wife. She watches every day.'' He smiled embarrassedly. ''I have to admit that we turn it on in the station sometimes, when things get slow. I didn't recognize you off the tube. I must say, Miss McFall, it's a real pleasure to meet you. You're even prettier in real life than you are on the TV.''

Nina flushed. ''Why, thank you, Mr. . . .''

''Logan,'' he said, ''Ben Logan.''

Turning to his backup officer, he abruptly became all business. ''Frank, get everybody's name, address, and phone number. Never can tell who we'll have to drag in—big shot like Mr. Meyer and all.''

To the group at large he said, ''Folks, I hate to detain you like this, but I must request that nobody leave until they're excused. We'll be taking names, asking questions and such. We'll make this as painless as possible, so please bear with us. It looks like Mr. Meyer died of natural causes, but we need to follow procedures just the same.'' He directed the sergeant to begin circulating among the guests, then turned back to Nina and Horst Krueger, ignoring Robin Tally and Noel Winston, who hovered anxiously at Nina's elbow.

''You're right, Mr. Logan,'' Horst said, seizing center stage again, ''it *is* cut and dried. Morty was known to be susceptible to heart problems. He's been under a lot of tension lately.''

''No,'' Nina interrupted, hard put to conceal her irritation at Krueger's pompous behavior, ''*not* cut and dried at all. There's something strange going on here that you should know about, Mr. Logan. Miss Gladys Parr, Mr. Meyer's personal secretary, is

32

missing, and her private quarters have been torn up.''

''*What*?'' Logan and Krueger blurted simultaneously.

Logan's brow furrowed. ''Hey,'' he growled, ''that *does* put a different light on things. When did you discover this lady was missing? Her quarters are all torn up? Does she live here?''

''Tell Mr. Logan, Robin,'' Nina said, ''what you and Noel discovered.''

Excitedly Robin told the dour-faced detective how she and Noel had scoured the house itself looking for Gladys Parr and how she'd finally led Noel to the small, four-room cottage situated some 200 feet behind the main house where the woman lived. ''It looked as though whoever did it was searching for something in particular. The drawers were all pulled out and her papers were scattered all over.''

''How did you know where Miss Parr lived?'' Logan asked. ''I thought you folks were all guests here.''

Robin Tally paused to gather her wits. ''I used to be a dialogue writer for the show,'' she explained. ''Mr. Meyer insisted that we do all our work at Leatherwing. There's a special writers' studio on the grounds. So I know Miss Parr, the entire layout, very well.''

''You used to work here, you say? And you don't anymore?''

''No. I got interested in the acting end of things.'' She faltered again. ''It's a long story. Anyway, I quit writing a year or so ago. There was a slide-in. The actress they had in mind got a movie contract. I tried out for it, one thing led to another, and—''

''A slide-in?'' Logan interrupted.

''A slide-in is when they introduce a new character into the show. They were facing a desperate deadline, and they gave me a chance on the spur of the moment—"

He cut her off again with a raised hand. "Okay, I get the picture. So what did you do after you found Miss Parr's place all ripped up?"

"We looked for her," Noel put in. "Not an extensive search, mind you. But around the cottage and behind the house. We found absolutely nothing. Robin tells me she seldom leaves the grounds. If she's gone, I'd say she left unwillingly."

"When was the last time anybody saw Miss Parr?" Logan asked.

"That's hard to say," Nina said. "I never saw her at all." She looked at the scowling producer. "Horst, did you see her?"

"She was in and out," he said. "I saw her before dinner. She and Morty had their heads together over some papers in his office."

"What time was that?" Logan asked.

"Five-thirty or so. I came early to discuss some business with Morty. Come to think of it, he seemed a little more agitated than usual."

"Anybody else see her?"

"Well, maybe some of the other guests can tell us something about her movements," Logan said. "We'll get to that in due course. But first—"

"And what," Krueger snapped, "does any of this have to do with Morty's death?"

"Your guess is as good as mine," Nina responded. "Probably nothing at all. But if he was upset, as you say, Horst, then maybe it had something to do with whatever happened to Miss Parr. It certainly warrants some double checking, don't you think?"

"Definitely," Logan answered for him, then went

over to the two paramedics, who were in the process of placing Meyer's body on a stretcher. "Leave him, boys," he ordered. "You'll just have to stand by for a moment or so."

Then he said to the guests at large, "Everybody sit tight. We have to do some checking around the grounds. Get yourselves another drink or something. Relax. It should only take ten minutes or so." His voice rose. "Nobody leaves, is that understood?"

Immediately an angry buzzing built up in the room, and groans and rumblings of complaint were heard. Several guests moved immediately toward Meyer's bar.

"Frank," Logan snapped, "come with me." And to the paramedics: "You guys tag along, too. No telling what we might run into." He turned to Robin Tally. "Okay, Miss Tally. We gotta see that cottage for ourselves. Lead the way."

The scene was exactly as Robin and Noel had described it. Gladys Parr's desk and files had been ruthlessly rifled. Articles of her clothing, lingerie, and hosiery were strewn all over the floor. The mattress and box spring had been dragged off the frame and slashed to ribbons. The pillows were similarly mutilated.

"Somebody sure had the hots for something," the cop named Frank said softly. "Surprised he didn't take the paper off the walls."

"Perhaps he would have if he'd had time," said Horst Krueger. Logan had suggested that he and Nina join the search party. "Maybe he was interrupted before he finished the job."

"Suppose Miss Parr came in," Nina speculated, "and caught him in the act. Then he put the knife to her throat and forced her to tell him where the object he was looking for was hidden.''

''And taking it one step further, Miss McFall?'' Logan said, a half-mocking, half-admiring smile on his lips. ''What happens next?''

''She knew who he was. . . .'' Nina paused. ''He? It could have just as well been a woman. Anyway, the fat was in the fire. There was only one thing left to do—get rid of Miss Parr.''

''Which means she could be anywhere,'' Noel said. ''On the grounds, under a convenient bed. In New York City, for that matter.''

''True,'' Logan said. ''The time element, the fact that someone saw her around five or six this afternoon, has to enter into it. If we follow Miss McFall's scenario and the woman *did* catch the perpetrator in the act, he could have taken her clear out of the state by now.'' He turned to the other cop. ''Frank, get the power flash from our cruiser. We better start looking in the immediate vicinity first.'' And to the paramedics: ''You got some lights in that emergency buggy of yours. Get 'em. Everybody spread out. Search the cars, the bushes, anyplace a body could be stashed. Move it!''

Nina, Robin, Noel, and Horst went with Logan, making a grand circuit of the house, inspecting every dark niche the rambling structure afforded, looking behind every bush, even lifting a black plastic tarp covering a huge woodpile in back. Nina wished she'd thought to bring her jacket. And her fragile, silver-strapped sandals were a terrible nuisance. The night had turned chilly, and the dampness seemed to seep into her very bones. She was thankful to be with friends; the darkness took on a threatening menace all its own.

As they came full circle and emerged in the vast

parking area to the east side of the grandiose pile of rock and aged cedar, they heard a faint cry in the distance.

"It's the bandage brigade," Logan muttered. "Down by the river. They're onto something."

"What've you got, Charley?" Logan wheezed as they reached the iron guard rail at the edge of the cliff, fighting to regain his breath.

By the way of answer the taller of the two paramedics wordlessly threw the beam of his power flash along the stairway that led down to the Hudson.

They followed the searching circle of light as it cut through filmy, writhing skeins of fog and settled at the base of the eighty-foot bluff. There, twenty feet to the right of the stair landing, among some huge boulders, lay the pitiful jumble of a human form, surrounded by a blur of color where a colorful print skirt had flowered one last time. An outstretched tangle of arms and legs had been arrested in a final desperate flailing. The prim Miss Parr would have been mortified beyond words to know she'd been found so disgracefully exposed.

Nina McFall found herself shuddering all at once, as though a skeletal hand were grasping her hair at the base of her skull, twisting viciously. Robin released a single, terrified wail. "My God!" Noel Winston gasped.

"That would be our lady, I imagine." Logan sighed resignedly. And after a respectful pause: "My job to go down, I guess. Will one of you . . . someone who knows her . . . go with me, please, to identify the body?"

Torn between revulsion and curiosity, all chose to accompany the police detective down the zigzag formation of wooden steps. When they reached the body, Robin clambered across the largest boulder that blocked their way. In tardy concession to modesty she rearranged Gladys Parr's skirt, but the obscene act of murder could not be so easily concealed. Nina looked once as the flashlight played across the bloody, crumpled body, then closed her eyes. She forced herself to take quick, deep breaths.

"Yes," Robin Tally said. "It's . . . it's Miss Parr."

One of the paramedics approached the body, lifted a limp wrist, held it briefly. "She's dead, all right," he said laconically. "We'll need an autopsy to determine whether the fall killed her, or if she was dead when she went over the cliff."

"I'm calling for an autopsy on Meyer, too," Logan replied grimly. "The two deaths have to be connected."

*Who*? Nina's mind raged as she continued to see the mangled remains behind her closed lids. How could one human being do such a ghastly thing to another?

For a long time no one spoke. The only sounds were the soft lapping of the river, the sibilant intake of collective breaths, as all fought to regain their wind after the long climb down and to reconcile themselves to the shocking sight of what was left of Gladys Parr.

"Well, that cuts it," Ben Logan said at last, his voice booming startlingly. "I'm definitely in over my head on this one. We're authorized to reassign jurisdiction, to go out of the county when a case gets as tricky as this one's bound to be. And since Mr. Meyer's more of a New York City celebrity than a local boy . . ."

He stared about the others, his eyes picking up eerie reflections from the flashlights. "I'm making a call as soon as we get back to the house," he announced. His shoulders seemed to slouch in defeat. "I'll let those hotshots at NYPD handle this one."

He turned to his sergeant. "Frank, you stay here with the body for now. The rest of you, up to the house."

# Chapter Four

Detective Lieutenant Dino Rossi, main ramrod of the NYPD's elite "silk stocking" squad—a special department that dealt exclusively with "show-biz" and celebrity crimes—was around six foot three, weighing a possible 180 pounds. Nina McFall was forced to admit that the dark-haired, muscular detective was one of the most attractive men she'd laid eyes on in months, on TV or otherwise.

Then why the antagonism? she asked herself, trying to overcome a long-time prejudice against overly handsome men. In her experience, they all came fully equipped with an overload of conceit. Did he have to be so blasted aggressive? Why the gratingly cocky, know-it-all attitude?

It was 11:35 P.M.; Rossi and his four-man team had been at Leatherwing for twenty minutes. How they'd driven all the way to the Meyer estate so fast, Nina had no idea. The detective had taken swift control of the situation, barking orders with machine-gun rapidity, using each flunky, even Ben Logan's crew, to peak efficiency.

The crime scene unit was scouring the house, Gladys Parr's cottage, the grounds, and beach at that very moment. Photos of the two corpses had been taken, vital tests had been conducted. Mortimer Meyer was already aboard the ambulance, awaiting transportation to Manhattan; Gladys Parr would shortly be trundled up the meandering stairs and placed beside him. Later the medical examiner would take over. It was hoped that there would be some hard answers before another dawn rolled around.

The majority of the party guests had been dismissed. Only the immediate family and Horst Krueger, Nina McFall, Robin Tally, David Gelber, Noel Winston, and Angela Dolan (who also recalled having a fleeting glimpse of Gladys Parr at 6:30) had been asked to remain. Off to one side, Rafe Fallone, much worried about Robin's involvement, had chosen to wait for her.

Helen and Byron Meyer were huddled on the couch, Byron with an arm around his stepmother. As forthright as Lieutenant Rossi was, he nevertheless hesitated when it came to direct questioning of these two.

Give him a gold star for compassion anyway, Nina conceded grudgingly, while simultaneously she pondered her ambivalent feelings about the savvy cop.

Rossi was wearing a medium blue twill suit. A black knitted tie hung loose at the neck, the top button of his lightly patterned plaid shirt undone. The glint of a gold detective's badge caught the light when his jacket fell open. His black loafers were polished to a dull gleam. His shoulders were impressive, and Nina wondered if he was a body building freak, perhaps a weight lifter. She guessed he was in his mid-to-late thirties.

His face was angular, with prominent cheekbones

that conferred a somewhat gaunt, feral look. His nose was large and slightly aquiline. A mass of black, curly hair set off his chiseled features, reminding her vaguely of Michelangelo's statue of David. Thick, dark eyebrows shadowed deep-set eyes of a cool and piercing gray. Combined with the seemingly perpetual frown on his face, the total effect was one of stubborn determination. This was one confident, take-charge guy, she decided. Arrogant, too, most likely.

Rossi had already questioned David Gelber, Robin Tally, and Horst Krueger. Now he and Nina sat on a couch located a discreet distance from the grieving family while a scarecrow-thin sergeant interviewed Angela Dolan across the room. Jotting notes into a buff-colored shorthand pad, Rossi reviewed the night's events one more time.

"Let's get this over with as quickly as we can, Ms. McFall," he said. "It's late, we all want to get home. How about some top-of-the-head reactions to what's happened here tonight?"

Nina, faintly dismayed at the disarray of her thinking processes at the moment, paused momentarily before answering. Instead of concentrating on the interview, she found herself wishing she weren't quite so grubby, that she might have found time to freshen her makeup, dab away some of the stains at the hem of her skirt. Her pretty party shoes were scuffed and caked with mud. Lord, she thought, I must look a mess!

"Ms. McFall?"

"Oh," she said, displaying small, even, white teeth in a confused smile. "Sorry. I was distracted, I guess."

"Apparently. As I understand it, you and Mr.

Krueger were the first to reach Mr. Meyer after he fell.''

"That's correct. He went down so swiftly. I could feel it through my shoes when he hit."

"Was there anything suspicious about the way he fell?"

"I'm not sure I understand what you mean."

"People who have heart attacks usually don't go down in the manner you described. Are you sure your observations were accurate?"

Nina frowned, annoyed. "What are you suggesting, Lieutenant?"

"I'm not suggesting anything, Ms. McFall," Rossi said patiently. "I'm waiting for the ME's report, and while I'm waiting, I'm trying to recreate the actual scene as best I can. To do this I must rely on eye-witness accounts." His glance was the slightest bit disparaging. "From people like you."

"I see," Nina said, bristling in recognition of the fact that she'd just been scolded. She glared at him, her sea-green eyes like chips of emerald ice.

"I repeat, Ms. McFall," he said, enunciating each word carefully, as if dealing with a learning-disabled person. "Was there anything the least bit unusual about the way Mr. Meyer fell? And do you feel there's any connection between the two deaths?"

"I certainly do," she said frostily, fighting to recover her composure. Why was she acting like such a dolt? "Two and two still do make four, don't they? When someone dies in his own living room from undetermined causes, and the next thing you know his personal secretary's body is found at the bottom of a cliff, of course there's a connection!"

Lieutenant Rossi smiled for the first time. "I tend to agree with you. And now what about the way Mr. Meyer fell?"

"Well, if you say there's a difference . . . He *did* fall hard, that's true. Almost like someone who'd been hit from behind."

"But there's no possibility that he *was* hit from behind, is there?"

"Hardly. Not with all those people around."

"Do you know of anybody who would have liked to see Mr. Meyer dead?"

She frowned again, took her time in answering. "I suppose there might have been a few people who might have wished to harm Morty," she said carefully.

He looked up expectantly. "So? Name one."

"Are you trying to set me up, Lieutenant? What kind of question is that? I'd be wise to plead the fifth."

Rossi's intense concentration never wavered. "But you won't."

"Well, let's see. . . ." She avoided those steely eyes, looking down at her clasped hands. "I'm sure you've heard all this already from the others. . . ."

"Suppose you tell me again, Ms. McFall."

Nina took a deep breath. "His own wife might be a possible suspect, I suppose. That *wasn't* a happy marriage, all the anniversary cakes in town to the contrary."

"Yes, her I've heard about. Anyone else I should get a handle on?"

Nina frowned, thinking. "Morty shafted a dear friend of mine recently," she said reluctantly. "She was one of the principals on *The Turning Seasons.* She was in the process of being phased out; it couldn't have come at a worse time financially for her. She and Morty—well, let's say they were playing house on the side. Only she believed it was for real at first, poor thing. And when she refused to put up with any more of his double dealings, he had her written out of the show. It was a rotten, underhanded way to treat someone who'd once loved him.''

''A real sweetheart, huh? Did Mrs. Meyer know about it, do you think?''

''I expect so. Helen watched him like a hawk. He always had another woman on the side. She learned to take it, look the other way.''

''She stands to inherit Meyer Productions?''

''I suppose so. I'd expect that Morty made generous provision for his son, Byron, as well. That's him over there, with Helen. Ordinarily they'd be at each other's throats. Byron's a possible suspect, too, I suppose. He and Morty didn't always see eye to eye.''

''Whew. The plot thickens. And sickens. I've got more leads here than I bargained for.''

Nina's smile turned bitter. ''And don't forget the greater New York TV business community and its cast of thousands. Mortimer Meyer didn't climb to the top of the soap opera heap without doing a lot of back stabbing on the way.''

''Can you prove any of this?'' Rossi asked sharply.

''Not a smidgin. But I imagine there are people who'd know where to start digging. As for Marta, even if I were willing to go public with her story, that would fall into the area of unsupportable hearsay, no doubt.''

''Marta?''

''The girlfriend he fired last March.''

''Oh, yes. Her. You're right, it would be pretty hard to make that stand up in court, since I gather she wasn't here tonight.''

''It's all conjecture anyway,'' Nina said. ''After

all, we have no proof yet that Morty *didn't* die of a heart attack.''

Rossi shook his head. ''Some kind of big, happy family you have on that set.''

''Happier than most TV crews,'' Nina said defensively. ''We have our thorns, of course. But what show, what organization doesn't? I'll bet there are a few guys at the department you'd like to get rid of. Right?''

He raised an eyebrow.

''You're quite a little philosopher, aren't you?''

''Don't be patronizing, Lieutenant,'' Nina snapped. ''I'm quite a little everything—actress, tax-paying citizen, woman. You asked, so I'm telling you. Actually, we're a pretty loyal gang on *The Turning Seasons*. I have a lot of good friends there, a lot of people I've come to love.''

His eyes suddenly became darker and, it seemed to Nina just then, drilled into her more penetratingly. ''I can appreciate that kind of loyalty,'' he said.

''Thank you, Lieutenant,'' she said, experiencing the first feeling of warmth toward this pushy man.

Rossi moved on to other things. ''What do you know about Miss Parr?''

''Absolutely nothing. In fact, I first heard about her tonight. Robin Tally just told me about her over cocktails. Robin's my best friend. She . . .'' Nina caught herself. ''But you just talked to her; she's already told you all this.'' She laughed. ''Very clever, Lieutenant.''

''Not really. It's standard police procedure. You never know what you'll hear when you pose the same question to several different people. Back to Miss Parr. You were saying?''

''That's all.'' She shrugged her shoulders. ''Robin

had some misgivings about the arrangement, as I recall. It leaves things wide open for some rather way-out conjecture, don't you think?''

"Exactly," Rossi said. "We'll be checking out the relationship between Mr. Meyer and Miss Parr very carefully, believe me." He flipped through his notes.

"Let's go back to square one, if we may, Ms. McFall. You were one of the closest persons to Mr. Meyer when he died. You are the only one so far to comment on the fact that he fell so heavily. I find that most interesting. We can all see that there's no evidence of foul play, certainly no gunshot wounds, no knives, no blows to the body. Any other ideas?''

"Ideas about what?"

"About the cause of death, of course, Ms. Mc-Fall.''

"That leaves only one thing. I've read enough mystery novels to know about poisoned drinks and all that sort of thing. But that's not possible, not with everybody there, with scads of people surrounding Morty. How would one go about poisoning his drink without his becoming suspicious? How would they do it without risking giving the lethal drink to the wrong person?''

Rossi's gaze became distant; he didn't speak for a few moments. "Not entirely impossible," he murmured, as if thinking aloud. "It could be done. It would take a lot of fine tuning, split-second moves. And, God knows, it would certainly muddy the waters with so many possible suspects on hand.''

Again he sent her that hard, penetrating look, but there was a glint of admiration in it this time. "Interesting thinking, Ms. McFall.''

"Not really, Lieutenant Rossi," she said. "It's the only other possible answer if Morty didn't die of natural causes. But, as you say, the circumstances . . .'' Her eyes widened. "You don't really think that—''

"I'm not ruling out anything, Ms. McFall. Think back again, please. Did you see Mr. Meyer make a face, as though his drink tasted bad? Anything that might even hint at the possibility of poison?''

"I didn't see him drink at all. I was talking to some other people. The next thing I knew, Morty was going down.''

Rossi changed tack, talking her through the visit to Gladys Parr's cottage and the discovery of the body at the base of the cliff. There was time for Nina to become aware of the sensitivity of his well-shaped, sensual lips. He *was* an attractive man. Was he really as tough as he pretended? Or did the hard-boiled exterior simply go with the territory?

"Okay, Ms. McFall.'' Rossi sighed wearily, rising. "That'll do it for now. Thanks for the very interesting input. You are quite an observant lady, if I may say so. I'll be getting back to you later. For now you're free to leave.'' Then he grinned. "Don't leave town.''

Nina was now sitting with Robin and Rafe, sipping a heavily iced Coke. They talked softly among themselves, trying to make sense of the night's happenings, all the while keeping an eye on Rossi as he questioned Noel Winston, and speculating on developments when various cops approached the lieutenant and muttered into his ear.

When Lieutenant Rossi chose to question even Rafe Fallone, simply because he was there, Nina decided to call it a night. She'd done all she could to help with the investigation; it was certainly going to drag on for some time yet. In the immortal words of

Scarlett O'Hara, tomorrow was another day. She'd no doubt hear from Rossi and company again.

"Are you coming?" she asked Robin.

"No, hon," Robin replied. "You go ahead. I'll wait for Rafe, drive back with him."

"Okay, then. Call me tomorrow." Nina stood up. "Let me know how things went."

She went over to where Helen Meyer sat, alone now, hunched over in exhaustion. Everyone had tried persuading her to go to bed, but the *grande dame* had remained adamant. She would wait for the results of the police investigation; she would have justice; she had to know who was responsible for her husband's death.

"Please, Helen," Nina tried a last time, "won't you let me take you upstairs? This has been a terrible shock for you. You need to recover your strength. A good night's sleep will make all the difference in the world. Come on, now. That detective isn't going to trouble you tonight."

"No!" Helen said firmly. "I'm going to sit right here and wait until I know who killed poor Morty." She began to sob anew. "That poor man—who would want to harm him? He never hurt a soul." She self-pityingly surrendered herself into Nina's arms, sobbing histrionically.

Yes, Nina thought, "that poor man." How could Helen ignore the innumerable hurts he'd inflicted upon her and upon everyone else he came in contact with? How could she be so hypocritical now, just because Sporty Morty was dead? Or was it all just an act?

"Well, Helen," she said finally, "if you're sure there's nothing I can do for you . . . it's past midnight, and I've got a long drive back into the city.

50

I'm terribly sorry. And please, Helen . . . try to get some rest.''

"Such a lovely party," she mimed wearily under her breath, as she gathered her jacket and bag. "Thanks so much for asking me."

A cold draft hit Nina when she got outside and began feeling her way across the darkened parking area. She shivered as she fit her key into the Mazda's lock, dropped into the driver's seat, snapped the door latch.

Her mind swarmed with confused thoughts as she drove. The evening's developments kept being replayed in her brain. Morty's death was bad enough, but who would want to murder Gladys Parr? Granted, according to Robin Tally, she was a prissy, over-officious busybody. And yet, some suspected her of carrying on an affair with her unlovable boss. But does one get murdered for things like that? No, there had to be more to the mystery.

And while the evidence seemed to point to a connection between her death and Morty's, couldn't it just possibly be that such conclusions were a bit premature? Couldn't it be that there was no connection whatsoever? Why complicate matters unnecessarily? Maybe Morty *did* die of the obvious cause—a heart attack. And what if Gladys Parr had simply experienced a giddy spell as Nina herself had earlier that evening as she had stood looking down on the Hudson and had gone over the edge all on her own?

But what about the way her living quarters had been torn up? How could one explain that? And just what could the ransacking intruder have been looking for?

Nina's thoughts spun faster and faster. And if Mortimer Meyer hadn't died of a heart attack, then what had killed him? There was apparently no indication that anyone had jabbed him with a hypodermic needle—no bruises, no blood, no marks of any kind. As she'd said to Dino Rossi, poison was the obvious conclusion. But again, how? In the midst of that mob of quests, how to pull it off without anyone being aware of it, without killing an innocent bystander by mistake?

Now Nina thought about her conversation with the handsome police detective in which she'd suggested a few possible perpetrators. She realized that she'd barely scratched the surface regarding people who might have hated Mortimer Meyer enough to kill him. Which suspect, if the decision was left to her, would she lean on first?

Ridiculous, she told herself sternly. Why was she fretting? It certainly wasn't *her* concern, at any rate, in not more than a superficial way. Yes, Mortimer Meyer had been her boss, and she should be upset over his death, and the puzzling circumstances surrounding it. But as for playing any real part in solving the murder, forget it.

No, after tonight, except for minor checkbacks by the police, she was out of the picture for good. As Ann Landers was fond of saying, MYOB—Mind Your Own Business.

Suddenly, a vision of Dino Rossi came back. Again Nina pondered the unsettling effect the man had had upon her. Why? Was she ready for a new romance? Thoughts of Clay Burgess briefly flashed across her memory, jarring her. No, she adjured, that's all over. Leave it on the shelf. She frowned. One thing was certain: If she was looking for a new romance, it wouldn't be with a super-macho male like Dino Rossi. She knew all about Italians and their women—keep them barefoot and pregnant, that was their philosophy, and that she certainly didn't need.

She sighed impatiently, leaned forward, concentrated on her driving. Who, she wondered, had gone and moved New York? It seemed like she'd never get there. Just then, like the Emerald City, she saw that first announcing glow on the horizon. "Run, Toto," she quoted aloud. "We're almost there."

Several hours later, in the bathroom of her spacious, super-luxurious Riverside Drive apartment, Nina McFall busied herself with her nighttime toilette. It was almost 2:30, and though she'd fixed herself a stiff vodka and tonic and had watched part of a soporific late-night movie, she still wasn't sleepy. Too many things kept churning in her mind.

She had hung up her clothes and now stood in the bathroom wearing just her bra and panties while she removed her makeup, tied back her thick red mane, and applied her nightly moisturizer. Just then her phone rang. She whirled, startled and apprehensive. What now? she wondered. At this hour?

"Ms. McFall?" the brusque male voice said. "Dino Rossi here. I hope I didn't wake you."

She flushed, suddenly aware of her near-nakedness. "No," she said, a little breathlessly. "I was just getting ready for bed. I wasn't sleepy. Too upset, I guess."

"I just thought you'd like to know. I rousted one of our docs, had him do an autopsy on Mr. Meyer."

"Yes . . .?" she said expectantly.

"One more question, Ms. McFall. You're one-hundred percent positive that you didn't see Mr. Meyer's face when he fell? An expression that might indicate a bad taste in his mouth?"

"I told you, Lieutenant, I was just turning when

he fell. There was no way I could have seen his face. Why do you keep asking?''

''Because Mr. Meyer did not die of natural causes. He was poisoned. What kind we don't know; we'll need further tests. May I offer my congratulations?''

''Congratulations?''

''For your fine detective work. Your comment about the possibility that Mr. Meyer had been poisoned got me to thinking. That's why I rousted Doc Pollard. You've got a flair, Ms. McFall, a real nose for crime.''

Nina momentarily fell silent. Was he paying her a compliment, or was he just being sarcastic? Did she detect genuine admiration in his tone? Was there perhaps a more personal motive behind his late-hour call?

''Well,'' she said finally, ''I'm glad I was able to help. It ought to be good for something.''

''Pardon?''

Nina smiled. ''My nose. Mom always said I was always sticking it where it didn't belong—in other people's business, mostly.''

He laughed. ''Is that right?'' And when she didn't reply, ''Another thing, Ms. McFall. Please keep this call, what I've said about the poison, completely confidential; no other member of the cast should know about this. I'm already off base to be informing a witness of inside information concerning a crime, but I feel confident that you'll keep this to yourself. I just wanted to let you know how useful your suggestion was. As I say, you're a natural, and I'd certainly like to have you on my side, if you know—'' he sounded confused—''what I mean. Please, not a word until I give you the green light. Is that clear?''

''Yes, Lieutenant Rossi,'' she said demurely, feeling an odd, tingling excitement. "I won't breathe a word."

"Good. I knew I could trust you. As I said before, don't leave town. We'll be in touch. Good night, Ms. McFall."

"Good night, Lieutenant."

Oh yes, she thought as she put down the receiver, his words still ringing in her ears. Certainly their paths would cross again—soon. They *would* be in touch. Yes, she'd like that very much

# Chapter Five

Late though it was, Nina found it impossible to fall asleep immediately. Instead, she lay in bed, thinking back over the series of events that had brought her to this time, this place, this situation. Sometimes the past seemed like a dream, or something that had happened to someone else. . . .

She had come to New York five years ago, when she was twenty-nine. Her life was in total chaos at the time, and the move was an impulsive decision, similar to a move to Mars.

Born in Madison, Wisconsin, to a physician father and a housewife/social-activist mother, Nina's had been up to then, a protected and prosaic life. Her interest in performing had first been piqued during high school plays, glee club membership, even a stint as a cheerleader during her senior year. But it hadn't been until her third year into her chosen career as a high school English teacher back at Walker High, still living at home no less, that she experienced self-discovery with a vengeance.

She finally realized that she was totally underwhelmed by her profession. Teaching Shakespeare, Wordsworth, and Keats to kids who'd never experienced anything more culturally stimulating than Sha-na-na, Captain Universe, and *Gilligan's Island,* she discovered, was about as much fun as slamming her fingers in a car door.

In an attempt to alleviate her frustration, she began helping with high school programs and plays, eventually accepting an assistant director's role in addition to her regular teaching duties—unpaid, of course—at Walker. In an amazingly short time she became director, even branching out into writing original scripts for her budding Marlon Brandos and Jessica Tandys. This, in due course, led to her participation in productions staged by the local little theater group. It was there that she met Clay Burgess.

The show was *The Most Happy Fella,* one of her all-time favorite musicals. Her whiskey-alto voice was tailor-made for the role of Cleo, the heroine's bosom buddy. Clay Burgess played the role of Herman, Cleo's foil.

At first, her startling beauty and no-nonsense, get-on-with-it approach to life put Clay off; and though she was attracted to him almost from the start, weeks passed before he could summon up enough courage to ask her out. A fledgling attorney, he was, at twenty-nine, on the shy side, unsure of himself. But once he relaxed, Burgess proved to be devastatingly witty and possessed of an oddball sense of humor. He was sensitive, cultured, and gentle beyond Nina's wildest expectations. She melted every time he looked at her with his dark, yearning eyes. And when he touched her, finally dared to kiss her . . .

Nina had never been to bed with a man before, though she'd had her share of offers over the years. She had always believed that a gold ring, accompanied by a wobbly rendition of "Oh, Promise Me" in the local church, was a mandatory prelude to immolating passion. However, with Clay, such Pollyanna notions quickly went out the window. It was she, in fact, she realized in retrospect, who had seduced *him*. One night at his apartment, after one glass of wine too many, things had definitely gotten out of control.

Afterward, Clay had been heartbreakingly contrite, begging for forgiveness. It had seemed her heart would explode from the love she felt for him at that moment. And, yes, she would respect him in the morning.

They talked of marriage, but not right away. Time—they needed time to savor their love, time to be sure. Give it a year. The following June, they promised each other ardently.

But as the popular old torch song had it, the romance was "too hot not to cool down."

Eleven months later, it was all over. As Clay's infatuation faded, he gradually became petty and querulous, and suggested they shouldn't be seeing so much of each other. Innocent that Nina was, she couldn't read between the lines, and only pressed harder. Perhaps she was being selfish, she worried. She wasn't giving enough of herself. Yet her devotion only drove him farther away. A basically superficial, selfish man, Burgess decided that he'd had enough of her smother love, and deliberately provoked a hysterical screaming match which effectively ended the relationship.

Nina had gone into deep shock after they split up. She had truly loved Clay; it was to her the bitterest of injustices that he couldn't love her back, that he didn't want her forever and ever.

Unable to bear another year of teaching, of living in the same town with her former lover, Nina had rejected her new contract. Ignoring parental advice, she'd gone to Milwaukee, where she joined a small repertory company. The monthly salary (when she could get it) was laughable. But at least she was doing something she loved; it would help her forget, give her wounds time to heal. Other opportunistic males tried moving in on Nina but received the royal brush-off for their pains. She wasn't ready for a heartbreak encore just yet.

Nina stayed in Milwaukee for fourteen months. Then opportunity knocked. Hank, a character actor, down on his luck, drifted in from New York. He knew a man who knew a man who knew that *The Turning Seasons*, one of TV's most popular soaps, was actively seeking a stunning actress for a slide-in role. The stunning part was easy. But finding a looker with acting talent was another story. Nina was a natural. Why didn't she take a flyer? He, personally, would put a bug in someone's ear. Someone influential.

Here's what she should do . . .

Nina McFall arrived in New York late on a Friday in early December and took a room in the fleabag hotel her friend had recommended. She had an appointment to read for a man named Spence Sprague on Sunday afternoon at 3:30 P.M. No advance scripts were available; she would have to audition cold. Walking the Broadway blocks, meandering into the theater district in temperatures of ten degrees, the wind cutting her exposed face like knives, taking in the glittering marquees of the Mark Hellinger, the St. James, the Majestic, seeing the affluent ticket holders thronging in, she was filled with excitement and anticipation.

But as she detoured into the seamier corners of Times Square, took in the adult-book and sex-toy stores, the peep shows, the porno theaters, the squads of cruising prostitutes, she had second thoughts. In and out, she told herself firmly. If she didn't win the role, she'd be on the first plane back to Wisconsin come Monday. She'd seen how the other half lived in the Big Apple, and if she couldn't be on the right side of the stage, then she wanted no part of it. Better to be a big frog in a small pond, she concluded.

On Sunday she appeared at the West Side Studios and timidly let herself in through the ornate door emblazoned with the words MEYER PRODUCTIONS. Four other women sat waiting in the luxuriously appointed reception area, all of them knockouts. Momentarily she quailed, considered skipping out, forgetting the whole thing. But her friend Hank had thought she had the stuff. He'd gone to the trouble of making the necessary contacts. Quickly the old confidence came back.

"Here's a copy of the script you'll be reading from, Miss McFall," the plain, mannishly dressed receptionist told her with a reassuring smile as she checked in. "The part starts on page forty-two. At least you'll have a little time to prepare."

Her appointment time went past. It was 3:45, then 4:00. Two of the other women were summoned into an inner office, each reappearing within ten minutes. The third woman was gone for almost twenty minutes. She's won the part, Nina concluded, her heart sinking.

Shortly the tall, beautiful, poised blonde came out, sweeping the room with a smug, condescending glance as she left. "Miss McFall," the receptionist said, "you may go in now. Second door to the right."

Spence Sprague was in his early fifties, balding slightly, his white hair wildly untidy. He had a sharp voice but kind eyes. "Good afternoon, Miss Mc-Fall," he said, rising behind his desk, his eyes registering quick approval. "So nice of you to come. Won't you sit down?"

He briefly explained the role of Melanie Prescott, whom they would be introducing into *The Turning Seasons* just before Christmas. She was a self-aggrandizing, ambitious, no-holds-barred career woman. Did Nina think she could handle a characterization like that?

Nina said she expected she could. And then, running lines with Sprague, she had proceeded to give the performance of her young life.

The director had been plainly impressed. "Very good, Miss McFall," he said. "Now if you don't mind, take a crack at this script. You play Kim Chessley, who is saying good-bye to a lover who's given her up. Let it all out. Be as emotional as you can."

That was easy to do. Immediately memories of Clay came flooding back. And with his memory came a suffocating tightness in her throat, a sharp, tearing pain in her heart. The loneliness that accompanied being a stranger in the big city helped, also. By the time she finished the six-page segment, her voice was quavering, her eyes overflowing with tears. "I'm so sorry," she choked, fighting for control. "I got carried away, I'm afraid. I . . ."

He stared with wide-eyed amazement. "I guess you did, Miss McFall. Marvelous! It's astonishing how you got into that role so fast."

Even so, the final decision wouldn't be announced until Wednesday or Thursday. There were still a dozen or so other candidates to audition. But she was definitely in the running. Would she be able to remain in the city a little longer?

Nina nodded, her heart pounding insanely.

Those four days of tension-wracked waiting had seen the last of Nina McFall's little-girl vulnerability go down the drain. And by Thursday, the day Mr. Sprague had promised to call, after exploring the tough city streets night and day, she was transformed. While she could hardly be taken for a hard-boiled native, she now had a tentative handle on the city's brawling, vital life-style. Win or lose, New York had, in her eyes, lost its power to intimidate.

Thursday came and went, and still no word. Remembering the timeless show-biz refrain "Don't call us, we'll call you," she was reluctant to dial Meyer Productions. Friday, she couldn't bear the uncertainty another day. At 10:30 A.M., just as she was about to give up and call Eastern, inquiring after the earliest Milwaukee flight, the phone rang. Counting to ten, foolishly striving not to appear too eager, she had carefully picked up the receiver. "Yes?"

"Miss McFall? Spence Sprague here. Can you come over to the office this afternoon at 1:30? I think we've got some good news for you . . ."

Could she? She could have walked on hot coals!

On Sunday morning, drinking coffee at 11:30 and biting into a chewy bagel as she idly riffled through the million-page edition of *The New York Times*, Nina found it hard to believe that in another five months, she'd have been in New York five years. Where had the time gone? From Miss Naïveté to hardened soap opera pro, just like that, in the seeming blink of an eye . . .

Well, hardly. In reality it hadn't been all that easy, that cut and dried. It had been a harrowing, mind-boggling, bone-pulverizing experience. Five days a week, rising at 6:00 A.M. to arrive at the studio in time for the first call at 8:00, going through the storyboard drills, the endless rehearsals, the action walkthroughs also known as blocking. Then late in the afternoon, in costume and makeup, the final tapings, with every nerve extended to its fullest to avoid fatal fluffs that would require more extra takes than were absolutely necessary. The day's episode was finally a wrap at 3:00 P.M. . . .

Even that wasn't the end of it. The next day's script already in hand, she would return to her apartment where, after a quick dinner, she would fill the hours before bedtime reading and memorizing tomorrow's lines.

At first the frenetic pace seemed unbearable, and Nina wondered if she weren't close to cracking. There were days—and lost salary be damned—when she was actually grateful to have Melanie Prescott written out of the script. If it hadn't been for friends like Marta Hollings, and later Robin Tally, to tease and laugh with her, to encourage her, to hold her hand when the tears came— A tough cookie she'd become, yes. But would she have survived without them?

At the outset, Nina had been hired on temporary status, receiving the minimum $500 scale for every episode she appeared in. Sometimes she'd be on-screen once a week; other times she'd be written in every day for two weeks. She averaged two or three days a week, however, which, in New York, turned out to be skimp-by money.

But during the second year, as the character of Melanie Prescott caught on, as Nina McFall's fan mail grew from a mere trickle to 50, then 100 letters weekly, Meyer Productions had been forced to up the ante. Nina's salary jumped to $2,500 per week, guaranteed, whether she appeared or not. Currently she earned $5,000 a week. The staggering sum made her head swim at times. Yes, it's really me. I'm still here. Dreams do come true.

Abruptly she sat upright on the peach-colored Buffoni davenport that graced the east wall of her sumptuous living room. Surely she had better, vastly more important things to think about this morning. These incredible goings-on at Leatherwing last night, for instance. What was happening? Shouldn't she have heard something from someone—anyone—by this time?

In characteristic fashion, she seized the initiative and reached for the phone on her chrome-and-glass coffee table, punching out Robin's number. "Miss Tally," she said, disguising her voice. "This is the front desk. You requested a noon call?"

"Come off it, Nina," Robin said. "I've been up for hours. Who could sleep, after what happened last night? What's shaking, doll?"

"*I'm* shaking—still, after what happened last night. Have you heard anything at all?" Nina asked.

"Not a word. But then, what did we expect? We don't rate. We're not even prime suspects."

"You have a point there." Nina paused, sipping her coffee. "Anything happen after I left last night?"

"No. Lieutenant Rossi was questioning Byron Meyer when we were excused. We finally got Helen to bed. There were no last-minute developments so far as I could see."

"How late did you stay?"

"It must have been one A.M. before we pulled away from Leatherwing."

"He was really thorough, I take it."

"Who do you mean?"

"That NYPD detective—what was his name? Dino somebody?"

"Come on, Nina, don't play games with me,"

Robin scoffed. "Dino somebody indeed! He made an impression on you, all right. Don't try kidding your old friend. He made *my* pulse rate go up, let me tell you."

"I take it that Rafe didn't stay over," Nina said archly, in a deliberate attempt to change the subject. "Otherwise you wouldn't be talking so freely."

"He's right here. He knows he's not irreplaceable." Her voice faded away as she called across the room to Rafe. "Isn't that right, lover?" Then she spoke into the receiver. "How about you? Anything to report?"

"Not a thing." Though Nina was dying to tell her closest friend about Rossi's early-morning call, she remembered her vow of secrecy, and managed to keep silent.

"I'm surprised. The way that detective zeroed in on you last night, I was sure he'd be in touch," Robin prodded.

"Oh, for heaven's sake! Nina scolded, feigning irritation. "The man had no designs on me. He was just doing his job."

"Oh, sure. We should all have jobs like that." Robin paused. "How did you like the charming little party last night? A load of laughs, wouldn't you say?"

"I'm still in a state of shock," Nina admitted. "I can't believe it all really happened. It's like a bad dream. Only when I wake up it's still there."

"What exactly did you tell Lieutenant Rossi?" Robin asked.

"Oh, probably the same thing you told him," Nina said, being deliberately vague.

"Why do I get the impression you're holding out on me? You two had your heads together for ages." Before Nina could think of an innocuous reply,

66

Robin continued. "You know, Rafe and I were talking on the way back home last night, and we agree there's something fishy going on. I mean, it's too bad about poor old Morty, though I for one am not about to shed any crocodile tears. I wasn't any fonder of him than anyone else. And I was never really friendly with Gladys Parr, but her death was a terrible shock just the same. Nina, level with me—don't you think it's a little strange that they both died violently within a few hours of each other? And what about the mysterious person who wrecked Gladys's cottage? Do you really think he—or she—might have done old Gladys in? That's what you suggested to Detective Logan. What I'm leading up to is, are we talking double murder here?"

Amazed to hear her friend voice her own suspicions, Nina attempted to hedge. "Robin, you've got to stop watching *Murder She Wrote*. I was talking through my hat. Who'd want to murder poor Miss Parr?"

"I haven't the faintest, but I can think of quite a few who'd have been overjoyed to see the last of Mortimer Meyer, including yours truly. Doesn't Lieutenant Rossi suspect foul play?"

"I really can't say," Nina said truthfully.

"Can't or won't?" Robin probed. When no answer was forthcoming, she sighed. "Okay, I give up—for now. What are you going to do today? Any plans? How about coming over for dinner? I can thaw something and throw it in the microwave."

Nina laughed. "Sounds like a gourmet treat. Thanks, Robin, but I don't think so. I have lots of chores to do, and there's the small matter of tomorrow's script, if you recall. Got your lines down?"

"Hardly. That's my ulterior motive. I thought we could run them together. Rafe's such a poop when it comes to running lines—he's more of a silent study.''

"Sorry, but I'll have to take a rain check. Some other time, okay?''

Robin reluctantly agreed, and the two women hung up.

Nina fell back onto the sofa, letting out a long, exasperated sigh. Keeping her vow of silence was going to be harder than she'd anticipated. She just hoped Dino Rossi appreciated how hard it was. She also hoped she'd have the opportunity of telling him in person.

Though she knew it was highly improbable that he would call today—he *was* up to his ears in a murder case, after all—she was a little disappointed that she hadn't heard from him. After all, if he'd been sufficiently impressed with her detective skills to call her in the wee hours of the morning and tell her her suspicions had proved true, it stood to reason he'd keep her posted on developments. Nothing personal, Nina reminded herself. Nothing at all to do with his broad shoulders, piercing eyes, sensual mouth . . . Now cut that out!

Nina rose from the sofa and moved into her kitchen, where she poured a fresh cup of coffee. Still in her peach satin negligee, matching mules on her feet, she leaned against the glistening tile counter, her long, slender fingers twined around the delicate Limoges cup. Eyes narrowed, she stared into space, thinking.

Lieutenant Rossi's question came back to haunt her: Whom would she pick as prime suspect in the Leatherwing murders? Who was behind all this? Who hated Mortimer Meyer enough to kill him? Granted, old Morty would never have even made runner-up in a popularity poll, but who bore so grievous a grudge against him that murder had resulted? And what about Gladys Parr? The woman was a cipher. What had she known or possessed that had made it necessary to kill her as well?

As Nina had told Rossi the previous night, she felt sure the two deaths had to be in some way connected. But if someone had been with Gladys Parr during dinner last night, tearing up her place, then dragging her, alive or dead, to the edge of the cliff and tossing her over, how could that same person have been inside the house poisoning Morty's after-dinner drink? Perhaps there were *two* people involved—the actual murderer and his (or her, Nina reminded herself) accomplice.

Nina kept coming back to the enigma that was—or had been—Gladys Parr. Her death seemed to indicate that there was some sort of business deal involved, something Morty was cooking up that Gladys was privy to. But what if it were purely personal? What if, as Robin had suggested, she and Morty had been carrying on a torrid affair, and Helen had found out? Maybe that had been the straw that broke the camel's back, the camel in this case being the "grieving widow," and Helen, berserk with jealousy, had polished them both off? But no, that was impossible. Helen had been very much in evidence every single minute, and whoever killed Gladys and tore up the cottage must have been away from the house for a considerable period of time. . . .

Nina's head spun, almost as if she were drunk. How could anyone hope to sort out all the loose ends? It was like nailing noodles to the wall! Another thought, totally out of left field, suddenly emerged. Could Gladys Parr have been blackmailing Morty? What if he was cooking up a really shady deal, one she knew about? Had she tried to extort money from him in exchange for keeping quiet, and Morty had hired someone to find the evidence and bump her off? But in that case, then who killed Morty, and why? Who put the poison in his drink, and how?

Putting down her coffee cup, Nina pressed her fingernail to her aching head.

I've got to stop this, she told herself, or I'm going to go stark raving mad! Leave it alone! That's what Dino Rossi's being paid for. Let him worry about it.

She strode purposefully from the kitchen, heading for her bathroom. I can't just sit around all day playing detective, she decided. I've got jillions of things to do. She'd shower first. Then she'd dress, go out for a late lunch. Or, no, she'd eat in. If Rossi called, she didn't want him to get her answering machine. She hoped she'd get through the papers before the day got away from her. Then, of course, there was that blasted script. Spence would be back tomorrow, and he didn't suffer fools kindly, especially lazy fools who overused the teleprompter. Thus far she hadn't abused that privilege, and wasn't about to start now, murder or no murder. God, with all this going on, how would she ever keep her mind on Melanie Prescott's problems? But she would, somehow. After all, Nina McFall was a pro.

At 9:30 P.M., the next day's script was committed to memory. Dinner had been finished hours ago, the dishes put away, the kitchen gleaming. *The New York Times*, as digested as it was ever going to be, lay in a neat pile by the door.

Dino Rossi hadn't phoned. And after she'd altered her plans, deliberately stayed in all day, just in case! She watched the last part of *Masterpiece Theater* with half an eye, her annoyance growing.

Nina was in bed by 10:15. Her late night on Saturday, the grisly excitement, the continual tumble of speculation in her brain, had taken their toll. She could hardly keep her eyes open. She sent a last jaundiced look at the phone on her nighttable. If he decided to call her in the middle of the night again, she'd give him a piece of her mind. Would she ever!

She turned out the lamp, snuggled under the covers, felt fatigue gather her in, cuddle her close like a weary child.

Dino Rossi, you jerk, she thought, just before she drifted off to sleep.

# Chapter Six

"Nina, darling," Angela Dolan cooed as the statuesque redhead crossed the main rehearsal hall on the way to her dressing room, "how lovely you look! That complexion of yours—always so clear and dewy. How do you do it at your age?"

Nina forced a smile. She'd hoped to avoid Angela, who stood with a cup of coffee in one hand, one of the gooey, sweet-roll monstrosities the management provided in the other. Angela was always the first person on the set, her seniority notwithstanding. Getting past her in the morning was akin to the day's first jump on a military obstacle course.

"By staying away from stuff like that," Nina replied, matching Angela's dulcet tone. "And you, my dear, should certainly be the last person in the world to be bringing up age at this hour of the morning."

Angela bridled.

"My, aren't we touchy today? Have a bad night?"

"No, darling," Nina said sweetly, "not at all. I had a good night, in fact. It's the mornings I find hard to cope with." And with that she headed for the stairs.

"Well!" Angela sniffed. "That's what you get for trying to be nice to some people."

There was no real malice in either woman's words. It was merely a ritual, a daily game they played, the obligatory acknowledgement of the long-standing rivalry between the two top female anchors on *The Turning Seasons*. Each prided herself on being able to conjure up fresh barbs to start each day off with a twinge.

In her dressing room, Nina locked her purse away, hung up her jacket, and glanced at herself in her large dressing table mirror. Her eyes seemed a bit haunted, but otherwise everything else was in all the right places. She wore a peach-colored silk blouse, tan whipcord slacks, and brown Ferragamo pumps. Sitting at the table, she fussed with her hair, tucking in an occasional unruly wisp.

Nina winced as she looked at the miniature writing desk near the door and saw the stack of letters that had accumulated over the weekend. She estimated the pile at thirty or so. All cast members were expected to skim through their mail, indicate an appropriate comment on each envelope, then return them to the publicity department for computerized response and a four-by-five photo. Truly outstanding letters were to be answered personally, another chore added to the cast's already overloaded day. Nina knew she should be grateful that her loyal fans cared enough to write, but there were times— Today was one of them.

At 8:00 A.M. sharp the fourteen actors and actresses on Monday call filed into the barnlike, script-littered rehearsal room, arranging themselves in a semicircle on decrepit folding chairs. While some directors split the cast into "scene" groups, Spence Sprague insisted on a "full" group first thing in the morning. He felt that each actor's grasp of the show's total continuity was essential. Later on, Spence, Bellamy Carter, and Assistant Director Nick Galano would take separate groups in tow. But for now, a full-scale line rehearsal was about to begin.

"Okay, Nina," Spence said, stopwatch in hand, "you'll be walking over to close your office door here. Give yourself—oh, say five seconds. Yes—then turn and deliver the line."

He turned to Bob Valentine, who was in the scene with her. "Bob, you've got to act *stunned* at what Miss Prescott is proposing," Spence said. "Do a double take if you have to, wait two or three beats, then start again. Okay, now. Deliver your line. C'mon, people! Let's get some life into this damn scene!"

Generally there were five scenes in each daily half-hour episode; each must be honed to razor sharpness, each movement choreographed to play on the exact second, with the cameramen, lighting crew and sound technicians on alert, all moving in rhythmic, split-second unison. It was a minor miracle, Nina McFall often thought, still awed after five years by the logistics of preparing a daily television show.

By 9:30 the principals had moved to the studio itself, where, using the "halfsets," they delivered their timed lines while actually moving back and forth, the camera dollies, the sound booms, the floods, and spots coalescing in magic synchronization.

As camera time neared, timing became more precise, and lines were added or pruned, replaced or removed again and again. Each actor was held accountable for every last-second change in the script.

All this was the responsibility of Sally Burman, the second writer, who, as David Gelber's resident surrogate, handled on-the-spot script changes where needed. A tough pudgeball, she was ruthless when actors got temperamental and complained that their lines weren't right. Mark Viner, her dialogue flunky, followed her around to carry the dog-eared scripts, and sometimes wrote extemporaneous lines himself.

During blocking, the cast and production crew went through the scenes two, sometimes three times. And though the pace was hectic, the life-and-death aspects—when adrenaline would truly pump, tension rise to a scream—must wait until after lunch. Small wonder some novices on a soap opera set verged on physical and mental burnout during their first weeks on the job. There were actually lifetime veterans of stage and screen who vehemently refused to consider even a cameo role on soaps, so grueling was the pace.

Finally, from 11:15 to 12:30, a lunch break was called: the cast scattered, some to favorite haunts, others to their dressing rooms where a sandwich and a soda passed for the noon meal. Some female leads, needing extra makeup attention or a new hairdo, skipped lunch altogether.

This particular Monday morning there was added aggravation as a direct result of the deaths at Leatherwing. Word had somehow gotten around that Mortimer Meyer had not died of natural causes and that Gladys Parr's death had been no accident. The entire cast was shaken, as attested to by constant fluffs, memory lapses, and loss of concentration by all concerned, including Nina. Sprague, Carter, and Galano were beside themselves; how would they ever get the day's show on tape with the cast so skittish? Hadn't those damn actors ever heard the old show-biz maxim, "The show must go on"?

"I just can't believe it really happened," Martine

Neilsen leaned over to whisper in Nina's ear. "It's like I expect Morty to come barreling through that door at any minute, being his old, obnoxious self."

"I know what you mean," Larry Spangler added. "God knows I wasn't crazy about the old goat—maybe he had it coming to him. But it's not the kind of thing you want ringside seats to, either. I couldn't get it out of my mind all yesterday."

"Same here," Nina said, keeping a watchful eye on Spence Sprague, who didn't like conversation below decks when he was critiquing a scene.

"*Please*, people," Sprague interrupted the small talk, his eyes focusing directly on Nina McFall, "*if* we could dispense with the chatter." And to Martine Neilsen, who had blown her entrance and her lines for the third time: "Please, darling? Try to concentrate? Now, let's run through that scene once more. . . ."

But the Leatherwing hangover wasn't that easily dispelled. Everywhere one looked the rest of the morning, cast members had their heads together. A perpetual buzz-buzz was going on, and the topic of everyone's conversation was Saturday night. Even more unnerving was the suspicious expression in everyone's eyes, as they stared furtively about at their fellow actors. The question was unmistakable: Could it be Rick, or Angela, or Rafe? Or even Robin, the reigning ingenue? Is it he? Is it she? Is it *you*? The paranoia became an almost palpable thing as the morning wore on.

Tension rose to a screaming pitch shortly after 9:00 A.M., when Lieutenant Dino Rossi, accompanied by a plainclothes assistant, appeared on the set. Spence Sprague nearly had a hemorrhage, but in the end, was prevailed upon to permit interviews with cast members in between scenes. "But get this,

Lieutenant," he stormed, "when they're paged, you let loose immediately. This studio has to be cleared by four-thirty P.M. *sharp*. This episode *must* be a wrap by then, understand?"

Detective Lieutenant Rossi worked deftly around the director's tight schedule for the next two hours, and between him and his sidekick, Sergeant Charley Harper, managed to corner Bob Valentine, Valerie Vincent, Martine Neilsen, the doughty Angela Dolan, Sirri Ballinger, Larry Spangler, and finally even Spence Sprague himself.

"Why me?" Sprague argued. "I wasn't even at the party. I was home in bed, getting over a gallstone attack. I was certainly in no position to do away with Morty. *Or* the Stone Virgin."

"Stone Virgin?" Rossi smiled slightly. "That's one I haven't heard yet. I assume you're referring to Miss Parr."

"The one and only. Pushy, officious little tyrant. Should have been a doctor's receptionist."

"Protective, huh?"

"Protective isn't the word. Paranoid was more like it. You'd think somebody was going to eat her precious Morty. Even Helen had her rounds with Gladys. But Morty couldn't fire her. She knew too much."

"Interesting. Do you have any off-the-wall theories as to why someone might want to push her over a cliff?"

Sprague shrugged. "Why did somebody kill her? Probably because she knew too much. She knew the bottom line on every shady deal Morty Meyer ever pulled."

"So how come Mr. Meyer bought it, too?"

"You're the detective, you tell *me*. And pardon me if I don't shed any tears over either of them—

write that in your little notebook. Parr especially. She just loved to keep people waiting, to misplace messages. I could have a national crisis here on the set, and if I needed two words with Morty, do you think she'd put me through?''

A snarl twisted Sprague's mouth. ''She was spiteful and mean. It was like she was trying to get some power into her life. Sure as hell God never gave her any. She died a virgin, or I miss my bet—unless Morty scored somewhere along the line. But I can't believe that even *Morty* could get that hard up.''

Sprague broke off, embarrassed at his outburst, then continued more temperately, ''Morty's funeral's scheduled for Wednesday. I'll be honest with you, Lieutenant. Showing up's going to be a real chore, for me anyway. I might just get a relapse of that gallstone attack.''

Dino Rossi made no comment, merely asking, ''So you didn't much care for Mr. Meyer, either?''

Sprague shrugged. ''He and I didn't cross swords that often. I answer to Horst Krueger and Ken Frost mostly.'' His lip curled disdainfully. ''And to Helen Meyer. She's always putting her oar in where it isn't wanted. No, if you're thinking I had any reason to kill old Morty, forget it. We moved on completely different tracks.''

''What about Horst Krueger?'' Rossi said. ''I've heard rumors to the effect that there was bad blood between him and Mr. Meyer. Know anything about that?''

''It's no big secret, Lieutenant. When Meyer first started out in the soaps, he and Horst were partners. Nothing on paper, mind you, but good buddies. They both came from somewhere around Newark, where they ran some two-bit radio station.

When they hit New York they were going to make it big, share fifty-fifty right down the line. Only somewhere along the way their deal went sour. Morty was top dog in a multimillion-dollar company, while Horst was left holding the bag it came in.''

''When did all this happen?''

''Back in 1967 or thereabouts. When TTS first came on.''

''TTS?''

''*The Turning Seasons*. Speed-speak, you know?'' He laughed softly, but there was a bitter undertone to it. ''Why Morty didn't tie a can to Horst's tail then and there, I'll never know. Maybe he enjoyed having Horst around, for a whipping boy perhaps. Morty was a real rub-your-nose-in-it kind of guy. Maybe Horst finally found a way to get even. With the Stone Virgin, too. Undoubtedly she was in on whatever shaft job was going on, too.''

''You trying to tell me that, after more than twenty years, Mr. Krueger finally got fed up enough to commit murder?''

Sprague shrugged again. ''What you see is what you get, Lieutenant. You read it any way you like.''

''There's talk about other show-biz types who might have had it in for Meyer,'' Rossi went on.

Sprague blinked, his face expressionless. ''I could probably name a dozen. But none of them would have been invited to Morty's big blast. If they wanted to finish him off, they'd have hired a man with a silencer to hit Morty on some dark street. Or they might have bought off someone at the party. No amateur hour stuff for these boys.''

''Mind naming a couple?''

''Not at all. Try Ralph Foy. He and Morty had a subsidiary production company on the drawing boards. Ever hear of Astra Features? *Big* bucks there. They put out *Clancy's Squad*, *Citizen Soldier*, and *Midnight Mission*. Top hits, all of them. That's Astra. Ralph was a stand-up, hand-shake guy, too. Guess who got zero percent of Astra?''

''Ralph Foy?''

''Precisely.''

''Where do I find him?''

''Foy Engineering. On Torrance Street.''

''Any other names?''

''I suggest you ask Foy. He keeps a list. Enough. I'm out of here. I've got a show to put on, remember?''

Dino Rossi watched Spence Sprague hurry off. He stared into space, a dour expression on his face. This case was beginning to sound like the story of the fabled Hydra. For every head you cut off, two more grew back.

Nina had spotted Rossi the minute he came through the door. He'd looked her way but hadn't smiled, hadn't approached her. Their eyes had locked for the briefest moment, and she'd felt a quick sense of excitement. Then he'd turned away and become involved in questioning the other members of the cast. Look me up before you leave, Lieutenant, she thought. I've got a couple of questions I'd like to ask you.

But the demands of the scene she was doing with Bob Valentine (Bellamy Carter directing) took precedence, and she turned away, momentarily forgetting about Rossi.

During a breather, Nina sat in the rehearsal room drinking a Coke. Except for Valerie Vincent and Rossi's assistant who was deeply involved in muted conversation with Bellamy Carter in a far corner, Nina had the room pretty much to herself.

Nina glanced at Valerie where she sat studying her script, trying to memorize a lot of last-minute line changes. Nina noticed that the girl looked a bit peaked. Her mother hen instincts coming to the fore, she wondered if Valerie might be coming down with something. At the party Saturday night she'd seemed to be in the bloom of health, a vision of youthful beauty in rose-colored silk. Granted, none of the actresses got made up until the afternoon dress rehearsal call, but there was no reason for Valerie to look so pale unless she were ill.

Valerie was twenty-four, and played the role of Polly Bissell, a teenage runaway, on TTS. One of the newest members of the cast, a pretty, voluptuously endowed blonde, Valerie seemed to have few friends on the set, and Nina always took pains to speak to her and pass the time of day whenever the opportunity arose. Concerned for the girl, she took the initiative and sat down on a folding chair beside her.

"Morning, Valerie," she said. "How are things going today? Are you feeling all right? You look a little down."

Valerie's smile was stiff. "I'm fine, Nina," she replied. "Just tired, I guess. Too much weekend— that awful party on Saturday. And then I was out again last night." She rolled her eyes in a feeble attempt at humor. "Some people never learn, I guess."

Nina frowned. Up close, Valerie looked even worse. Her skin was pasty, her eyes lifeless. The makeup crew would really have their hands full with her later. So would wardrobe—the girl was also putting on weight. "You know, Valerie," she said, going into her sisterly act, "sometimes we forget just how demanding this job of ours can be. You have to pretend you're an athlete in training, and take care of your body the same way an athlete does. Exercise, watch your weight, get plenty of rest . . ."

"You're right, Nina. Thanks." The girl smiled wanly.

"Have you talked with the police yet?" Nina asked.

"Yes. That guy over there. We finished a minute ago."

"Did he give you a hard time?"

"No, not really. I'm new—I don't know many of these people very well. I'm the last person the police should be questioning."

"They questioned me Saturday night—wanted to know if I had any ideas about who might have pushed Gladys Parr off that cliff. And about Mr. Meyer."

"Who do *you* think did it?" Valerie asked, her eyes registering animation for the first time.

"I really don't know. I can't believe it's anybody from the show, even though none of us were particularly fond of Mr. Meyer."

"I don't know why people didn't like Mr. Meyer," Valerie said. "He was nice to me, those few times we bumped into each other on the set. Always friendly and smiling, always full of little wisecracks."

I'll bet, Nina thought darkly. Sweet young thing like you. Had Morty made a move on Valerie? She wasn't the brightest kid in the world. Valerie was an adequate actress, but possessed no real depth. She seemed somehow unformed as yet, unsure of herself.

Nina touched Valerie's hand. "Are you sure

you're well, dear? You look awfully pale. Maybe you should see a doctor.''

Valerie stiffened, her expression becoming guarded. ''I'm okay, Nina. Honest. I told you . . . too much to drink last night, that's all. I'll be in fine shape by tomorrow.'' Abruptly she jumped up, closed her script. ''Catch you later. Another damned runthrough.''

Nina sat there for a long time after Valerie left. She couldn't shake a strong feeling that something was out of synch. There was something wrong with Valerie, something she was trying to hide. But what? Or was she, in reality, just hungover? Could it be drugs? Kids today were exposed to so many dangers and temptations, and Valerie seemed so vulnerable. She would have to try to get to know Valerie better. If only she could head her off before she got totally messed up . . .

Come off it, Sherlock, she scolded herself. You're getting to be just like Lieutenant Rossi—eternal bloodhound. Drop it, will you?

She rose. It was time she reviewed some script changes of her own. That crazy seduction scene was especially tricky, a departure from Melanie's established character pattern. It would require a lot of extra study before camera time. Nina turned and sought the solitude of her dressing room.

Nina had decided to play it cool, if and when Dino Rossi saw fit to grant her five minutes of his time. She would be all business. ''Ms. McFall,'' he said, coming up from behind her as she came away from her second rehearsal, ''may I have a few words with you?'' His smile was somehow boyish—there was nothing at all arrogant or threatening about him to-day.

"Yes, Lieutenant?" she said, raising her eyebrows. "What can I do for you?"

"I intended to call you yesterday," he said, his voice warm, even intimate, "really I did. But every time I started for a phone, something came up. And then at eleven, when I finally called it a day, I figured it was too late."

"It would have been perfectly all right," she said coolly.

"Not all right at all. Especially since I'd kept you up so late the night before. This job of yours can be extremely demanding, I expect. You need your rest."

"Why, thank you, Lieutenant," she said, a strange melting sensation building in her heart. He could be awfully charming when he wanted to be. "How considerate. Most people think soap opera actors sit around reading their press notices all day. But it really would have been all right, I assure you."

He drew her to a far corner of the main studio and let his voice drop to a near whisper. "Cyanide," he said.

"Cyanide?" she blurted. "What are you talking about?"

"The poison," he said, glancing about guardedly to see if any of the other cast members were watching, "that killed Meyer. That's what the autopsy turned up." Another look over his shoulder. "You haven't mentioned my call to anyone, have you?"

"Not a soul, Lieutenant. But it's been very difficult. I hope you're going to give me the all-clear soon."

"Not yet. I'm working on some definite angles." He paused. "I just might catch somebody off guard."

Nina frowned. "Let's stop right here, Lieutenant.

Something's been bothering me ever since you called the other night.''

''What's that?''

''*Why* are you telling me all this? Isn't this privileged information . . . my being a witness and all?''

Rossi gave her a penetrating look. ''I've got my reasons, Ms. McFall,'' he said, ''believe me. More on that in due course.''

''Well . . . okay. If you're sure you won't get into a jam later . . .''

''Believe me, I know what I'm doing,'' he said. ''Once I check out a few more suspects—''

''You'll have it solved?'' she asked eagerly. ''That *is* fast work.''

''No. Not solved by any stretch of the imagination. Suspects, I said. There's a far piece between that and preferring charges.''

''What's happening? What did you find out?'' she asked.

''Nothing all that earthshaking,'' he explained. ''I spent the best part of Sunday tracking down the various members of the catering crew—the waiters, the chef, the coordinator, the clean-up people. I was trying to figure out how the cyanide got into Meyer's brandy snifter.''

''From what little I know about poison,'' Nina interjected, ''I'd expect it would have taken longer for Morty to die. I read a lot of mystery novels, when I'm not studying scripts. There would have been sweating and dizziness beforehand, then convulsions when it took final effect.''

''Not if someone slips you five hundred milligrams.'' His expression turned grim. ''You go down like a sledgehammered ox. Just as Mr. Meyer did.''

Rossi then summarized his thinking on the investigation to date. How, he reviewed for Nina, had the brandy snifter containing the cyanide been delivered to Mortimer Meyer? After all, the drinks were being passed on a tray. And, if there *was* an accomplice among the waiters, how was the man going to keep someone else from picking up the poisoned drink?

"Good questions," Nina said. "What did you find out about the catering people?"

"Not a blasted thing. They all checked out; there's no way under the sun any of them could be in on it. Plain, everyday working stiffs, no police paper on any of them. No connections whatsoever between any of them and any of the guests. So far as they knew, nobody else at the party ever came into the kitchen, or hung around the bar when the glassware was being set out, when the drinks were being prepared."

"What does it mean?"

"What it means is that somebody at the party, somebody who'd been standing nearby at the time Meyer picked up his drink, had to be responsible. But there's another thing. The stuff comes in capsule form. How could he get that whole capsule down, literally in one swallow? Why didn't he see it in his drink? I'll grant you the room was dimly lit, but it wasn't that dark."

"And if the capsule itself didn't go into his glass," Nina offered, "if the contents of the capsule had been stirred into his drink, why wouldn't he taste the cyanide with his first sip?"

"Now get this. We figured we'd recover that glass, maybe find the cyanide residue, even some helpful fingerprints. But there were no usable prints, and the cyanide traces were virtually nonexistent. And why?"

"Tell me!"

"Because, in the immediate crush, just after Meyer went down, someone conveniently managed to step on that glass and grind it into a thousand tiny fragments.''

''This gets spookier by the minute. So where are we?'' Nina caught herself. ''I mean, where are *you*?''

''I'm stuck with Krueger. He was the only one close enough to Meyer to slip the capsule into his glass. But how he'd do it without Meyer or anybody noticing, I can't begin to imagine.''

''Horst?'' Nina was astonished. ''No, that can't be. Not Horst, circumstantial evidence to the contrary. He's a sweetheart, one of the few really decent men we have among the top echelons. I don't buy that at all.''

''Well, Ms. McFall, despite your high opinion of the man, a picture is beginning to form. Krueger definitely had reasons to do his old partner in.''

''Old partner? I thought I knew everything about everyone on this set, but I never heard that one before. What sort of old partner?''

Lieutenant Rossi shook his head. ''Later, Ms. McFall. Not everything at once.'' He glanced around again, then turned back. ''Is there any chance we could have lunch together? I want to explain all this, but not here in front of everybody.''

Nina's heart skipped a beat, her mind raced. ''Lunch?'' she finally answered, her expression wary. ''Yes, I suppose that could be arranged. There's a place . . . Corrigan's Pub . . . just around the corner from the studio. We could go there.''

''No, that won't do. Too close. Someplace where your crew doesn't go. They mustn't see me with you. I've got something important to tell you. You know where The English Garden is? About five blocks west on Sixty-sixth? What time?''

''We break for lunch at eleven-fifteen. . . .''

''Great. I'll meet you there at twelve.''

"Meet me? Why can't you pick me up?"

Rossi sighed. "Because, Ms. McFall, I want this to be a secret. I'll explain later. Besides, if we drove away in the radio car, everyone would think I was taking you in for booking. Would you like that?"

Nina's green eyes widened in alarm. "I'll meet you," she said.

Nick Galano had taken the final blocking rehearsal. A schoolmaster type, he insisted on yet another motivational. "Okay, folks," he said, "we're getting close to movie time. Let's fine-tune it, shall we?"

He then went on to flesh out the scene Nina and Bob Valentine would be doing, describing the radical departure for the character, Melanie Prescott, who is encountering some hard knocks at this point in her life. While she is a hard-driving, career-woman type, he explained, she is an inherently moral person who succumbs to a temporary short-circuiting of her otherwise high standards, a lapse that she will live to regret. Which lapse the home viewers—always eager to forgive a sinner—would eat up.

In the scene at hand, Melanie, depressed because of a career setback, plus a serious argument with her lover, would actually attempt to seduce Gregg Thomas (Bob Valentine), a marketing subordinate and a much younger man. When her overtures are rebuffed, the pain cuts too deeply, and she lashes out, threatening his job if he doesn't do as she says.

"I don't like it," Nina said, frowning. "Serious character distortion. Whose bright idea was this?"

"Guess," Galano said. "Sally Burman told me Helen Meyer dreamed it up, insisted it be written in."

Nina rolled her eyes. "Wouldn't you know?"

"I know it sounds like pure meller-drama," Nick

said with a conciliatory grin, "but it's gonna work. So? Shall we give it our best shot, kids?"

Despite the queasy repugnance she felt, Nina vowed to do just that.

At the climax of the scene, as Melanie/Nina moved woodenly toward the door, closed and locked it: "I mean it, Gregg." She forcefully chewed out the words. "I need someone. Right now. And you're it. Over here. On the couch. Yes, that's it . . . put your arms around me. Kiss me." Her voice grew thick with deep urgency and longing. "Yes, Gregg! Kiss me! Kiss me like you meant it, damn you! Oh, I need someone to love me so badly!"

And as Bob Valentine took her in his arms, leaned her back into the cushions, both positioning their heads precisely for the best camera angle, Nina found herself becoming aroused. For some crazy, unexplainable reason she found herself imagining that it was Dino Rossi who was holding her.

"Oh, wow, Nina!" Bob Valentine laughed when Galano called the cut. "You were really getting into that. Talk about chewing up the scenery! We'll knock 'em dead this afternoon."

"Great stuff, Nina," Nick agreed enthusiastically. "That ought to melt the sprockets right off the cameras. Whoever you were thinking of, sweetheart, keep it that way for the final take."

Nina McFall blushed furiously and ran off the set without a word. *Idiot,* she raged, ducking her head in shame. *What's happening to you? You're a big girl now. So get in control. Good Lord! Dino Rossi! What's the matter with you?*

"What do you mean, Nina?" Robin Tally protested. "You've got another engagement? You're coming to lunch with Rafe and me, and no arguments."

"No," Nina said firmly, unable to look her best friend in the eye, "I can't. I've got some shopping to do. I'll grab something quick at a fast-food place."

"What's this sudden shopping trip, hon? Who do you think you're conning here?"

"Something's come up, Robin. Personal business. So drop it, will you? You and Rafe go ahead without me, okay?"

As the grumbling pair went out the door, headed down the street to Corrigan's Pub, Nina waited until she saw them go around the corner. Only then did she dart from the front door of Meyer Productions and flag down a convenient taxi. As she fell into the backseat and told the driver her destination, she wondered at the crazy thing she was doing. Why was she meeting Rossi in the first place? And more importantly, why did she feel like such a fink, like a downright traitor to her friends?

# Chapter Seven

Dino Rossi waved to Nina from a booth halfway to the rear of the crowded, plant-filled restaurant, and she hurried down the aisle, sliding into the seat across from him. "I feel like Mata Hari or something," she said, smiling nervously. "All this hush-hush stuff. My friends were a trifle miffed when I canceled out."

Today Rossi wore a gray shirt, a burgundy-colored tie, a forest-green blazer, and gray flannel slacks, an outfit Nina thought very attractive. She knew momentary concern as she saw how haggard he looked. Do all of New York's Finest work this hard? she mused. "Well," she said, smiling tentatively, "what's this all about?"

Rossi signaled a waitress. "Why don't we order first?" he said, sidestepping the question.

Nina chose a chef's salad with bleu cheese. Dino settled for a club sandwich. Black coffee for both.

She looked at him expectantly, but if she hoped for continuation of the warm rapport she'd felt earlier, she was disappointed. Rossi was edgy, evasive.

"I've got an appointment with Mr. Horst Krueger

after lunch," he said. "We're gonna play a little hardball."

"Please, Lieutenant, don't." She reached across the table, touched his hand supplicatingly. "I think you're wrong about Horst. He'd never kill anyone, believe me."

"Perhaps not. But he's the closest thing to a hot lead that I've got. And with the new information I have about him—"

"Which is?"

Tersely he recapped his interview with Spence Sprague. And despite his reassurances that it was okay, Nina still felt uneasy being on the receiving end of these confidences. Nevertheless, she remained silent while he finished. By then the waitress had arrived with their food; conversation lapsed while she served them.

"I intend to check out some of these other business connections of Meyer's also," Rossi went on, taking a bite of his sandwich. "I think we're into mother lode here."

Nina pushed her introspections aside. "Aren't you jumping to conclusions? Chasing the first rabbit to jump out of the bushes?"

"Rabbit? Bushes?"

"Well, you implied yourself that this is a much more complicated case than you originally thought. So, just because Horst was the nearest person to Morty that night, just because you got a tip about his losing out on some business deal with Morty, off you go without keeping the larger picture in focus. Is that the way police work's done these days?"

"Now listen, Ms. McFall, I—"

"And will you stop the 'Ms. McFall'? I was Ms. McFall when I taught school. Please call me Nina."

"Good." He raised a quizzical eyebrow. "A

teacher, huh? I'd never have suspected it." He laughed. "And you might as well call me Dino. Since we're going to be partners and all . . ."

Nina stared at him. "We are?"

He held up his hand. "Later. As I was saying, I've got a gut feeling about Mr. Krueger. Most of the time instinctive reactions like that pan out for me. It's a truism in the cop business that if you don't solve the average murder within seventy-two hours after it happens, your chances of ever solving it go out the window in ninety percent of the cases. The clock is running."

They concentrated on their food again. He looked at her with a mocking grin. "So? Who do you like in the third race?"

"Pardon?"

"If you don't like Krueger, then who do you favor?"

"Is it supposed to be that cut and dried? Aren't you supposed to do a little more homework?" She grinned and carried his analogy a step further. "Shouldn't you study your tote sheet?"

He scowled at her. "C'mon, Nina. You're fudging. Give. Who do you think did it?"

"Someone we haven't even thought of yet," Nina said promptly. "Someone not even in the picture. And it all goes back to Gladys Parr. I think she was murdered as an afterthought, when someone else's bluff didn't pay off. It's all so complicated—I can't really explain it. If I were going around asking questions the way you are, well, then I could . . ."

"But you aren't." His expression became condescending, and Nina felt her hackles rise. "So you just leave that part of it to me."

"Yes, sir!" she said in exaggerated deference.

He ignored her sarcasm. "But there is an important part you *can* play, Nina."

"Oh? And what is that, pray tell?"

"I know you've been thinking that my behavior reflects a certain breakdown in police ethics."

"Now that you mention it, Dino, it *is* making me a bit anxious."

"I need your help, Nina," he said quietly, his eyes boring into hers and giving her butterflies. "I guess, down deep, I'd have to agree that there's a missing quotient in this case that I can't begin to get a handle on. I can ask questions all over New York, I can interrogate until doomsday, and it won't get me any closer to an answer. Something's going on beneath the surface here, something on the TTS set itself. And there's only one way to crack it."

He attended to his food again, letting his words sink in, then continued. "What I need is a pair of ears in the studio, someone to nose around, to report on any oddball things that might be taking place. Someone who—"

"Me?" Nina interrupted, her pulse racing.

His voice was patient. "*Someone,*" he said, "who has a nose for detective work. And you, Nina, *do* possess that rare quality. I saw it the other night at Leatherwing." He paused. "What do you say, Nina?"

Confusion warred with elation on her exquisite face. Elation switched to chagrin, back to elation again. Chagrin won out. "You mean you want me to be a stool pigeon? To rat on my friends? Oh, no, Dino—Lieutenant Rossi—I couldn't do a thing like that!"

"I'm sorry you look at it that way, Nina. It's not really being a stool pigeon. It's more like being an observer, sharing the things you see with an outsider. An outsider, who, by nature of his job, can't do it himself.''

''But I'd feel so—so sleazy. Just knowing that I—''

His eyes became hard. ''Look at it this way, Nina. A murder—two murders—have been committed. Two people closely involved with *The Turning Seasons* are dead. Who knows, more may die. Don't you want to help catch whoever's responsible?''

''It's just that I'd feel—crawly somehow, doing that. What if I discovered that it was one of my close friends in the cast who did it? My friend Robin, for instance. How could I turn her in?''

''That's exactly what I mean,'' he pressed. ''Can't you see that paranoia's already building? People are looking around at one another on the set, thinking, 'Is it he? Is it she?' Paranoia like that can cause long-time relationships to unravel overnight. Do you want to see that happen? It could, in the long run, even doom *The Turning Seasons*. The show could die. And all because one rotten apple was allowed to spoil the barrel. You understand what I'm saying, Nina?''

''I suppose I do. And I suppose you're right. But when I see myself fingering friends . . .''

''Friends? Do friends poison each other, push each other off cliffs? No, those aren't friends.'' He made a placating gesture. ''Think about it at least, won't you, Nina? If something should jar a nerve, put you on guard, all you have to do is call me, any time of day or night, and we'll thrash it out, see if it means anything. And if it does, you'll know you've done a good thing. No one will ever know the part you played except yourself.''

He dug into his back pocket, withdrew his wallet. He laid one of his official police cards on the table, wrote another number on it. ''My home phone,'' he said. "Letting that number out is an absolute no-no. But as a sign, a gesture of trust . . ." That melting earnest expression shone in his eyes again, and Nina was helpless to refuse.

"Okay," she said with an explosive sigh, "you win. Maybe it's all wrong, but you've convinced me, Dino. It's a good thing you don't sell encyclopedias!"

He reached across the table, gravely shook her hand. She felt actual regret when he released it. "Thanks, Nina. I'm truly grateful."

"How far does this—ah, partnership, of ours go, Dino?" She was careful to keep any note of intimacy from creeping in. "Do I get to go along when you close in on whoever it is? Or am I just set dressing?"

"A silent partner," he said firmly, his mouth set in a thin, determined line. "The department would crucify me if harm came to a civilian I'd brought into a case. It would mean my badge. You feed me the tips, leave the muscle to me. All you do is look, listen, and report."

"That's no fun." She feigned a small pout. "I'm a big girl now. I can take care of myself. One thing's certain, if I get onto a lead and you aren't available, I certainly don't intend to let the criminal get away."

Dino sighed. "You've been watching too many TV shows. That isn't the way it happens in real life—unless you'd like to quit your job and take a stab at the Police Academy." He smiled. "Please. Leave the hard stuff to me. If anything ever happened to that lovely face, I'd never forgive myself."

Nina flushed, dropped her eyes. "Oh, all right. But as I said—Dull City." She wiped her mouth with her napkin, pushed her salad bowl away. "And just what is it I'm supposed to be looking for?"

"You'll know it when you see it. Something out

of synch. Hell, you know those people you work with better than I do. Just keep your eyes open. When the vibes aren't right, go to work. A question here, a raised eyebrow there. I think you know how that goes." He snorted. "Women! They're past masters at intrigue."

"You sound like a man who's been there."

"I have. I was married for five years." Nina detected a hard note of cynicism. It was reflected in his eyes, revealing a deep hurt. "I know the route."

"You *were* married?"

"Yeah. Divorced seven years ago. I got the kid. Peter. He's twelve. That should tell you something." He sighed heavily. "Oh, I know the games women can play."

Nina fell silent, resisting the urge to counter his wholesale condemnation. Instead she said, "I'm sorry things didn't work out. And Peter?" she probed, her intrinsic compassion coming to the fore. "What's he like? Tell me about him. How did he take the . . . divorce?"

"He's a tough kid. He was quiet for a while, almost like he knew there was no other way around things. But he's come out of his shell of late. Car crazy . . . listens to all that racket kids call music these days. He does okay in school." He shrugged. "He could do better. But what're you going to do? I'm not around as much for him as I should be."

His offhanded attitude didn't fool Nina. She saw the haunted light in his eyes, knew there was more— much more—to the story that he wasn't telling her. "Does she have a name?" she said. "Your former wife, I mean."

"Carla," he snapped. "C'mon, Nina, let's change the subject." He forced a smile. "Why should you be subjected to all this?"

Her eyes sparkled with a soft mischief. "We're partners, Dino, aren't we? Doesn't that go with the territory?"

"Does it?" he challenged. "So let's start in on *your* story. You're not married, I guess. At least I don't see any rings."

"No, never married," she replied with a faint smile. "I'm one of your hard-core career women. Too busy, I guess."

"Burned you good, huh? Afraid to put your hand back in the flame?"

"Okay, Dino, you win. Can we change the subject?" Her expression became cold. "It's time I was thinking of getting back. Another time, maybe."

"I hope so," he said softly. He reached out, pressed something into her palm.

"What is this?" she said, opening her hand to reveal a ten-dollar bill.

"Cab fare," he said.

He saw Nina to the curb, whistled a taxi down for her. His hand lingered on hers for just a split second longer than was necessary as he helped her inside. "Call me if you hear anything. Leave a message if I'm not in. Otherwise I'll give you a ring later tonight." His eyes burned hers. "I mean it. Scout's honor."

The cab pulled away from the curb. Nina sighed as she looked back, saw his figure swiftly grow smaller. She shivered lightly and was struck by an almost eerie sense of loss.

Poor guy, she thought sadly. It can't be any picnic for him. A single man, a cop besides, trying to bring up a live-wire son all by himself. Who took care of the boy while he was on duty? She hadn't thought to ask. Well, she decided, next time.

What was his ex-wife—Carla—like? Did she keep

in touch with Dino? Was there contact with Peter? What had caused the split? Something very unpleasant, more than likely, if Nina could judge from the abrupt bitterness that Dino Rossi had exhibited once the topic had arisen. Next time, she concluded, more than a little surprised at the interest she felt for the man. The mother of us all, Nina thought dryly, closing out her introspections.

From 12:30 to 1:00, the runthrough took place. Here all props and all sets were used, with cast, technicians, and directors on deck, utilizing the entire studio. Timing and final blocking were honed to split-second precision.

Following this there was a wild scramble to get into makeup and costume for the dress rehearsal at 1:45. Around the edges, the separate scene groups came together with their individual directors to do ''notes.'' This was perhaps the most creative hour of the day, as cast members, camera, lighting and sound crews exchanged ideas on every phase of the work they'd done up until then. All would contribute to the excellence of the final taping. One final time lines might be changed, interpretations shaded, set positions realigned. Different lighting angles, music, new camera angles—all were subject to scrutiny during these intense brainstorm sessions.

The dress rehearsal ran from 1:45 to 2:15. Again timing, lines, lighting, and camera positioning were major concerns. Each actor's face was checked on the monitors, the makeup, hair, and wardrobe crews taking notes feverishly. Angela's lipstick was too dark; Larry's bald pate needed more talc; Robin's dress called for a tighter pinning at the waist. The clock ticked inexorably on. The only thing that could go wrong now was a major line flub, or a camera or spotlight breakdown.

Now, at 2:30, after frenzied last-second fixups, came the final take. The video cameras began to roll. Every eye was on the set in use, either on the fringes of the set itself, or near the banks of monitors where Spence Sprague watched, his hands waving, gesticulating like an orchestra conductor's, his lips moving nonstop as he spoke into his mike, cueing the production people. Every iota of creative energy was totally focused . . . 2:45, then 2:50. They were on the home stretch. The last scene was Nina's surrender to carnal need . . . 2:55. Now, at long last, 2:58. The crawl—the slow progression of names, actors, producers, directors, writers. And bingo! At last 3:00 tripped over on the studio clock.

"Tapes are good—it's a wrap, gang!" Spence Sprague exulted with a chuckle, his shirt drenched with sweat. "Go pick up tomorrow's scripts."

Still, there were those who lingered to appraise their performance one last time, watching over the various directors' shoulders as the episode unreeled yet again (it would air three weeks later) on the monitors.

Nina McFall, after all these years of zero-hour tension, was drained, yet pleased; for her crucial interpretation of Melanie Prescott's breakdown had gone without a hitch. She received many compliments as she came off the set.

But the feeling of self-fulfillment was short-lived. As she entered her dressing room, her breath caught in her throat. Someone had been rummaging through the things on her dressing table. Bottles of perfume, cans of hair spray were scattered helter-skelter. What in the world? she thought, her brow furrowing.

Then she saw it. Her newest lipstick, the tip mashed, lay on the floor at her feet. Her eyes took in the crude scrawl of letters slashed across her mirror:

NINA, she read, DON'T STICK YOUR NOSE WHERE IT DOESN'T BELONG. UNLESS YOU WANT THE SAME THING GLADYS PARR GOT!

Nina gasped, caught the edge of her dressing table for support. Apparently someone had discovered that she was cooperating with the police. She felt suddenly cold; she actually shuddered. It hadn't occurred to her that she herself might be in danger. For the first time in her life, Nina felt real fear.

# Chapter Eight

Instantly, realizing what a damning indictment the bizarre message on her mirror would be if someone should walk in just then, Nina McFall ran to the door, closed and locked it—After the horse is stolen, she scolded herself. How many times had Ken Frost railed at the cast for neglecting to lock their dressing room doors?

But that was neither here nor there. If she'd locked the door, whoever it was would have just got the message to her in another way.

*Whoever it was.* The words echoed ominously in Nina's brain. Nobody had ever barged into her dressing room before, nothing had ever been disturbed. Who indeed? There were probably more than eighty people in the building—everyone from custodial to secretarial, from technicians to actors—all involved in putting together each episode of *The Turning Seasons*. Just where did one start to look?

First things first, she decided, grabbing a handful of tissues and scrubbing vigorously at the lipstick on her mirror. It took three batches to do the job. It was only after she had finished that it occurred to Nina that she should have tried to find a camera, taken a

Polaroid photo or something. Had the crude lettering been done by a male or female hand? She'd heard there were experts who could decipher such things. Well—too late now.

Her mind raced in an attempt to decipher the logistics of how her meeting with Rossi had been discovered. Robin and Rafe were the only ones who knew her routine had varied today. And she'd seen them go around the corner; there was no way they could have tailed her to The English Garden. So, who else among the cast or the production crew could have known she'd sneaked off to lunch with Rossi?

There could only be one answer. *She* hadn't been followed. Someone, perhaps an accomplice to a cast member, was watching Dino; there was no other way to figure it. Nina's puzzlement grew. Whoever it was had taken a huge risk, for shouldn't a cop be quick to tumble to the fact that he was being tailed?

She discarded the last of the tissues, stirring up the papers in her wastebasket to conceal the fire-engine–red mess. Suppose someone had followed Rossi to The English Garden, had been on the street watching when she'd gotten out of the cab and gone in. For all she knew, the person might have come in, watched them from another booth while they ate and talked. The grim possibility gave her a fresh case of shivers.

Now Nina checked the drawers of her dressing table, especially her handbag. There were no signs of tampering; the drawer was still locked. No, theft had not been on the intruder's mind. Nina breathed a brief sigh of relief. Though she never carried much cash, a thief could have a field day with her credit cards. The heartwarming little message had obviously been the only reason for the stranger's visit.

Whoever the interloper might be, Nina realized

that he or she had to be familiar with on-the-set routines. The intruder knew just when Nina McFall's dressing room would be vacant and for how long, and that Nina never locked her door. The person also apparently knew just when the majority of the cast members would be too intensely engrossed in rehearsal or performance to notice someone prowling about.

*Fingerprints!* Nina's head jerked upright. The lipstick! Instantly she lowered her eyes to the tube on the floor. Her heart sank as she saw that the case was wrapped in a piece of tissue. Smart, she conceded with grudging admiration. So much for Mickey Mouse detective work.

Rossi. Shouldn't she call him, tell him what had happened? Not yet, she decided. Get your head together first. Check things out.

Her heart still thumping, perspiration pearling her forehead, she took a stance in the middle of her cramped dressing room and turned with studied slowness, her eyes searching for—

What? Nina snorted impatiently. She didn't know. Had the intruder dropped anything, left telltale footprints on her beige-carpeted floor? Any respectable clue at all? Nothing. There were no signs whatsoever that anyone had violated her private space.

Her breathing slowly returning to normal, Nina sank into her chair, frowning in concentration. What would Dino Rossi do in her position? Ask questions, she supposed. But how could she do that? Whom could she talk to without arousing suspicions, blowing her feeble cover? To Robin, next door: ''Hey, babe, have you seen anything suspicious, anyone fooling around my dressing room?''

"No, Nina," she would respond. "Why do you ask? Has something been taken?"

"No, nothing like that. It's just that someone wrote a threatening message on my mirror."

Forget it. Interrogation was definitely out.

So what did it all mean? she asked herself. Was Rossi so close to paydirt that the murderer was running scared—and dangerous? Fresh shudders swept her. Could it be that the murderer had actually been on the set today, was somebody she'd rubbed elbows with perhaps only minutes ago? Or perhaps the murderer had an accomplice on the set, someone he'd told to sneak into her dressing room and warn her off. That was equally scary.

So how had this hypothetical person contacted his hypothetical accomplice? By phone, possibly. It occurred to Nina to approach Myrna in the front office and inquire about incoming calls to cast members. After a moment's thought, she discarded the ploy. Too risky. Myrna would be suspicious, or tell her it was none of her business. Perhaps it was best to wait, ask Dino Rossi what to do. But the idea of delay gave her the screaming meemies.

Just who could these two characters be? she went on, her mind tumbling nonstop. What could the linkup be?

Nothing came to her at first. Then she thought of Horst Krueger. But he hadn't been anywhere near the set today. Dino was way off base on that one. And besides, he and Dino would be finishing up their interview at this very moment. Ridiculous.

Who else? Business colleagues whom she knew nothing about, not even their names? If you really want to get off-the-wall, what about Robin Tally? Maybe something had happened during her writer's stint at Leatherwing that she'd deliberately kept from Nina, something so gross that she'd never been able to bring herself to share it with her closest friend, something that might drive her to such a drastic measure as murder. Oh, sure, she and Rafe had engineered the whole thing in plain view of Nina and the entire entourage. Now *that* was stretching things to the breaking point.

She branched out. How about ghosts from the past, like Marta Hollings, Nina's friend, whom Morty had dumped as mistress number forty-two last March? She still had friends on the set. Nina shook her head. Pathetic, frail, little Marta could leap the Chrysler Building more easily.

Angela Dolan came to mind. Rumor had it that Morty had lately been moaning about falling audience shares, the eternal TV-biz plaint, and saying that it would take a major infusion of younger characters on TTS to build them up again. And since Angela was one of the show's oldest mainstays, she must certainly feel threatened. A wry smile twisted Nina's lips. Yes, Angela was mean enough, but hardly smart enough.

She ticked off several other possibilities. Chet Kelsey had been head writer until two months ago, before David Gelber was moved up. A drinker, he'd pushed his luck one time too many. Justified though the firing had been, Kelsey was known as a volatile, brooding type. And while in reality it was pressure from Helen that had cost him his job, what better way to get back at his nemesis than to murder her loving hubby? No, too farfetched. Kelsey had climbed into a bottle, never to be seen again.

Of course, there were always Byron and Helen Meyer. Both, as Nina had admitted to Dino Rossi, had more than ample reason to plot Morty's demise. In the first place, both stood to inherit millions. Besides, Byron had always volubly resented the fact that his father treated him like a child, giving him no real say in Meyer Productions affairs. Who could tell what other grudges the pampered brat might have nursed?

As for Helen, Nina thought, perhaps a particularly gamy (and recent) dalliance of Morty's had finally pushed her over the brink. Why wait for Morty to die of natural causes before stepping into her share of the Meyer millions? Why shouldn't she lend a helping hand?

Nina discarded these speculations also. Both Helen and Byron had been too obviously devastated by the murder; it would have called for some truly top-drawer acting to bring up performances like those she'd witnessed on Saturday night, and that kind of talent they didn't have. Again, if such schemes festered in either bosom, they'd had all the time in the world to do Morty in, and in private. Where was the logic of doing it with forty guests present?

Abruptly Nina's dark ruminations ended. She was tired. She was sick of thinking about it, immediate threat or not. She would call Rossi, let him carry the ball from here on out. Yes, call. Right now.

She rose from her chair, testing her wobbly legs. There were pay phones down the hall. . . .

Suddenly she changed her mind. That's all she needed, to have someone, possibly the very person who'd left the message, overhear her talking to Rossi on the telephone. No, it would have to wait; she'd call from home. She sighed and began changing from her costume, a gray tailored suit, into her own clothes. She'd return the suit and blouse to wardrobe, pick up her copy of tomorrow's script from

Myrna, and be on her way. It was only 3:40; she'd be home by 4:15 at the latest.

Coming out of her dressing room—carefully locking it this time—she peered down the long hall. The emptiness and silence, the sight of so many closed dressing room doors stretching out of sight was suddenly unnerving. If her unknown enemy should jerk open one of those doors, confront her, drag her inside . . .

Nina shivered and walked faster, her heels making a sharp tattoo on the steel steps as she went down to wardrobe.

# Chapter Nine

Later that afternoon, the taping completed, Nina McFall stretched out on the custom-made curved couch in her palatial living room, enjoying the rich, soothing sensation of its raw silk pillows beneath her head. She had showered and put on her favorite at-home garment, a powder-blue crushed velvet hostess gown, and had artfully applied her makeup to create a "natural" look rather than the glitzy image of a soap opera star. Set off by the soft, loose waves of her red-gold hair, her face had a positively ethereal glow despite her tiredness. Thank goodness for pink blusher and lip gloss, she thought wryly, particularly after a long, hard day like this one!

Then, sitting up, she tucked her bare feet beneath her and reached for the crystal goblet of champagne on the chrome-and-glass coffee table by the sofa. As she sipped, she was very much aware of the ambivalent feelings at war within her. In the first place, she wondered about the wisdom of having invited Dino Rossi to her apartment. Equally disturbing were her conflicting thoughts regarding the subliminal motives that underlay the invitation.

Though ostensibly they would discuss this afternoon's dressing room episode, Nina would be less than truthful with herself if she denied the emotional cross-currents that had buffeted her ever since she'd met this disturbing man. It was less than forty-eight hours since their paths had first crossed. Amazing! And yet so much had happened; it seemed that she'd known him much longer, that he was a more important part of her life than she cared to admit. And while she told herself repeatedly to relax, that his impending visit was strictly business, she had a hard time making herself believe her own words.

All right, face it, she thought. She *was* interested, her initial antagonism to the contrary. Their brief working relationship, the effect of their undercover complicity, could not be denied. People get to know each other very fast in these situations.

And while we're being honest, let's go one step further. It wasn't the propriety of having Rossi come to her place that was foremost in Nina's thoughts. What was really worrying her was speculation about the impact her apartment would make on Dino. Would her luxurious, obviously very expensive surroundings, the white, peach and chrome Art Deco opulence, put him off? Yes, she *did* have designs on the handsome detective, vague and confused though they might be, and she wanted no distractions, now of all times. Men could be so foolish sometimes. Nina had no idea how much detective lieutenants were paid these days, but she was sure it was nowhere near what soap opera principals commanded. And if the woman was earning five or ten times as much as the man—if her super-elegant apartment rented at $5,000 a month—well, macho types like Dino Rossi could be easily spooked.

Just then the buzzer sounded, cutting her muddled thoughts short.

"There's a Lieutenant Rossi here to see you, Ms. McFall," the security guard said over the intercom.

"Yes," Nina said into the speaker. "Send him up. I'm expecting him."

It was 6 P.M. She'd contacted Rossi's office when she got home from the studio and left a message. He'd called back, and she'd briefed him on what had happened. "Can we talk about this, Dino?" she'd requested. "Everything's happening too fast for me. I'm—I guess I'm a little frightened." It was then that she'd asked if he could stop by, and he'd agreed.

As she waited for Dino to come up, she glanced around the apartment. Everything was, as usual, in perfect order—perhaps *too* perfect? The stereo was playing Rodgers and Hart. A small tray of hors d'oeuvres, glasses, and the ice bucket containing the open bottle of Dom Perignon were ready. There was no need to be uncivilized, she rationalized. After all, he *had* bought her lunch.

Her doorbell sounded, and Nina slipped her feet into satin slippers the same shade of blue as her robe. She glanced at her reflection in the large mirror that hung in the foyer, filled with sudden misgivings. Was the blue robe too seductive, too elegant? Should she have done something different with her hair? Oh, well, too late now.

She pressed the button that controlled the set of electronic locks on her front door, and Dino stepped inside.

"Ms. McFall . . . Nina . . ." he said, his eyes widening ever so slightly as he looked at her, then beyond her at the spacious room. "How—nice you look."

"Why, thank you. Please come in." As Nina re-locked the door, she smiled warmly at him. "I appreciate your coming, Dino, particularly on such short notice."

Normally at ease in any social situation, Nina felt undeniably tense, even awkward. Keep it light, she warned herself.

"I told you I would, didn't I?" he said brusquely, apparently almost as ill at ease as she was. He kept glancing around the room, then back at Nina. It was clear that both her apartment and her appearance had impressed him. "It's all part of our arrangement, remember?" he added.

"Were you followed?" she asked anxiously.

"Followed?"

"Yes. I told you on the phone, Dino. Somebody must have followed you this noon. How about now?"

He smiled patronizingly, as if calming an overimaginative child. "No, Nina. I checked, but I didn't see anyone."

"Are you sure?"

"Positive."

He moved farther into the room and stood with his hands on his hips, silently appraising the exquisitely appointed area. After a silence that lasted almost thirty seconds, he said, "Wow! This is really something. I've seen places like this on TV—that show about lives of the rich and famous—but I never thought they were for real." He went over to the picture window that took up most of the west wall and stared out at the magnificent view of the Hudson River, a rapt expression on his face. "Some view," he said, sighing. "Blows you away."

Nina smiled. "I'm glad you like it. I find it therapeutic at times. I just sit here and look out for hours—the sunsets are phenomenal. Won't you sit down . . . ? No, here," she patted a cushion next to her on the sofa, "so we can talk without shouting. Will you have champagne, or would you prefer something else?"

"Gin, if you have it. Martini, very dry."

Martini, very dry. I'll remember that, Nina thought as she fixed his drink, then poured some more champagne into her empty goblet. Sitting down next to him, she leaned over the coffee table and slid the tray of Brie, crackers, raw vegetables, and dip closer to him. Dino raised his glass in a brief salute. "Cheers," he said briskly. Though his posture was relaxed, there was a defensive quality about him that disturbed her.

"Cheers," she replied, feeling her heart sink. This damned apartment, she thought. It *is* turning him off. I was afraid it would.

"So"—he sighed, putting the glass down with exaggerated care—"you had yourself a little adventure today." He frowned. "So much for all those good friends you were talking about."

She made a face. "It looks as though one of them wanted to show me how much they care."

He quickly became all business. "Suppose you start at the top, Nina. Tell me every detail, right from when you returned from lunch. Try to remember everyone you talked to, every person who might have been hanging around the dressing rooms. Somebody had to be watching you from the moment you got back."

Nina matter-of-factly recounted the studio's typical afternoon routine. Other than a few clarifying questions, he let her talk without interruption. "And then," she concluded, "when I walked in and found that message on my mirror . . . I froze, went cold, even looked around, as if whoever did it might have been still hiding in the room.''

Rossi stared into space for long moments when she finished. ''You have to be right,'' he said finally. ''About somebody tailing me. There's no other way they could have discovered our working arrangement so fast.'' He took another sip of his drink, tried a cracker and some Brie. ''See anybody suspicious hanging around afterward?''

''No,'' Nina answered. ''It was late when I left—the place was deserted. Spooky, almost. I got out as fast as I could, raced home and called you.''

''Any ideas at all? Anybody acting strange?'' he prodded.

She shook her head. ''No stranger than usual. No, there wasn't anyone who was doing anything out of the ordinary. I don't have a clue. But it's obvious that you're being watched very closely, Dino, and now I've made somebody's list, too.''

She shuddered slightly, feeling an uncharacteristic urge to be comforted, to be cuddled like a frightened child. ''I'm scared, Dino,'' she admitted in a small voice. ''I guess I had no idea of what I was letting myself in for.''

Genuine concern ignited in his eyes. ''Do you want out?'' he asked. ''I was obviously wrong to get you involved. It could get messy, if today's any indication.''

Pulling herself together, Nina jutted her jaw out determinedly. ''No way,'' she insisted. ''I'm in for the long haul. I've never been a quitter, and I'm not about to start now.'' Her face became perplexed. ''But tell me, Dino—are you really close to solving the case?''

''Hardly. I'm just going through the motions, following every possible lead. Why do you ask?''

"Well, it just seems to me that whoever is behind these murders must think you've got some really hard evidence lined up. Otherwise they wouldn't be watching you, and trying to scare me out of cooperating with you."

"Guilt causes people to act dangerously irrational at times. I'm not knocking it, however. That kind of risk-taking could eventually work in our favor."

Nina became more agitated. "Dino, do you suppose that whoever was tailing you came into that restaurant with us, and we didn't even know it?"

"It's possible."

Nina grimaced. "That really gives me the creeps!"

"What about Angela Dolan?" Rossi said, taking a different tack. "You hinted at some feud between you. She wouldn't be a possible suspect, would she? What's the line on her?"

Nina quickly laughed off the daily game-playing that she and Angela indulged in, but told him about Angela's fears of being replaced by a younger actress.

"Is there a legitimate possibility that she'll be written out of the show? Would that be enough to give her ideas about killing her boss?"

Nina shrugged. "Everybody worries constantly about being written out—occupational paranoia. Audience share drops three points, and we all get the shakes. With Angela, it could be a serious thing."

"How about her love life? Has she got somebody on the string? She's still a very attractive woman."

Nina laughed, ignoring a fleeting stab of jealousy. "Oh? You noticed? No, Angela's unattached. She's a dedicated career woman—like me. She's not about to let some *man* mess up her tidy little existence. When she's not on the set, she sits in her luxurious apartment with her TV, her stereo and her three cats, playing show music by the hour. She's actually a frustrated musical comedy star.''

"So the threat,'' he repeated, ''of being written out could be like a shiv in the gut.''

"I guess so. But I don't think she's smart enough to engineer a murder—correction, two murders. She doesn't have the nerve.''

"That's why I asked you about the boyfriend angle. If a gal like that had some help . . .'' He switched the subject. ''What about that girlfriend of yours,'' he mused aloud, ''Marta Hollings, was it? You mentioned her on Saturday night. She was supposedly one of Meyer's back-street numbers. Any possibility at all that she could be back in the picture?''

Nina assured him that there wasn't, convincing him that Marta didn't have the courage necessary to pull the murders off. ''I did think of another person this afternoon,'' she volunteered. ''An alcoholic named Chet Kelsey. But he's very marginal, probably doesn't mean anything.''

"Tell me anyway.''

Again she briefed Rossi, downplaying the possibility of Kelsey's involvement. When she finished, he agreed with her evaluation, but wrote the name in his notebook just the same.

"And what did *you* find out today?'' she said. ''You said you were going to corner Horst and get back to the Meyers. Anything?''

"Not so's you'd notice. Krueger admitted that there'd been some bad feelings once upon a time, but said that over the years he'd learned to sublimate his distaste.''

"I see,'' Nina murmured. ''I never knew that any bad feeling even existed between him and Morty.'' She noticed that Rossi's glass was empty and lifted

120

it in a "want more?" gesture. He nodded, and she poured herself some more champagne as well.

"Well, no longer, or so Mr. Krueger told me. Time mellows, and all that. He was mildly amused that I even suspected him. As for his being close to Meyer when he fell, he says he noticed nothing. He swears he didn't do it." He nodded his thanks as she handed him a fresh martini. "So unless we come up with some stronger evidence, I'll be vigorously canvassing Meyer's contacts in the business community."

"What about Byron and Helen?" Nina asked.

"Well, that was awkward. Is Byron Meyer on the slow side?"

"In some respects. Not a moron, mind you, but not exactly swift."

"He was reasonable, after a fashion, and realized I was just doing my job. But Mrs. Meyer . . . How that man lived with her for fifteen years, I'll never know!" He paused. "You're not number one on her dance card, you know."

Nina smiled wryly. "I don't suppose anybody is. If she could stop the world and tell us all to get off, I'm sure she would. What's stuck in her craw this time?"

"I couldn't exactly pin it down—she was going off at so many different tangents. But the essence is that she thinks you're altogether too . . . assertive."

Nina noticed the hesitation. "*Pushy* was the word she used, wasn't it?" And when Rossi nodded: "She's right. I simply won't kowtow to Dame Helen, and she knows it. We've more or less agreed to disagree. She's tried to get me fired any number of times, but the fans like me for some reason. They'd scream bloody murder if I were written out. There's a little bit of union clout that enters into it as well.

No, Helen doesn't intimidate me. Although with Morty gone and Helen in charge, things could change in a big hurry. I guess I'll have to cross that bridge when I come to it.''

Nina was beginning to feel a little fuzzy around the edges. Apparently the champagne was going straight to her head. She'd have to be careful—nothing more unattractive to a man than a sloppy drunk.

"So?" she said. "What else did you learn from Helen, aside from her feelings about me?"

"A lot of second-rate theatrics—how could I ever even begin to question her devotion and loyalty to Meyer. The usual what's-the-world-coming-to buzz-sawing. Bottom line, Nina, is that I frankly don't think she did it, or Byron either." He grinned, saluted her with his glass. "Hey, you make a mean martini."

"Thank you, kind sir. Care for another?"

"No, I guess I'd better pass. I don't want to disgrace myself. I'm not what you'd call a hard-core drinker."

"I'm not, either," Nina said. "But after what happened this afternoon, I feel I have a few coming." And it's not every day that I have such interesting—and handsome—company to drink with, she added inwardly. She stood up. "As a matter of fact, I think I'll just have a drop more champagne. . . ."

"Okay—you twisted my arm. As long as you're up, might as well fix me a short one."

Upon returning to the sofa, Nina determined to sip her drink slowly, to bring things back into focus. "By the way," she said, lowering herself carefully onto the sofa, "do you have to check in at headquarters or anything? The phone's there, to your right. . . ."

"No." Rossi smiled, displaying even, white teeth. "Enough is enough. I'm signed out for tonight. If anything comes up at home, Mrs. Bartolucci knows where to call."

"Mrs. Bartolucci?"

"My housekeeper. She lives in, rides herd on the kid. She's like a second mother to Peter."

The reminder of Rossi's domestic situation and his unhappy past jarred Nina momentarily. In an effort to brush away the intrusive thoughts, to disarm the idiotic little fantasies that kept popping into her mind, Nina forced her thoughts back to practicalities. "And so we're still on square one. I thought things would move much faster than this. With so many murders going on in the city, how do the police ever clear up any of them if each one takes so long?"

"Some of them are pushovers. But this one's different—too many important, highly placed people. We can't lean on them the way we do with other suspects." He smiled, his eyes locking with hers, holding that extra second. Nina felt strange—giddy, all at once.

"Be patient, Nina. It's not the only case I'm working on, you know. And it's only been two days. I'll keep asking questions until I'm hoarse, then I'll ask some more. We've got forensics experts trying to pin down where that poison came from, how it could have been administered without Meyer tasting it or anyone noticing."

"I'm not exactly looking forward to going to work tomorrow," Nina admitted. "Not that I want out, you understand. I'm just a little—nervous."

"Play it by ear. Don't take any unnecessary risks. Keep in touch. And by no means go off playing detective on your own. Leave that stuff to me and my men. If anything happened to you, I'd never forgive myself." Nina's heart seemed to swell until it felt huge in her chest. When she was unable to come up with a flip reply, an awkward silence ensued. Then abruptly, out of nowhere, in a foolish attempt to fill the gap she blurted out the most inopportune words of all: "Dino?" she asked in a quavery, smoky voice. "What is your ex-wife like?"

His gray eyes seemed to darken, to become opaque. "You really want to hear about Carla?" he said, his voice hard, flat. "What's to tell? We were married. And we aren't anymore." He looked away and took a hefty swallow of his drink.

"I'm sorry, Dino. I shouldn't have asked that. I just thought I'd like to know more about you. It's really none of my business."

His smile was tinged with bitterness, but it was a smile all the same. He knew Nina was embarrassed, and that bothered him. That bothered him a lot. He shrugged. "No harm done, Nina. It happened; there's no reason why we shouldn't talk about it. It was just one of those things. Happens every day, in divorce courts all over the country. Carla didn't love me as much as I loved her, I guess. She got too— anxious."

"What do you mean by that?" Nina blundered on, unable to let it go. "Anxious how?"

Dino rested his elbows on his knees, leaning forward in a hunched, seemingly defeated pose, turning his glass between long, tapered fingers. Staring at the floor, his voice muffled, he told her the whole story. It was a familiar tale—about the hard working ambitious husband and the restless, impatient wife. Rossi had dropped out of his second year of business administration at NYU. Borrowing ten thousand dollars from relatives, he opened his own business, a wholesale shoe outlet. But when racketeers attempted to muscle their way in, he pulled out, ate his losses—and those of his relatives. Becoming a police officer seemed to be the most appropriate means of getting revenge. He graduated with honors at the police academy and became a beat cop, moving his way up in the PD echelons.

"I guess I was one of your typical horny kids," he said, "and maybe I married Carla for all the wrong reasons. But at the time it seemed like a super idea; I was sure I was in love with her. I was twenty-four, she was twenty-two. I'd known her since we were kids; her family and mine went back a long way. One of those arrangements, you know."

They had a child, Peter, a year later, and life quickly became boring for Carla. In her eyes, her husband was going nowhere fast, destined to be a flatfoot the rest of his life. Not only that, but his dedication to his job had changed him; he was dour, preoccupied, no longer fun to have around.

And then one day he came home early, to find her in bed with another man. Though furious and heartsick, he forgave Carla—until the next time he caught her cheating. That time he filed for divorce. Peter was six at the time.

Two months later, in the midst of final custodial negotiations, Carla was killed in a car crash on her way to yet another assignation. . . .

"Crazy," he said, avoiding her eyes, "but I haven't talked about it to anyone since it happened. And now, with you, a complete stranger . . . I just let it all hang out." His emotions warred dangerously on his twisted features, and he drew in a deep, trembling breath. "Sorry. I didn't mean to dump on you. I told you, I don't drink much. Must be the booze talking. . . ."

Nina had all she could do to keep from reaching out to him. "It's all right," she whispered, her heart aching. "Sometimes it's good to let things out, or they can eat us up from the inside. I feel privileged that you chose to tell me, that you didn't shut me out. And I'm *not* a stranger. . . ." She lost control momentarily. Her voice almost breaking, she said; "Dino . . . I don't want to be a stranger. . . ."

Good Lord, she admonished herself, get hold of yourself! What's wrong with you, anyway? A patsy, that's what you are. Anybody comes along with a sad story, and over the edge you go.

When she could speak coherently once more, she said, "And how did things . . . your life . . . go afterward?" she said, testing her voice warily. "How did you . . . and Peter . . . cope?"

"A day at a time," Rossi replied, realizing how precariously close to full breakdown he had come. "Peter, of course, was devastated by his mother's death. I hadn't told him about the divorce, that we were breaking up. He was too young to understand. I haven't told him to this day. As far as Peter's concerned, Carla was a saint." His voice blurred slightly. "He was just a little kid . . . such a little kid. . . ."

Compassion filled Nina. "Are you close?" she asked. "Do you have time for him? *Enough* time?"

"Not as much time as I'd like. I feel guilty about it, but I do the best I can. As you know, I *do* have this damnable dedication to my job—that's basically what started the trouble between me and Carla. Even now, no matter how hard I try, I know I sometimes lose sight of what really matters most. Sometimes I get so scared . . . when I see that terrible loneliness in Peter's eyes. . . ."

His voice broke then, became ragged, and he turned away from Nina in an attempt to hide his emotions. Moving almost without her own volition, she reached out for him, put her hand on his shoulder, gently turned him to face her. And when she saw the bleakness in his eyes, the way his mouth was set in a grim line as he fought for control, she drew Rossi toward her, astonished at how yielding that big, hard body was. Sympathy for the man overpowered her. She needed to give him comfort, take away the pain.

His dark, curly head fell against her shoulder, slid into the concavity there just above her right breast, seeming to burrow into her flesh for solace. As abruptly, Nina felt the muscles of his back stiffen. Hardheaded male, he musn't surrender to such womanish grief. But Nina's arms held him, holding him close to her soft warm body.

"It's all right, Dino," she soothed. "It's all right. Don't go away. Let me help, if I can. . . ."

She wasn't sure when the subtle transfer occurred, when she was no longer the earth mother, granting comfort to a grieving child. All she knew was that suddenly she was in his arms, pressed tightly to his hard, muscular chest, feeling the insistent pounding of his heart that echoed that of her own.

She was amazed at the mind-obliterating sense of comfort and completeness she felt as she lay wrapped in his arms, breathing in his masculine scent, as she felt him gather her more closely to him, his fingers caressing her shoulders and back in involuntary expression of physical need. She felt him tremble, heard his breathing becoming harsh and rapid.

She raised her face to his, her lips slightly parted, her eyes closed. Then he kissed her, tentatively at first, then fiercely, greedily. Their lips fused, clung,

127

became molten, as if they were seeking desperately to consume each other.

Nina's eyes filled with tears as Rossi continued to kiss and caress her, and she surrendered willingly, pressing her body almost greedily to his. It seemed her very bones would crack from the ardor of his embrace, yet she wouldn't have exchanged that sweet pain for anything in the world. So long, she crooned to herself, it's been so long. It can't be wrong, it isn't cheap. "Yes, Dino," she whispered. "It's all right. Yes, touch me there . . . !"

"Oh, God, God!" His words were a throaty, strangled cry. "Nina," he muttered, "You're beautiful, so beautiful—I can't help myself!"

"It's all right," she repeated breathlessly.

Then Dino was standing up, lifting her in his arms. "Where?" he gasped.

She nodded toward her bedroom, her arms entwined around his neck. She was amazed at his strength, at how small, how utterly helpless she felt at that moment. It was a feeling she'd never had before.

Now he was moving through the bedroom door, gently depositing her on the bed. . . .

# Chapter Ten

Nina was alone in her dressing room. It was 7:30 in the morning of the following day. Sitting at her dressing table, a cup of black coffee in her hand, she stared at her image in the mirror, daring anyone to knock on her door. Just the least bit hung over, she knew it would be rough to face first call in thirty minutes. Until then, coffee and more coffee. Trespassers will be violated. She smiled wanly at her feeble attempt at humor. And just what, she asked herself wonderingly, was last night all about? There had been no chance to talk to Dino this morning— He'd been gone when she'd awakened sometime near 2:00 A.M. What, exactly, had triggered last night's minor forest fire? Short rations? she questioned caustically. Too much to drink? Right on both counts, she supposed. But that wasn't all there was to it, at least not on her part. She had never gone in for one-night stands—she respected herself too much for that. But what about Dino? Had she been the latest in a long line of women Dino Rossi loved and left? The thought made her cringe.

Lord knows, Nina's life was complicated enough already. Did she need Dino Rossi in her life? Here she was, a TV personality known to millions of soap opera fans across the nation, a soap queen with tons of lines to learn, a woman whose life had been threatened yesterday, who was in the thick of twin murders. The last thing she needed was a messy love affair.

She combed her fingers through her hair and slumped forward dejectedly. How had she come so totally unglued?

What must Dino be thinking, experiencing at this very moment? Guilt? Remorse? Hardly. Tough cop type that he was, he'd probably be gloating, congratulating himself on his easy conquest. Another notch on his bedpost. Women and cops—pushovers every time.

Nina groaned aloud. Dino, you bastard! To take advantage of me that way . . .

And in the next breath, No, put the blame where it really belongs. It takes two to tangle, remember? Who was it, actually, who set the whole thing off? Dear God, what must he be thinking?

In the dark, lying in his strong arms, her face pressed to his broad chest, she had told him about Clay, about the years of celibacy that had followed. Her exact words had been, ''You're the first man in all this time . . .'' What a chuckle he must have gotten out of *that* weary warhorse!

Tears welled up. Damn it, she raged, it's true! There have been no others. I'm *not* easy! I don't believe in casual flings!

She dabbed at her eyes, trying not to smear her mascara all over her face. It was the old, old story—''Will you respect me in the morning?'' And how would she find out, since he'd faded into the night like some gypsy rover?

Another twist of the knife. What about their

newly established working relationship, their so-called partnership in crime-solving? Would last night compromise that? Could Rossi ever take her seriously again, seek out her input and counsel after she'd fallen into bed with him so readily?

No, she railed inwardly at the injustice of it all, he can't let last night change that. She *wanted* to be involved in the murder case, wanted to help discover whoever it was who'd killed Morty Meyer and Gladys Parr. In spite of her trepidations, her fear for her own personal safety, she'd actually been enjoying her new role of amateur sleuth. She'd never dreamed their ''partnership'' would evolve into a love affair.

*Love*? she repeated. *Who said anything about love*? Who needed love, if it left you feeling like this? She was content just being the famous Nina McFall, soap opera queen; that was enough for her—wasn't it? She didn't need any more emotional involvements, Dino Rossi and his problems notwithstanding. I don't want to be in love with anybody, she told herself vehemently. I'm happy exactly the way I am. And if I do need someone in my life, it will damned well be someone I get to know gradually, someone I can trust, someone who doesn't desert me in the middle of the night.

Which made Nina feel even more miserable. Her confusion multiplied. She didn't really know *what* she wanted. Oh, Dino, why don't you call? she agonized. Can't we talk, straighten all this out?

Oh, goddamn men anyway!

''Good news, gang,'' Spence Sprague announced as the cast gathered at 8:00 for the day's first line rehearsal. ''Early call tomorrow. Everybody be ready to go at seven bells.''

A chorus of groans arose. "Why?" a dozen voices called.

"We've got a funeral, remember? We pay homage to our dear departed boss and mentor. As a gesture of our solidarity and family unity, Dame Helen has commanded that we *will* appear at Brinston and Hedges Mortuary on Madison Avenue, at eleven tomorrow morning. There will be a reception—I figure we'll lose two to three hours at least."

The protestations were more muffled now, but were protestations just the same.

"So we'll do a little crowding today, dispense with a rehearsal here, a rehearsal there, see if we can stay on schedule," Sprague went on. "Tomorrow will be a bitch, and you all know it. Everything we can clear today, the better off we'll be."

With that, he plunged into the group line rehearsal, the hurry-up tension already obvious in his voice. No mention, Nina noted, had been made of the hapless Gladys Parr. What would happen to her? Would she, perhaps, bury herself?

As she waited for her scenes to come up, scanning lines feverishly to make up for precious hours squandered last night, there was still time to look about at her fellow actors. Robin smiled at her from across the circle, obvious concern in her eyes. She'd apparently noticed that Nina wasn't in top form.

In particular, Nina sent covert glances at Angela Dolan, indulging in further speculations about the woman. Was there even the faintest possibility that she could be involved in the murders? Yesterday's ruminations had fermented overnight, providing increased cause for concern. Angela could, after all, have an ally that Nina didn't know about, someone who could do the real dirty work for her if pointed in the right direction.

Nina even gave Spence Sprague a hard look. Dino had mentioned questioning him yesterday. Spence had been very quick to point the finger at others when his own possible motives were challenged. Maybe he deserved watching, also. Sprague was cynical and short-tempered. His tongue could peel varnish when he was crossed, but he was more bluster than brawn. Nina did a quick mental rerun of what had happened when Morty had inveigled TTS principal Wilma Gorman out of Sprague's bed into his own, all in a matter of two weeks. Instead of fighting, Sprague had simply caved in. Still, when Morty had tossed Wilma back, Sprague had seen to it that a gradual write-out of Wilma's character was commenced. Wilma, still dazed from Morty's rejection, had never known what hit her.

Nina felt a sudden chill down her spine. Why, she thought, didn't I remember that cute complication before?

She caught herself up short. Why was she bothering with speculations like this now? Most likely, after last night, her involvement with the case was at an end.

Abruptly her ponderings were interrupted by Sprague himself. "Wake up, McFall," he snapped. "Show time, honey."

The day roared into high from that moment; there was no time for further thoughts of her tempestuous night with Dino Rossi. Business with a capital H, for Hurry.

Now, her lines out of the way, the group breaking up, Nina was following Nick Galano into the studio to run the actual scene. Bob Valentine trailed along behind.

As she came into the vast arena, stepping carefully over the welter of TV and sound cables, which

133

resembled myriad, slithering snakes, she was once more struck with the enormity of this dream factory in which they daily transformed fantasy into reality. The heel of one of Nina's pumps caught between two cables, causing her to step out of her shoe. As she leaned on Valentine's shoulder while replacing it, she happened to glance upward along the black, light-deflecting screens that hung from the second level. She saw canted sound panels. Still her eyes climbed to the third level, taking in a vague impression of balconies, catwalks, cables, and girders. Then the black, vaulted dome gave way to total, impenetrable darkness, and she could make out no more.

All this, she marveled, just to put out a soap opera. The gods *must* be crazy.

They came to the long alley of shallow booths where tacky, budget-built depictions of scenes stood face-to-face across the cable-cluttered aisle, or back-to-back, with doors, windows, and flats doing double duty when necessary. The outer wall of the boardroom set was painted to represent a street exterior. A door announcing the entrance of Luigi's Italian Restaurant served as an exit from the kitchen set on the opposite side.

"Half-sets" of the Allender living room, the garage where Billy Hinton eked out an honest living for his grasping, unappreciative family, a grocery store, the office belonging to the high-powered Melanie Prescott—all these and more stood waiting for the magic of the cameras, the appearance of glamorous actresses and handsome actors to spark them to life. Now, however, under the dull glare of the work lights, the sets were revealed in all their tackiness. The walls of Melanie's office were a prime example. Constructed of rough canvas over plywood, spray-painted a doughy gray, the "take wall" boasted a single, bargain-basement Utrillo print. Her secondhand desk, with an arrangement of fake flowers on it and a chair behind it, took up one corner. The infamous couch and another artificial plant occupied the other. It all looked so cheap, so fake. And yet, once the cameras dollied in, once the steamy action of these "everyday" lives rolled, it became a veritable temple of dreams.

"Okay, kids," Galano broke into her reverie, "let's block out today's action and take a peek at tomorrow's while we're at it. Strictly aftermath, with Melanie trying to gloss things over with Gregg, while Gregg sees a chance to pull a few creepie-crawlies of his own. Okay, Nina. You're sitting behind your desk, your head in your hands, unable to face yourself after what you've just done. . . ."

Cinema verité, she thought bitterly. It all comes back to haunt you.

There was a break around 9:30, and despite her misgivings about her status as inside contact for Dino Rossi, Nina seized the moment, seeing it as a golden opportunity to implement a plan that had been in the back of her mind since yesterday afternoon. If she struck out, so what? It was certainly worth a try.

Shaking off her mild hangover, Nina feigned a cheerful demeanor as she entered Myrna Rowen's office, an inner sanctum just behind the reception area. Myrna was the show's general secretarial slavey who spent most of her time screening calls the receptionist couldn't slough off, typing out the eternally changing shooting schedules, the sign-in sheets, photocopying, and passing out the daily scripts, minor payroll, and such. An amiable kid, Myrna had "soap" in her eyes also, and finagled like a bandit whenever there was an "extra" call.

Thus far she'd played in three full episodes, and dreamed of a slide-in someday.

Realizing that networking was the name of the game, Myrna was always friendly and accommodating to every member of the standing cast. You could never tell who might whisper vital advance notice in her ear. And yet she was cautious—there was no end to the unauthorized privileges the opportunistic principals tried cadging from her. In short, she had a sixth sense when someone tried a con, as Nina knew full well.

"Morning, Myrna," she said brightly, sinking into a convenient chair. "What's happening?"

"Nothing much, Nina," Rowen said, her eyes wary. "How are things going back there? Everybody all excited about the early call tomorrow?"

"Absolutely delighted. Funerals are our favorite thing. I suppose you were drafted, too."

"Everybody. Camera, audio, the whole nine yards. The receptionist is the only one excused."

"I suppose Helen can't force us to go, but . . ."

"She can make it darned unpleasant if we don't," Myrna finished with a grimace.

"Do you suppose Byron will call the roll? It'll be just like being back in first grade." And then, concluding that this was warmup enough, Nina said, "By the way, Myrna, did I get any calls yesterday after lunch? I was expecting word from a certain Mr. Wonderful—I gave him the inside number. I was sure he'd follow through. You didn't slip up on any messages, did you?"

Myrna was momentarily perplexed. "Not that I can recall," she said. "But I'll check."

Nina watched intently as Myrna opened the second desk drawer on the right side, withdrew a log book, and studied it. "Gestapo stuff," she grumbled. ''They demand that we record all this, to see who's abusing phone privileges.'' Then with a bright smile, ''No calls for Ms. Nina McFall.''

It was all Nina could do to restrain herself from asking point blank, or seizing the note pad from Myrna's capable hands. ''And do we?'' she asked.

''Do we what?''

''Abuse the privilege. Pass out the inside number too freely.''

''Not really,'' Myrna said. ''There are a few, but for the most part . . .''

Nina raised an eyebrow. ''For instance?''

''It's best that I don't mention names,'' Myrna said primly.

''Well, like yesterday afternoon, for instance. How many calls came in?''

''Why do you want to know?''

Nina assumed her most artless expression. ''Just curious. I wouldn't want my guy getting caught in any traffic jams.''

Myrna Rowen shrugged, pulled out the pad again. ''Slow day,'' she said. ''Only four all afternoon.''

And right after lunch? Nina was dying to ask. Someone must have called in early to alert her dressing room vandal. But she restrained herself. Instead she rose and sighed melodramatically. ''That's what you get for counting chickens. Thought I had a live one. How quickly they forget!''

*Clever*, she congratulated herself as she breezed from the office. Just right. How could Myrna even begin to be suspicious of a stellar performance like that?

During the lunch-hour crush, as Myrna trotted back and forth into the studio on last-minute errands, Nina found it easy enough to sidle into her office. Her heart pounding, she darted behind the desk and pulled open the drawer. The pad was lying right there; she didn't even have to pick it up.

Instantly her eyes scanned the entries, paying special attention to the times noted. *Angela Dolan, Rick Busacca, Valerie Vincent.* All three calls were between 12:30 and 1:30; thus all could be considered suspect.

She barely escaped the office in time. She was on the stairs, heading up to her dressing room, when Myrna came around the corner a mile a minute, waved gaily at Nina, and disappeared into her office. Nina loosed a sigh of relief.

All through a light lunch at Corrigan's Pub, with Robin chattering a blue streak, Nina was distracted. She sifted the names through her mind again and again. Who, of those four, could have invaded her dressing room yesterday afternoon and left the grim warning? Even more disturbing, which one of them had already been given or would shortly receive an update on last night's activities, and move accordingly? What if someone had been watching her apartment building, had seen Rossi enter at 6:00 and leave during the wee hours of this morning?

"Are you listening to me, Nina?" Robin interrupted plaintively. "If you could just help me decide. The blue dress at Saks is a dream, but there's a pink one at Bloomie's I like, too, with a kind of a cowl-turtleneck effect. Very smart and . . ."

Nina nodded and tuned out again. Of the three, only Angela Dolan was on Dino's suspect list. Rick Busacca hadn't the vaguest connection to anything. And as for poor, haggard little Valerie Vincent, forget it. She'd more than likely forget to return any call she received.

But even so, where had each of them been yesterday afternoon? Could Nina figuratively place them as she was taping that last scene? They all had reason to be upstairs; the dressing rooms, male as well as female, were in the same wing. It would take no real cleverness, in the midst of the end-of-day rush, for someone to slip into her room. Who would have been paying attention, after all?

Angela Dolan returned to mind. He case would certainly require careful thought, and some further snooping. Who did Nina know who'd ever gotten close to Angela? She'd have to ask Dino how to approach a thing like that . . .

Abruptly the sick pain was back. *Dino*. Where was he, anyway? Was he going to drop her, just like that?

"Nina?" Robin Tally was waving her hand in front of her face. "Hello? Are you in there?"

And when Nina pulled herself out of her daze, "What is it, hon? Something wrong with the food? You've hardly eaten a thing. You don't look well. Have a bad night?"

Nina smiled tiredly. "Yes," she said. "Bad night. Hardly slept a wink." Don't ask, Robin!

But Robin wouldn't let it go.

"Problems, Nina? Tell old Aunt Robin."

"Who, me? Problems? No more than anybody else on the set. The murders have got me down, I guess. I can't seem to stop thinking about them."

"Same here. Wouldn't you think the police would have figured it out by now? I keep looking around at all these people, wondering which one of our old buddies might have done it. I'll bet everybody else is doing the same thing. It drives me crazy."

"I know what you mean," Nina agreed with a weary sigh. She wished the damnable day was over.

When I get home, she told herself, I'm going to crawl into that shower and never come out. She picked up her check and rose. "I think it's time we got back to Happy Acres. The nice people there are waiting to slide us into our cute little rubber suits."

"But aren't you going to eat *anything*?" Robin protested.

"I'm really not hungry." Nina headed for the cashier. "Come on, Robin. Let's go." She had more detective work to do—the hell with Dino Rossi!

Almost immediately after returning from lunch, Nina ran into Angela coming from her dressing room. "Angela, darling," she said on the spur of the moment, "did you want to see me about something yesterday afternoon? Someone told me you were looking around in my dressing room."

Catch the suspect off guard—that's how they do it in mystery novels. Watch her eyes, the way she moves her hands. Things like that can reveal a lot about a person.

Angela wheeled around—regal, strikingly beautiful, fresh from wardrobe and makeup. "Why, Nina," she cooed fatuously, "whatever would I be doing in your dressing room when I have a much *nicer* one of my own? Besides, I was with you all afternoon. Why go upstairs looking for you?" Her teeth, all perfectly capped, flashed in a distinctly mocking smile. "Besides, how would I get into your dressing room when you weren't there? You *did* have it locked, didn't you, dear?"

There was no wavering of that brilliant blue gaze. Angela's hands never fidgeted once. Nina felt deflated, but she didn't back down. Matching smile for smile, she said, "Tsk, tsk, Angela—pull in your claws. You just might scratch yourself. Perhaps I was misinformed, if you say it wasn't you. Sorry to trouble you. Oh, and Angela,'' Nina couldn't resist adding, ''better check your makeup. Your false eyelashes look a little crooked to me.''

As Angela scuttled back up the stairs to her dressing room, Nina grinned. Score one for the home team!

She tried a similar approach later with Rick Busacca, but without the sarcasm this time. Again there were somewhat mystified denials—no incriminating body language, no guilty looks.

Next on Nina's list was Valerie Vincent. For a long moment after Nina spoke, the girl was mute, avoiding Nina's eyes. ''No, Nina,'' she said at last, ''I was nowhere near your dressing room yesterday afternoon.'' Then, regaining some composure, she added, ''I talked to you in the morning, remember? Why should I have been looking for you in the afternoon?''

Nina shrugged elaborately. ''That's what I was wondering. But the fact is, someone came into my dressing room while I was taping, and I heard it was you. You're absolutely positive it *wasn't* you?''

Valerie's pale eyes widened, registering—what? Astonishment? Fear? ''I—I don't know what you're talking about. What's wrong? Was something stolen?''

''Oh, no, nothing like that,'' Nina said quickly. ''I believe you, Valerie. Sorry if I upset you.''

Valerie stared at her for a brief moment, then, her gait somehow awkward, turned and disappeared into the studio.

Nina looked after her, frowning slightly. The girl had seemed upset, all right. Had she been lying? Or was she just generally jittery because she was unwell? Nina tucked those questions away for future pondering.

Because of the funeral, Spence Sprague announced that they would skip dress rehearsal and go directly to the final taping. Immediately after that, the cast would be given tomorrow's scripts, have half an hour for lightning study, then proceed to abbreviated line rehearsals on the upcoming episode. "Everyone on your toes," he bellowed. "With total cooperation we can make this work and not get off schedule by so much as one goddamned hour. Move it, now. Places!"

His crude pep talk accomplished its purpose. The taping went off without a hitch. Sprague was generous with his praise. The cast was flushed, proud. Weary as they were, all were almost eager to plunge into the next day's pages. With any kind of luck, they could tape Wednesday's work immediately after the funeral and reception, which would give them the rest of the day off.

Nina was especially bushed. The events of the preceding night had definitely taken their toll. As she sat alone in an isolated part of the studio, studying her script in a director's chair situated near the edges of the mini-amphitheater, she nearly dozed, waking herself once when her head actually began to nod. Tired as she was, it never occurred to her to be concerned for her own safety. There were too many other things on her mind.

She was doggedly focusing her eyes on the script, going over a particularly troublesome line, when she heard a muffled clatter overhead. Technicians, she thought, dismissing it.

"Look out!" a male voice to her right boomed suddenly. She became vaguely aware of a faint

142

rushing sound. Instinctively Nina leaped out of her chair in response to the jarring outcry.

Just then a one-foot section of I-beam, a piece of ballast normally used to anchor floating flats, whizzed past her, missing her by mere inches. Forty pounds of torch-cut steel hit the right arm of her chair, shearing it off as if it were so much paper, then struck the concrete floor with a solid *whump*! The impact, felt through her feet, set up jarring reverberations in the pit of Nina's stomach. For a moment, she thought she was going to faint.

She screamed once, then began to sob, collapsing into a shuddering ball in what was left of the chair.

"Jesus H. Christ!" Spence Sprague stormed as he ran over to her. "Those things are supposed to be wired down!"

"It was," Rick Busacca said as he squatted to examine the piece of I-beam. "But it almost looks as though someone took a wire cutter to it."

Nina strained every nerve to regain her composure. She struggled to fight her mounting hysteria as well as she could. Watch, she commanded, almost as if she were out of her body, looking on from the sidelines. Be alert. This is crucial.

As she stared about her, bringing all the faces into focus—everyone was there—she realized that Angela Dolan, Susan Levy, and Valerie Vincent, along with Rick Busacca, had been among the very first to reach her side. So none of them could have been upstairs, cutting the ballast wire.

It was Valerie who held her in her arms, crooning, "There, Nina. There, now. It's going to be all right. It was just an accident. You're going to be just fine. . . ."

What in Heaven's name, Nina asked herself, is going on here? If they're all here—

Then who had been up there?

An hour later, Nina was alone in her apartment, staring absently into space. Robin and Rafe had just left, after bringing her home and making sure she was really all right. Robin had volunteered to stay the night, but Nina had declined her offer. Alone— she needed to be alone. Otherwise, how would she ever get her head straightened out? She had to think, or rather rethink the entire situation.

Somehow she must have dozed as she sat on the sofa, for dazedly, as if coming out of a drugged sleep, she thought she heard the phone ringing. She jerked up, glanced at the Tiffany clock on the mantel. It was 7:10. Apparently she'd slept for a long time.

Dino, she thought immediately, her heart leaping. Yet, stricken with ambivalence, she delayed picking up the phone. She both did and didn't want to talk to him. She was desperate to tell him what had happened, desperate to have him hold her in his arms again, protect and comfort her. But on the other hand, his neglect of her all day after last night's encounter continued to rankle. Though she'd narrowly escaped being killed, it was her wounded pride that was bothering her now. She'd be damned if she'd ask Dino for help and protection when he'd treated her so badly!

Still, she decided she had to answer the phone. If it *was* Dino, he might come over uninvited, and she just wasn't up to dealing with her mixed feelings about him in a face-to-face confrontation. She picked up the receiver.

''Hello?''

There was a strange buzzing sound in the ear-piece, like a dial tone yet somehow different.

"Hello?" she repeated, becoming annoyed.

Then a gravelly male voice spoke. "Now will you lay off, McFall? Will you get it through your thick head that we mean business?"

"Who—who is this?" she gasped, but there were no more words, only a soft *click* as the line went dead.

Trembling violently, Nina dropped the receiver onto its cradle as though it were red-hot, then sank back onto the couch. In spite of her terror, her mind was churning rapidly. There was no way to identify the caller from his voice, but couldn't phone calls be traced? What if she called the phone company? Maybe they could tell her at least where the call had been placed. . . .

But before she could do so, the phone rang again. Anger mingled with fear as she snatched the receiver and shouted into it, "Listen, you creep . . ."

This time it *was* Dino. "What's going on?" he demanded brusquely. Nina went limp with relief. "I called the studio, and they told me you'd gone home early. Something about an accident. What happened?"

Breathlessly, Nina told him about the attempt on her life and about the phone call she'd just received.

"I'm coming right over," Dino said grimly. "You're in no shape to be left alone."

Glad though she was to hear the concern in his voice, Nina still refused. She wasn't prepared to face him tonight, no matter what. She needed to rest, to think. Yes, she would call him first thing in the morning. They could discuss the whole thing then. No, she did *not* want him to come over. She was perfectly safe—what could possibly happen to her in her own apartment with its burglar-proof locks?

Finally, realizing she was not to be budged, Dino gave up. "But call me immediately if there's any further trouble," he insisted, sounding annoyed. "I'll be at home. You still have the number?" Nina did. "Good. Keep it by the phone where you can get it at a moment's notice. I won't call again tonight, so I advise you to screen all calls with your answering machine." He paused. Then, "You're sure you don't want me to come over? My housekeeper's here with Peter."

Firmly Nina said, "I'm sure. I'll be fine, Dino, really I will. We'll talk in the morning."

After they had hung up, Nina decided to fix herself a light meal and go to bed early. Nervous exhaustion plunged her immediately into a deep but far from restful sleep, in which dreams of Dino alternated with nightmares of falling steel, and an unseen hand wrote garbled messages all over her walls—in blood this time, not lipstick.

# Chapter Eleven

Mortimer and Helen Meyer were not affiliated with any particular religion. Therefore Morty's funeral service was conducted in the plastic-fantastic, non-denominational chapel at Brinston and Hedges. The clergyman who officiated apparently specialized in the fabrication of only the most finely spun cotton candy, which had no more to do with reality than *The Turning Seasons* did.

To Nina's mind, he said nothing that anybody—certainly not Nina herself, coming as she did from a conservative Roman Catholic parish on Madison, Wisconsin's west side—could derive any sort of comfort from, provided one needed comforting. Tedious platitudes and clichés, the broadest of generalities, were all delivered in mellifluous, brain-numbing tones. Nina wondered if perhaps the preacher had been supplied by Central Casting.

The chapel was packed with show-biz, government, and business dignitaries. These, plus a few Hollywood executives, were shoulder-to-shoulder with the cast and production crews of the various shows under the aegis of Meyer Productions. The casket was almost totally obscured by floral sprays,

147

wreaths, and blossoming plants. As Nina glanced about the room, appraising the mourners, she noted with no surprise that there was not a wet eye in the house.

Helen Meyer, flanked by Byron and a mixed bag of assorted relatives, had shed her tears previously. Today, a patrician among the serfs, Dame Helen retained her dignity. No widow's weeds for her. Beautifully got up in a silver-gray designer creation that emphasized her still-trim figure, a black straw hat with a heavy veil, and matching silver-gray pumps, she looked every inch the grande dame and played the role to the hilt.

Nina couldn't help feeling sorry for the woman, despite her airs. Though Morty had been no prize, the couple had been together for fifteen years. For putting up with Morty that long, she deserved every consideration and sympathy. And picking up the pieces of the Meyer Productions empire wasn't going to be easy, especially since Byron would most likely be totally useless. She'd need all the help she could get. Nina, for one, given the chance, would do her part.

Nina started as she saw Dino Rossi standing in the back. Their eyes locked briefly, then darted away. She had phoned him earlier that morning at her apartment, and they had agreed to ignore each other at the funeral so as to carry on the fiction of their noninvolvement. But Nina had accepted his dinner invitation for this evening. Just the thought of being alone with him again gave her an extreme case of the jitters. How would he handle it after that craziness Monday night? How would she?

Nina had awakened shortly before dawn and had frantically gone over the day's lines. Little by little she'd managed to control the fear that had followed the attempt on her life and the threatening phone call. Later, at the studio, as frenzy became hysteria, she moved through the abbreviated rehearsals like a robot. Under the circumstances, she felt she'd done remarkably well. The cast would return to the studio for one last hour after the services for the final take, and Wednesday's episode would be history.

But there had been a definite distance between Nina and some of the cast this morning. Though on the one hand everyone expressed warm concern for her well-being, on the other, Nina got the impression that no one quite knew what to make of yesterday's "accident," as the incident with the falling beam was officially being called. But there were those, like Rick Busacca, who weren't buying the accident theory. Nina saw unspoken questions in many pairs of eyes—if it had actually been a murder attempt, why had Nina been singled out? And when might the attacker strike again, and at whom?

Now Nina looked over at Byron Meyer. He still looked very rocky—Helen seemed to be supporting him rather than the other way around. Nina found Byron's obvious agitation puzzling, considering what she knew of his character—or lack of it.

Two rows ahead, almost directly behind the Meyers, she caught a glimpse of Valerie Vincent, looking paler and puffier than ever. Yes, the child had to be ill, unless she indeed *was* on drugs. Remembering Valerie's kindness to her yesterday, Nina felt a surge of sympathetic concern.

To her right and several rows ahead, Nina spied Angela Dolan, funereally dressed in a dark blue suit.

Suddenly everything went into fast-forward, revving up to a kaleidoscopic blur. *Who* had dropped that lethal piece of steel? Nina shriveled inside, imagining the phantom stalking her in the studio's upper reaches, moving stealthily in the gloom until he (or she?) could get a clear angle on the wide-open target she had unknowingly provided.

She'd previously eliminated virtually all her major suspects among the cast and crew, but had the murderer(s) recruited outside help? How could an outsider be smuggled into the studio without being seen?

Through the fire doors, of course. Someone was always propping one or another of them open for quicker access to the street at lunch, or at day's end. It would have been no trick at all for an intruder to sneak into the building and climb into the flies, especially during the confusion reigning on the set yesterday afternoon. All the person had to do, after installing himself in the crow's nest, would be to wait until his obliging victim stationed herself where he could draw a bead on her.

And once the grisly deed was done, in the ensuing confusion and uproar, what could be easier than slipping out the same way the attacker had entered?

But still, Nina decided, under the circumstances, it definitely *had* to be an inside job. The timing had to be precise, the attacker had to know exactly where he was going in the dark, rambling upper stories of the vast soundstage. No total stranger or hired hit man would be so familiar with the studio layout. No doubt about it, someone in the TTS "family" was masterminding the whole thing, and that person had to be guilty of complicity in the double murders, even if he (or she) had not actually done the deeds.

Now as Nina's eyes unglazed, she saw the funeral home personnel putting up a screen to conceal Morty Meyer's casket. A heavyset, sweaty-browed man appeared to announce that the mourners were all invited to a reception, to be held in the Dorchester Hotel's Somerset Room beginning at 12:45 P.M. All wishing to pay respects to the family were respectfully requested to . . .

The interruption didn't completely exorcise Nina's introspections. Had the attempt on her life really been that? she mulled as she threaded her way out of the chapel between Robin and Rafe. Or should it be taken as another warning? Maybe they'd *intended* to miss her. Someone had to be running very scared indeed to believe that she knew anything crucial about the murderer's identity.

"Shall we walk?" Robin said as they emerged from the funeral home, jogging Nina's elbow to get her attention. "It's only five or six blocks. Such a lovely day—the exercise'll do us good. We can do a little window shopping on our way over."

The lure of a free meal and the availability of excellent liquor, combined with a chance to catch up on some high-powered gossip or wrap up a choice business deal proved irresistible, and the spacious reception room was jammed. It seemed to Nina that there were more mourners at the Dorchester than had been at the services.

The buffet was elegant and bountiful, and so was the bar. The guests enthusiastically availed themselves of both. The prevailing keynote seemed to be, "Last chance to stick it to old Morty."

Which, Nina decided, was the saddest of epitaphs.

Even after a weak vodka-and-tonic, Nina remained subdued. She spent her time observing, her tension causing her to read menace into every move the honored guests made. Off and on, her gaze returned to Valerie Vincent, who was sticking close to Coletta Haney and Bob Valentine. Why, she wondered, did she feel so protective of the girl? And why, in spite of this feeling, did she still harbor a nagging suspicion that Valerie had indeed been in her dressing room?

Then her attention was distracted by Angela Dolan, who was deeply engrossed in animated conversation with Horst Krueger. Animated? Any closer and she'd be in his pocket. Perhaps, Angela, Nina thought, her eyes narrowing, I've been underestimating you—and Horst as well. Though Ken Frost and Dave Gelber were in the group, Horst and Angela were concentrating exclusively on each other. Her eyes overbright, her smile slightly askew, Angela held a half-finished Manhattan in one hand, possessively touching Krueger's elbow with the other. It was obvious she was on her way to being sloshed. I'm glad I'm not playing any scenes with you this afternoon, Nina thought wryly.

She couldn't help being amazed at seeing Angela acting like a starstruck schoolgirl. Imagine Angela Dolan condescending to bestow flirtatious smiles on a mere man! Granted, they did make an attractive couple, Horst so tall and lean, and Angela's aristocratic, blond svelteness playing so smartly off that hard, craggy masculinity. . . .

Quickly the matchmaker glow faded, giving way to suspicion. If Angela and Horst were an item, perhaps there were unfathomed motivations to be considered. Another country heard from.

Nina's train of thought was abruptly derailed as she watched a stern-faced Spence Sprague come over to Angela just then, forcefully removing the cocktail glass from her fingers. "Enough, little girl," he said, employing his pet phrase for Angela. "You've got some heavy declamation to do this afternoon." Ignoring her protests, he added, "Take charge of the wench, Horst. See that she gets some food into her."

Nina's attention was distracted from this little scene when she saw Helen and Byron Meyer coming toward her.

"Enjoying yourself, Nina?" Helen said, her lips forming a gargoyle smile. "Everything up to your usual high standards?"

Nina was surprised by the open antagonism in the woman's tone, and thought for a moment that Helen, too, had had too much to drink. "I'd hardly use the word *enjoy*, Helen," she said guardedly. "It's not that kind of an occasion." She reached out and touched Helen's hand impulsively. "I'm very sorry about Morty. Things won't be the same without him." Which was true—she hoped they'd be better.

"Spare me the crocodile tears," Helen snapped, shaking off Nina's hand. "I know there was little love lost between you . . . between the entire cast, for that matter, and my beloved Morty. You're all just going through the motions."

"That's not so, Helen. Where in the world did you get an idea like that?"

"I'm not entirely stupid, Nina. Now that he's gone, I'm getting an entirely new angle on the way things were going at the studio as far as Morty was concerned. He should have fired the whole lot of you long ago."

Nina glanced at Byron. And I'll just bet I know who's been bending your ear, lady, she thought. Vengeance is mine, eh, sonny? Byron forced a vapid smile, looking straight into Nina's eyes. My turn now, his look said. Nobody brushes off Byron Meyer and gets away with it. But Nina kept her temper in check. "Helen, you can't mean what you're saying," she soothed. "You're understandably upset; you're letting your emotions cloud reality." She sent Byron a beseeching look that said, Take her home; don't let her make a fool of herself before everybody. Byron, however, only continued to smile.

"I'm in perfect control!" Helen Meyer flared. "More in control than I've been for a long, long time. And I'm telling you right now, Ms. McFall, that if you and the rest of the cast thought things were difficult in the studio when Morty was in charge, you haven't seen anything yet."

"Please, Helen," Nina said, noticing that others were staring, "we had no problems with Morty. He wasn't even in the studio very much. Believe me, you're mistaken."

Helen's eyes narrowed. "I heard about your little . . . *accident* yesterday. Or at least, that's what it's being called. But I have my own ideas about it, and I wouldn't be surprised if someone had a score to settle with you, considering your outrageous behavior. Don't think I don't know about you and Morty, and that you've tried to seduce Byron as well. Oh, yes, he's told me all about it!"

Nina could only gape at her, too stunned for words. So Helen thought Nina had been one of Morty's playmates, and Byron had apparently regaled her with his own version of how things stood between himself and Nina! She felt positively ill, then enraged. But she managed to control herself.

"What a cruel thing to say, Helen," she said softly. "And untrue, besides. There was never anything between Morty and me, and as for Byron, the idea is simply ridiculous."

But Helen didn't seem to hear. "Just watch your step," she snapped. "And I'll be watching, too. One false move, and you'll find yourself back on the street—where you belong, if the truth were known!" With that, Mrs. Mortimer Meyer turned on her heel and strode purposefully away, becoming swallowed up by the crowd.

"Please, Byron," Nina said to Helen's lingering stepson, "take her home. She'll be so ashamed of herself later. If she goes popping off to others the way she has to me . . ."

"Aren't you forgetting who's in charge now?" Byron said with a smirk. "I think that Helen can say and do exactly as she pleases. She *is* the new head of Meyer Productions, in case it still hasn't registered." His tone turned insinuating. "And when it's all over, Nina, and you find yourself out on your ear, remember who offered to help you the other night, and remember who was too busy playing Mother Superior to listen." His eyes took on a dark cast. "You had your chance, Nina. It's too late now."

Nina stood frozen as she watched Byron swagger over to join his stepmother. Had the whole world gone crazy?

At 7:40 P.M., Nina and Dino were seated at a table in a secluded corner of The Quatrefoil, a posh West Side restaurant. Nina, very hungry, had ordered a generous cut of prime rib, and was in the process of demolishing the last of it. She looked up with a quizzical smile, wondered when, if ever, Dino was going to refer to their night together. So far, the subject had been studiously avoided by both. And if Dino wasn't going to mention it, she certainly wouldn't bring it up. Instead, she said, "Speaking of funerals, what ever happened to Gladys Parr?"

"She's gone," he replied matter-of-factly. "Her

family . . . an uncle in White Plains, I think . . . finally claimed the body. She was buried yesterday.''

''Poor thing.'' Nina sighed. ''What was the final determination as to the cause of death by your medical examiner?''

''I thought I'd mentioned that previously. Just as I suspected the night we found her body on the rocks, she died from skull injuries. Someone bashed in her head with an unknown blunt instrument. We still haven't found the murder weapon. She was dead a good hour or so before she went over the cliff, or so the ME estimates.''

''And the reason she was killed?''

''Your guess is as good as mine. Somebody wanted something she had hidden in her cottage, no doubt, but we won't know what it was until we corner the person or persons behind all this. They forced her to tell them where it was, I suspect, and when they got what they wanted, they finished her off.''

Nina grimaced. ''What a horrible way to die!''

A momentary pause ensued. Then Nina gave Rossi a brief rundown of the weird developments at the funeral reception. ''I just can't believe that Helen could have said the things she did,'' she finished. ''It was *unreal*.''

''And you think your run-in with Mrs. Meyer has something to do with the murders?'' Dino said, a touch on the patronizing side, which annoyed Nina. ''I tend to go with your original premise—that the shock of her husband's death has put her temporarily over the edge. Either that, or one drink too many. She'll probably call to apologize tomorrow, you'll see.''

''*Helen* apologize? They'll ice-skate in hell first!''

Nina frowned. ''Then you're attaching little if any significance to her behavior this afternoon?''

''Frankly, I attach more to your item about Angela Dolan falling all over Horst Krueger. That's something I can get my teeth into.'' He paused to eat more of his steak—a porterhouse, well done.

Nina's ears perked up. ''Really?''

''I've discovered that Krueger's been doing a bit of investing in the stock market—commodity futures, stuff like that, something no amateur should ever monkey with. He's lost some very big bucks in the past six months. Would you believe four-hundred thousand?''

''My goodness! I had no idea Horst could afford investments like that. But where does Morty enter into it?''

''Pressure was being brought to bear on Krueger. The only out was doing business with his friendly neighborhood loan shark. Faced with a no-win situation like that, he hit up Morty for the money. And Morty turned him down cold, all but laughed in his face. Truth of the matter is that Morty was a bit 'overextended' himself. You've heard of Screen Features?''

Nina nodded. ''It's one of the new production companies. Aggressive as all get-out. Was Morty involved with them?''

''He was offered a healthy piece of Screen Features. Apparently it was too tempting a proposition to pass up. Trouble is that Screen Features was in financial hot water as well, and Morty got caught holding a lot of worthless paper. Given time the company will recover, but until then . . .''

''Fascinating! I thought that Morty was too smart to get caught in a crack himself. Where did you learn all this?''

Rossi shrugged. "We hear things. A friend of a friend who knows this lawyer and that one. At any rate, I got Krueger to admit it just this afternoon. Of course he insists that was the end of it; it never went any further. Only I happen to know better."

"What do you mean?" Nina pressed.

"I don't have this part of it solid yet, but I will by late tomorrow. Sam Corwin's flying in from China at noon, and I've set up an interview for three. You know who Sam Corwin is?"

"I haven't the foggiest."

Sam Corwin, he explained, was one of NYC's best known "greenmailers," a specialist who infiltrated well-established companies, engineering takeovers. Getting wind of Mortimer Meyer's temporary financial insolvency, he'd moved in for the kill.

When Corwin had confronted Meyer with his offer, Morty had thrown him out of his office. Thus, a mole was needed, someone inside the Meyer organization, to relay daily temperature readings. Enter Horst Krueger. Corwin had offered to bail Horst out, loan him the necessary funds plus the prospect of healthy stock options if the deal went gold in return for insider cooperation.

"But would Horst murder Morty over a thing like that?"

When the alternative was financial ruin, Rossi emphasized, Krueger very possibly would. In addition to that, Morty had uncovered Horst's involvement with Corwin. But instead of firing him, he'd enlisted him as a double agent. Back in Morty's confidence again, there had been ample opportunity for Krueger to do some plotting of his own, to set Morty up. With Morty dead, only Helen and Byron would be in Corwin's way, and they'd be sitting ducks; the company would fall to Corwin within two weeks.

"And Angela?" Nina broke in. "Where does she fit?"

"Well, assuming she's playing house with Horst, this works to her advantage, also. If she's stewing over the possibility of being written out of the show, she might be more than willing to become his contact on the set, and try to scare us off." He smiled broadly, verged on rubbing his hands. "I tell you, a few more days and we'll have this case sewed up. Once I hit Corwin with the news of the murder and tell him his stoolie buddy's involved . . . Oh, he'll be most cooperative, I assure you."

Nina's confusion grew. How, she wondered, do detectives ever keep all their information straight? "That's it?" she asked. "You're just writing off the possibility that Byron and Helen Meyer might be mixed up in this? Whatever happened to that open-minded approach detectives are supposed to have?"

Again that amused, patronizing smile. "I'm not writing anything off, Nina. But right now the Krueger angle has to take top priority. I appreciate your interest and concern, but—"

Noting the gathering storm clouds in Nina's eyes, Rossi changed the subject. He reached across the table and gently laid his hand over hers. "How did it go last night, Nina? Did you have nightmares? I hardly slept, thinking of you going through all that alone. I . . . wish I'd never let you get involved." A strange, yearning look sparked in his eyes. "But then, if I hadn't, I'd never have gotten to know you"—he seemed to be floundering—"as well as I have."

Nina was in no mood for pussyfooting. "Why don't you just come out and say it, Dino?" she said quietly. "What you mean is we wouldn't have gone to bed, isn't that right?"

159

"Nina, please. You make it sound so . . . Like something premeditated and . . . crass."

"Well, wasn't it? In your eyes anyway? A one-night stand? You didn't even have the decency to say good-bye. You crept off like a thief in the night! Wham, bam, and no thank you, ma'am!" She shook her head and pulled her hand away, fighting back quick tears. "Oh, Dino, if you only knew how much that hurt."

He said nothing, only stared down at the table. Finally, "I know, Nina. I've been kicking myself ever since. It wasn't one of my finer moments."

"Then why did you do it? After I told you everything, about . . . Clay, and about the fact that you were the first man I'd been intimate with since he and I—"

"I don't know. I was just all messed up inside. It all happened so fast—it was all so *good*. You were so loving and beautiful and upfront." He paused, fought to regain control, remorse visible on his face. "I didn't want to hurt you . . . get hurt myself. I knew I was in over my head, because I *cared*. And I didn't want to care, not ever again."

He looked up, his dark eyes searching hers. "I acted like a jerk, Nina, and I'm sorry. I'd give the world to undo the damage. Can you ever bring yourself to forgive me?"

Nina didn't flinch from what had to be said. "You were thinking of Carla, weren't you? Admit it—you were comparing me to her. And because I—was so incredibly—easy. . . . You tarred us with the same brush, didn't you?"

He didn't speak for a long time. "I—I guess I did, Nina. God, I'm sorry! I knew I was one-hundred percent off base, but I did it just the same. I was all

160

mixed up, crazy with wanting you—and *not* wanting you. And then . . . Oh, hell, let's drop it!''

''Then what? Dino, tell me,'' Nina pleaded.

''That place of yours, all that glitzy stuff, stuff I could never afford in a million years. That high-powered job of yours. Where did I get off thinking I could fit into a situation like that? A dumb cop, for Christ's sake!''

Nina released a tremulous sigh. ''Here we go again. Men! Dumb Neanderthals! You're all alike.'' Now she took his hand, clutched his fingers fiercely, looking deep into his eyes. ''Oh, Dino, she *did* hurt you, didn't she? She undermined you, tore you up so badly, in so many different ways. When you have to resort to fussing about trivial things like that—''

''Maybe trivial to you, but not to me. The way I was brought up, the man is the head of the house, and the woman lives on what he brings in. Prehistoric, okay, but that's the pattern. And if I couldn't hold on to Carla, who came from sort of a deprived background to start with, what chance would I have with someone like you, with *your* standard of living?''

Nina wanted to laugh and cry all at the same time. This was absolutely ridiculous! Did all men think like that? From bed to marriage, in one fell swoop? After one night together? She took a deep breath. ''Tell me something, Dino,'' she said. ''Am I still on the team?''

He frowned, perplexed. ''Team?''

''Yes—are we still working together on this case? If I told you that the other night was just a fluke, that I honestly and truly *don't* fall into bed with every guy I meet, could we still be—friends? Partners?''

He was slightly abashed. ''Partners? Well . . .

sure. I never said anything about changing our working relationship.''

''And our other relationship? Do you see any future for us there?'' she asked softly.

''I don't understand all this stuff, Nina. I just know I'm crazy about you. If you can't see that, then . . .''

''Crazy about me? You sure have a strange way of showing it!''

His face twisted as he sought to come up with the right words; he spread his hands placatingly. ''Hell, Nina, I think I'm falling in love with you. What else can I say?''

Nina could hardly believe her ears. She didn't know whether to laugh or cry. ''You *think* you're falling in love with me? What's that supposed to mean? Can't you be any more definite than that?'' Her lips curved into a teasing smile, the words rising above the happy clamor in her heart.

His voice thickened. ''I *do*, Nina. What happened the other night . . . it wasn't just a one-night stand, even if I did cut out on you. Believe it or not, I *cared*. I cared so much—it's the first time I've cared in years. You think you're the only one who's been going without? And when I really care for someone, I want to say, 'I love you.' ''

Nina's heart melted even more to see how difficult this declaration was for him. ''In my own crazy way, honey, I think I love you. And until I'm surer than that . . . until we're both sure . . . that'll have to do. That's about as close to high romance as I can get.''

Nina touched his lips fleetingly, resisting the impulse to lean toward him for a kiss. ''Oh, Dino,'' she breathed, her spirits soaring, ''that's close enough for me!''

162

* * *

It was as Nina returned from a trip to the ladies' room that an unsettling thing happened—a non-event, in all probability, but upsetting just the same. As she came around a small copse of tall, dense ferns and headed for the table where Dino was preparing to pay the check, she happened to glance to the right, to one of the tables against the shadowy west wall. She saw a most unattractive man, swarthy, dark haired, wearing a rumpled white suit, who appeared to be watching Rossi intently.

When the man looked up and saw her, his quick return of attention to his half-finished meal was too obvious to be ignored. Or was it? Paranoia again, she wondered, working overtime?

Had the man followed them to the restaurant? Nina pretended to ignore him, proceeding to her table. But it couldn't be. She and Dino had both checked repeatedly on the way there to see if they were being followed, and not once had they seen anything to cause suspicion.

Forget it, she told herself as she and Dino headed out the door. She decided not to mention the mystery man to him. He'd only say her imagination was working overtime. By the time they reached Rossi's car, she'd put the man out of her mind.

They were quiet as they drove back to the Primrose Towers on Riverside Drive, Dino obviously still shaken by his just-completed soul-baring and Nina anxious about what would transpire when they reached her apartment.

Should she invite him in? How would she handle it if she did? More to the point: Why the ambiguity? If she was as crazy about Rossi as she thought and he was as crazy about her as he said, then why was there the least question? They would embrace, kiss, take up where they'd left off on Monday night; it was as simple as that. Just the thought of being in his arms again, his hard body pressed against hers, his hot lips devouring her mouth, made her pulse race.

When he parked and insisted on seeing her to her door, Nina's tension mounted. She imagined the drowsy, gentle conversation, the endearments, those first tentative touchings . . . Just the same, she kept the conversation light as they rode up in the elevator and approached her apartment door. She felt absolutely light-headed by the time she surrendered her key and watched him insert it in the lock.

"I feel lousy about last night," he muttered as he opened the door, "leaving you alone the way I did. I should have come over, no matter what you said, stood watch on the street myself. I'd plant one of my men outside your door around the clock, but I don't have anybody to spare right now."

"Really, Dino, it's not necessary," Nina assured him. "I was all right then, and I'll be all right now."

"Maybe I'll just hang out across the street for a while, make sure nothing happens," he suggested.

Or you could spend the night, Nina thought but did not say. If you do, I know exactly what will happen!

"I want you to know I'm not taking any of this lightly, Nina," he continued. "I'm worried about you."

"I appreciate that, Dino." She took a deep breath. "You can worry about me much more comfortably inside." Her voice was seductively husky. "Coffee? A nightcap?"

He avoided her eyes. "I don't think so. I've got a lot of paperwork to take care of—and some heavy thinking to do, about you and me. If I came in, you know as well as I do that neither of us would get anything accomplished.''

''On the contrary,'' Nina teased. ''I think we'd accomplish a great deal!''

Suddenly Dino drew her into his arms and kissed her. It was a violent kiss, hard, almost brutal, expressing more directly than words his pent-up desire, and Nina responded as passionately. She felt herself going limp in his arms—then he pulled away, breathing hard, battling for control.

''I'll call you tomorrow,'' he said huskily. ''Let you know the latest developments. Take care of yourself, and don't take any unnecessary risks.'' He touched the tip of her nose, a rueful smile on his face. ''When this damn Meyer mess is over, we'll be able to concentrate on each other for a change.''

''Mmmm,'' Nina sighed. ''I'd like that very much.''

He waved once at the elevator, and then he was gone. Nina closed and locked her door behind her, wandering dreamily into the living room. It was going to be a long, lonely night.

# Chapter Twelve

Where the headache came from, Nina didn't know. She blamed it on the day's frantic pace, the residual tension from Helen's astounding and unwarranted attack at the reception following Morty's funeral, and the increasing pressure she'd been under since the murders and the attempt on her life. And then there was the necessity of learning tomorrow's lines—she hadn't even glanced at the script. Whatever the reason, shortly after Dino left, her head was splitting, and a quick search revealed not one aspirin in her medicine cabinet. In desperation, Nina made herself a cup of herb tea, but it had absolutely no effect—if anything, it seemed to make her head throb even more unbearably. There were no two ways about it. If she expected to be able to concentrate on her lines, she'd have to go out in search of an all-night drugstore.

It was past midnight, Nina was startled to realize, and she was not about to prowl the crime-ridden streets of upper Manhattan on foot. Even if her neighborhood drugstore around the corner on Broadway had been open—it wasn't, due to a fire that had demolished several stores on the block—

she would have taken her car. As it was, she'd have to get the Mazda out of the underground garage and drive around until she found an open drugstore. ''Don't take any unnecessary risks,'' Dino had said. Well, this was a *necessary* risk, Nina decided, and actually, the element of risk was very small. The elevator would deliver her to the garage, where security personnel were on duty night and day, and once she was on the street, she'd be only one of thousands of drivers cruising New York's ever-wakeful streets.

She briefly considered changing out of the sea-green silk dress she'd worn to dinner and putting on something more casual, but it seemed just one more effort that, in her pain-wracked state, she felt unable to make. Throwing a lightweight cashmere jacket over her shoulders and tying a Hermès scarf around her aching head to conceal her distinctive red mane (so much for impenetrable disguise, she thought wryly), Nina left her apartment, locking the door securely behind her, and headed for the elevator.

Piloting the Mazda down Riverside Drive a few minutes later, as a cool, fresh breeze off the Hudson blew through the car's open windows, Nina began to feel a little better. Driving had always relaxed her but, New Yorker that she was, Nina preferred to hop into a taxi or avail herself of the studio limo to get from one place to another rather than contend with endless traffic jams. Tonight, however, the Drive was relatively empty, and on impulse, Nina turned north, heading uptown on the West Side Highway rather than south toward Broadway. The sight of the moon and occasional lights twinkling along the Jersey Palisades reflected in the black waters of the Hudson had a soothing effect on her. Her paranoia easing, Nina didn't even bother to check for a possible pursuing car.

For the first time in days, she felt free, unconfused, unafraid. And her head was definitely feeling better by the minute. As she drove, passing Fort Tryon Park and the Cloisters, then admiring the jeweled span of the George Washington Bridge, Nina sank into what was almost a trancelike state.

It was only when her headlights picked up a sign saying YONKERS that she realized how far afield she'd gone. She left the highway then, aware of a sudden sharp twinge of pain in her head which reminded her of the reason she'd gone out in the first place, and after driving around aimlessly for a few minutes, she spotted a small, almost deserted shopping center. The only establishments still open at this hour were a pizza parlor, a restaurant, a bar, and, Nina saw thankfully, a drugstore some distance away, at the end of a row of darkened stores. She parked the Mazda next to a cluster of cars near the restaurant, got out, locked her door, and headed briskly for the pharmacy.

Once inside, she quickly found the section she was looking for and picked up a large bottle of extra-strength headache remedy, then, remembering she needed several other items as well, added toothpaste and facial tissue to her collection. As she came out clutching the bag containing her purchases, she noted that there was not another human being in sight. She snugged her jacket more tightly around her and started for her car. She had just stepped off the sidewalk and was crossing the parking lot when, to her left, a dark shape seemed to materialize out of nowhere. A rapidly moving automobile, its lights extinguished, was hurtling toward her at top speed.

Nina's breath caught in her throat, stifling a scream. For a moment she froze in her tracks, too terrified to move. Then, galvanized into action, she leaped aside with only seconds to spare. She actually felt the car's back fender lightly graze the backs of her thighs.

"Dear God!" she gasped. Someone *had* followed her, and that same someone was trying to kill her!

Her terror multiplied a hundredfold as she saw the brake lights of the car flash to life, heard the squeal of rubber. Then, motor roaring, power steering shrieking, it executed a wide arc and started for her again. Nina began to run. If she had been in any condition to think clearly, she would have made for the brightly lit safety of the drugstore, but in her terrified confusion she darted around the corner into the service alley that ran behind the complex, desperately seeking some place to hide.

She heard the car screech around the corner after her in hot pursuit. Nina's high heels (if only she'd changed her shoes!) beat a frantic tattoo on the asphalt; her breath was a scorching fire in her chest. Behind her, she heard the car's engine drawing closer. Ahead she saw the dark, brooding shapes of dumpsters and, with her last ounce of strength, sprinted to conceal herself behind them.

Suddenly Nina's heel caught in a crack in the pavement and snapped off, wrenching her ankle with a white-hot stab of agony. She fell to her knees. Wildly scrambling to her feet, she hobbled painfully behind the nearest dumpster.

Momentarily safe, Nina sucked in air, struggling to control the panic that consumed her. Peering cautiously out from her hiding place, she saw that the car had sped right past her. But even as she watched, it skidded into a sharp turn and started back down the alley. Now the lights came on, and her pursuer slowed to a virtual crawl, searching for his victim.

Heart pounding, Nina tried to reconstruct in her mind's eye the layout of the building in the shopping center. If she remembered correctly, the dumpster behind which she cowered ought to be in back of the pizza parlor—or maybe it was the restaurant. If only she could reach the back door, just a few feet away—if only the door wasn't locked—if only she could get somebody's attention . . .

She had somebody's attention, all right, but not in the way she'd hoped. The car had stopped, and Nina heard the echoing "thunk" of a car door closing. Her attacker was going to pursue his prey on foot, and with her injured ankle, there was no way Nina could escape.

But her terror was only beginning. As she heard the soft, stealthy tread of footsteps moving toward her, the automobile began to move again, to the end of the alley where it stopped, becoming an effective roadblock. Seconds later, the headlights went out. There were two of them! If she'd had any insane hope of somehow evading the first man, that hope died instantly. She was cornered, no doubt about it.

What could she possibly do? she thought frantically, on the verge of total hysteria. Take her chances, run for that door, pound on it, scream? The possibility of raising anyone was slim; nobody would be likely to be in the back room at this time of night.

Driven by desperation, she pulled off her other shoe and held it in her trembling right hand, the heel extended like a spike. She might be outnumbered, but she wouldn't be taken without a fight! Again she listened, heard the low thrum of the idling car engine, the rasp of shoe leather on asphalt coming closer, closer. Cautiously, she peered around the corner of the dumpster.

In the dimness of the alley, Nina couldn't get a clear view of the stalking man at all. He wore a billed cap, a dark windbreaker, dark pants. His face was completely hidden in shadow. Quickly, she withdrew—but not quickly enough. Even huddled as she was in the deepest shadow she could find, the stalker caught sight of her and headed in her direction.

Nina dashed, limping, toward the next dumpster, her breath raw in her throat. Instantly the headlights flicked back on, the car's engine revved up, and it moved inexorably toward her. It swerved close to her, missing her by inches as she darted behind the garbage receptacle. She glanced up and for the first time caught a glimpse of the figure behind the wheel. Her blood froze in her veins. Though she couldn't see the driver's face, she definitely recognized the rumpled white suit. There could be no mistake. It was the same man, the man from the restaurant! Before she could recover from the shock and try to plan her next move, Nina heard the crunch of gravel behind her. She gasped, whirled, saw a dark shape bearing down on her. She screamed as his hand closed on her shoulder, dug in, spun her around.

With all her strength, she lashed at the hand with her pump, the sharp heel chopping into flesh. Her assailant's bellowed curse and cry of pain rang in her ear as he released her, clutching his injured hand.

Then she was up and running, screaming with all the force left in her lungs. She heard the man running behind her, heard the car's engine roaring. Suddenly one of the doors in the alley swung open, and a husky six-footer, his arms loaded with empty boxes, emerged. The scene before him stopped him cold. He saw the running, wild-eyed woman, the man in full pursuit, the car moving in for the kill.

"What the hell?" he roared. "What're you guys doin' out here?" The boxes tumbled to the ground, and the man strode toward Nina. From the corner of Nina's eye she saw her would-be assassin wheel, stumble toward the car. A moment later he was inside, and with the squeal and stench of burning rubber, the car blasted down the alley and disappeared around the corner.

"Miss," her burly savior gasped, "what the hell's goin' on? You okay?"

It was all Nina could do to keep from bursting into grateful sobs. But she managed to control herself sufficiently to say, "Yes—yes, I'm all right. It certainly was lucky for me that you came out when you did!"

"Yeah, guess so." The man looked at her, taking in Nina's dress, torn and spattered with blood, the heelless shoe on one foot, the other shoe clutched in her shaking hand. "Lady, you don't look so good to me. You better come inside, have a cup of coffee or something. Then I'm gonna call the cops. What happened, anyway?" He peered at her more closely now, in the light that spilled from the open doorway. "Hey, you look kinda familiar. Haven't I seen you somewhere before?"

"Oh, no, I don't think so," Nina said quickly. All she needed now was to be questioned by the local police—the story would be all over the front page of the *Daily News*: "Soap Opera Star Attacked in Yonkers Alley!" Nina shuddered. "Look, I appreciate your concern, I really do, but I have to be getting home," she babbled. "Those men tried to steal my purse—they followed me from the drugstore. But they didn't get it—I dropped it behind one of those garbage things.'' She waved vaguely toward the dumpsters. ''They're gone now—I didn't see their faces, or the license plate of their car, or *anything*.''

As she spoke, she was edging away inch by inch.

''Really, I'm eternally grateful to you for scaring them off. You're a hero—a real hero,'' she continued. ''My car's parked right in front of the restaurant. I'll just be on my way. . . .''

''Hey, lady, wait a minute. . . .'' The man started after her, but just then a woman's shrill voice carried into the alley.

''Richie, whatcha doin' out there? We got a drunk in here, making waves. You're supposed to be the bouncer, so come and *bounce*!''

Richie hesitated, obviously torn, then started for the door. ''Don't go away, lady,'' he called over his shoulder. ''I'll be right back!''

The minute he disappeared inside, Nina hobbled as fast as she could in the opposite direction, stopping only to retrieve her purse. What had happened to her purchases, her jacket, and her scarf, she didn't know and didn't care. There was only one thought in her mind—to get home as fast as possible, lock her door, and then indulge herself in a well-earned fit of hysterics.

# Chapter Thirteen

Though Nina had feared that her assailants might have been lurking somewhere around the shopping center, waiting for another shot, there was no sign of the car—a Mustang, she now believed it had been, vaguely remembering the chrome hood ornament— and her drive back to Manhattan was without incident.

Her first impulse, as soon as she was safely inside her own apartment, was to call Dino Rossi and tell him of this second attempt on her life. But then she decided against it. In the first place, he'd no doubt be furious at her for taking off in the middle of the night, deliberately exposing herself to possible danger, and if he hollered at her, she knew she'd blow a fuse. In the second place, she had absolutely no hard information to give him. She hadn't seen either man's face, wasn't even sure of the make of the car let alone its license plate. The only thing she was relatively sure of was that the driver of the car was the man she'd seen at the restaurant earlier that evening, and she had a sneaking suspicion that Dino would not consider a brief glimpse of a white suit to be admissible evidence.

Besides, Nina rationalized, the whole thing was really his fault. If he'd stayed with her, she was sure she'd never have developed the blinding headache; and if she hadn't gotten the headache, she wouldn't have had to go out for aspirin, and if she hadn't gone out for aspirin, she wouldn't have been followed and attacked. If Dino really loved her, he would have stayed. But then, she reminded herself, he'd only said he *thought* he loved her. . .

Exhausted and drained, Nina undressed, throwing her ruined shoes and torn, stained dress into the garbage—expensive garbage, she thought ruefully, recalling the price she'd paid for both only a few weeks ago—then sank into a hot bubble bath. By the time she got out and toweled herself dry, the pain in her ankle had subsided, and all vestiges of the headache were gone. Nina crawled into bed and immediately fell asleep as though she had been drugged.

The following morning at the studio, as she tried to study her lines while waiting for the first call of the day, Nina realized that last night's little episode had had at least one positive result: It proved her theory that there were two parties involved in the murders of Morty Meyer and Gladys Parr. The man she'd seen in the restaurant who, she was convinced, was also the driver of the car, was definitely not a member of the TTS cast or crew, and though she hadn't seen the other man's face, she was sure that he, too, was a stranger to her. Which meant that they had to be in cahoots with somebody on the inside, somebody who regarded Nina as a threat.

And *that* meant that her amateur snooping had, unbeknownst to her, brought her dangerously close to discovering the truth. But what *was* the truth? And since they hadn't succeeded in finishing her off last night, they'd undoubtedly try again.

Nina shivered. The fact was that she was a sitting duck, fair game for the next attack. Once again, she considered calling Dino. Shorthanded or not, he'd be sure to provide police protection for her in light of this most recent attack. But if he did, the murderer would go even further underground, and they might never flush him (or her) out.

A sitting duck, Nina mused, staring sightlessly at the script in front of her. How about a decoy? If she could just keep her wits about her and her eyes open, force him to reveal his hand. Then, when she had concrete evidence, something Dino couldn't brush aside as imagination or paranoia, she'd turn to him. . .

If, said a nagging little voice inside her head, you manage to stay alive!

Nina didn't like that thought at all, so she forced herself to concentrate on her upcoming scene for several minutes. When she'd committed several pages to memory, her mind wandered again.

All right, so there was a mole on the set. There *had* to be. Who, then, were the prime suspects? At the reception yesterday following Morty's funeral, Angela Dolan had definitely moved up a notch in the list. And though Nina had discounted Helen and Byron Meyer at first, their obvious antipathy and virulence gave her reason to reconsider. Could the grieving widow and son have combined forces, impelled by jealousy and greed, to polish Morty off? Though brains were not Byron's strong suit, Helen was far from stupid. She might have arranged Morty's oh-so-public demise in the midst of that sickly sweet anniversary celebration deliberately in order to divert suspicion from herself. And she might have directed Byron to take care of Gladys Parr while making it appear that Miss Parr's death was connected to a frantic search for something that very possibly might not even exist.

Good Lord, Nina chastised herself, this is beginning to sound like one of the worst soap opera plots in history!

Glancing out the open door of her dressing room, Nina saw Valerie Vincent passing by, shoulders slumped, looking—if possible—even more bedraggled than usual. Nina had a sudden, truly bizarre, thought. Valerie had been looking peaked ever since Morty's death. Was it possible that this youngster had been one of Morty's conquests and, having been cast aside in typical Meyer fashion, had engineered his murder? Was she suffering the pangs of remorse?

Ridiculous! Nina decided. It was indeed possible that Morty had lured the girl into his bed, perhaps with the promise of a bigger and better role on *The Turning Seasons*—Morty's casting couch had seen so much mileage that the odometer must have turned over years ago—but Nina simply could not picture Valerie as a vengeful murderess. She might, however, be a very good mole. . .

Nina sighed. This was definitely not top-drawer detective work, but it was the best she could do under the circumstances. All she had to go on were hunches, impressions, observations, and gut reactions; but these were the very things she'd always relied on as an actress to develop and enhance her characterizations. So far, they'd stood her in good stead.

At that moment, the p.a. system blared in the hallway. "Full cast call," Spence Sprague's voice announced. "Main rehearsal room."

Clutching her script, Nina left her dressing room, looking furtively up and down the hall before she turned to lock her door. Any further messages would have to be delivered in person. Nina wondered with trepidation just how her enemy would approach her next.

During the rehearsal, Nina felt last night's headache coming back. Her ankle was beginning to throb a bit, as well; so at the first break she headed for the lavatory on the studio level, intending to take some aspirin from the communal first aid kit there. Satisfied that no one had followed her, she entered the room, to be greeted by the sound of someone throwing up in one of the stalls. Nina downed two aspirin and was about to leave, but when whoever it was continued retching, she became concerned.

"Hello, in there," she called softly. "Can I get you a drink of water or something?"

The woman mumbled something unintelligible. The only words Nina could understand were "Go away!" She glanced down beneath the door to the stall and saw a pair of white Reeboks, which weren't much of a clue to the person's identity. Many of the women in the cast and crew dressed casually. With a helpless shrug, Nina returned to the set for a scene rehearsal. It was only later in the morning when she realized that the only woman wearing white Reeboks was Valerie Vincent.

Which set off a chain of conjecture, beginning with the possibility of a major hangover and ending with the sudden conviction that the girl was pregnant. All the symptoms fit—the lassitude, the puffiness around the eyes, the weight gain.

Poor kid! Nina thought. Poor, dumb kid. If Valerie were pregnant, it would only be a matter of time before her condition became obvious to everyone on the set, and when that happened, the girl would be written out of the script so fast she wouldn't know what hit her. Susan Levy was TTS's resident mother-to-be, and Gelber certainly wasn't about to write in another pregnancy. And where would a pregnant, unemployed actress find another job? Valerie Vincent's career would be over before it began. . . .

"Ms. McFall, would you *kindly* pay just the *slightest* bit of attention to what's supposed to be going on in this scene?" Spence Sprague's acid voice cut into Nina's thoughts. "That's the third time you've blown the same line!"

"Sorry, Spence. Wool-gathering, I guess." Nina pulled herself together. "Can we take it from the top one more time?"

"*Some* people," Angela Dolan said, with an audible sniff, "have *no* consideration for other members of the cast who have taken the time to *prepare* for their scenes."

Nina bit back a sharp retort—for once in her life, Angela was right. She forced herself to concentrate on the business at hand for the rest of the rehearsal, but as soon as the scene was over, she resumed her thoughts on the subject of Valerie Vincent.

If Valerie *were* pregnant, was it possible that the child's father was someone in the TTS cast? Or possibly even the late Mortimer Meyer himself? If so, and if Morty had refused to provide for the child or to ensure Valerie's future on the show, it would certainly give the girl a strong reason to loathe him. And though Nina still couldn't believe that Valerie was capable of engineering the murder of Morty and Gladys Parr, she was becoming more convinced by the minute that Valerie might very well be the actual murderer's "inside" contact.

180

Talk about gut reactions and going off half-cocked! Nina said to herself. Yes, it was a neat little scenario, but it all hinged on Valerie's pregnancy, of which Nina had no evidence other than the girl's appearance and the fact that she'd been throwing up in the lavatory. Poor kid . . .

Poor kid, my foot! If that "poor kid" was hand in glove with the murderer, she was indirectly responsible not only for two deaths, but for the attacks on Nina herself, in which case, appearances to the contrary, she was a very dangerous person. Time to stop playing mother hen and settle into her Nancy Drew role. Take the bull (or in this case, the heifer) by the horns and see what you can find out.

Nina's opportunity came after the blocking rehearsal. Galano called a break, and Nina joined Valerie by the coffee maker. She poured a cup for herself and asked, "Coffee, Valerie? You look as if you could use a jolt of caffeine."

"N-no . . . no thanks, Nina." The girl edged away, picked up a teabag. "I'm off coffee these days. It seems to . . ."

". . . Upset your stomach?" Nina supplied smoothly. "I know how it is. Are you feeling any better?"

"What do you mean, feeling any better? I'm feeling just fine!" Valerie said belligerently.

"I'm so glad." Nina's voice fairly oozed sympathetic understanding. "I was worried when I found you throwing up in the restroom."

"Something I ate . . . must have been the bacon I had for breakfast . . ." the girl mumbled.

"That'll do it, all right," Nina agreed.

Clutching her cup of tea in a shaking hand, Valerie moved away, but Nina kept pace with her. "You know, Valerie," she said, "I really *am* worried about you. Whatever it is that's wrong is affecting your performance on the show. And makeup and wardrobe can do only so much to conceal puffy eyes and some additional pounds. I really think you ought to see a doctor, dear. You're new in this business, and you've had a fantastically lucky break, being given a nice, juicy part on TTS, a part that hundreds of struggling actresses would sell their souls to play. The camera's very fickle, believe me—it loves you when you're looking good, but it also picks up every little flaw. If you won't consider your health, at least think about your future, your career.''

''Lay off, Nina!'' Valerie cried. ''Just leave me alone, okay? I don't need you or anybody else snooping around, telling me what I ought to do! Believe me, I don't have to worry about *my* future.'' She was trembling violently. ''If I were you, I'd try minding my own business for a change, because if you don't stop sticking your nose in where it doesn't belong, one of these days somebody's going to chop it off!''

Nina didn't blink an eye. ''There, there, dear,'' she soothed. ''Maybe you ought to lie down and rest for a few minutes, or you'll never be able to concentrate on your next scene.''

Flustered, Valerie whispered, ''Yes—maybe I will. Sorry I blew up like that, Nina. My nerves are kind of shot, I guess. Honest, I'm really sorry.''

''I understand,'' Nina replied sweetly. ''I understand perfectly.''

And, watching the girl hurry off, she narrowed her eyes in intense speculation. Valerie was running scared, that was for sure, and very near the breaking point. Yes, Valerie was definitely the weakest link in a chain that just might connect Nina to the murderer—unless the murderer connected with Nina first. The old cliché in cases of this kind, Nina knew, was *"cherchez la femme."* In this instance, however, it wasn't a woman she had to find, but a man. The man in Valerie Vincent's life.

During the next break, Nina joined Robin Tally, casually maneuvering the conversation around to the subject of Valerie. Had Robin noticed how peaked the girl had been looking lately? Nina was increasingly concerned about her. Did Robin have any ideas about what might be bothering her? Was she perhaps using drugs? Or how about boyfriends? Perhaps an unhappy love affair?

When Robin admitted she knew virtually nothing about Valerie's private life, Nina asked if there was anyone else on the set who might give her some insight into the actress's problems.

After a moment's thought, Robin said, "Well, there's Tom Bell. He had kind of a mild case on Valerie when she first joined the cast about six months ago. He might be able to come up with something." Robin shook her head in exaggerated dismay. "Nina, honey, when are you going to stop trying to take care of every lame duck that comes your way?"

"Oh, I don't know," Nina said brightly. "Guess I'm just a natural-born do-gooder—but don't you dare let that get around—it would ruin my image as Melanie Prescott with my fans!"

And she set off to corner Tom Bell.

Tom, in his early thirties with a slightly receding hairline and a lean, somewhat foxy face, played a ruthless advertising executive on the show, but he was actually a gentle man with a boyish sense of humor.

"No," he said, smiling diffidently, when Nina posed her query, "I never got to first base with her.

I asked her out a few times, but she was always busy. Guess I didn't turn her on.''

''Do you think she was seeing anybody? Someone from the cast, maybe?''

''Nobody that I can think of. She's kind of a strange girl—a loner type. She never has much to do with anyone on the set.''

''You're sure, Tom? Maybe you saw her with somebody somewhere along the line. Think. This is important. That kid's in trouble of some sort, and I'm trying to help her.''

Bell's face became perplexed. ''Gee, Nina, I'd like to help you, but . . .'' He looked up suddenly. ''Hey, wait a minute! Come to think of it, I *did* see her with somebody, one night down in Times Square. A real sleazeball type—older. A foreigner maybe, one of those Middle Eastern types.''

Nina was instantly alerted. ''An older man, you say? How *much* older?''

''Hell, that was so long ago, and it was dark and rainy. They were hurrying along as if they had an appointment or something. When they passed me, she just said hi—didn't bother introducing me or anything. She was wearing high, leather boots and a leather coat. Looked kind of kinky, I thought at the time.''

''This man, Tom. Please, take a stab at it. How old? In his sixties? Forty? What?''

''Oh, no. Between thirty and forty, I'd say. If you nailed me down, I'd say thirty-five, thirty-six.''

''And you say he was on the dark side? Maybe Levantine?''

''Yes, that's right. He didn't look like the kind of guy Valerie would go out with—but then, like I said, she didn't go for *me*, so maybe that's her type.''

"And that was the only man you've ever seen her with?"

"Right. She's a real strange girl—hard to talk to. Acts like she's afraid of something all the time."

"Okay, Tom. Thanks. And please don't say anything to Valerie about this, all right? I can't help her if she thinks I'm sneaking around behind her back."

Tom shrugged ruefully. "That won't be hard. We hardly ever speak anymore."

Nina walked away, script in hand, looking for a quiet place to review her upcoming scene. But the words blurred before her eyes. Yes—a dark-complexioned, unkempt man, the man in the white suit. The age was right. What role would someone like that be playing in Valerie's life unless there was a lot more to Valerie Vincent than met the eye?

The period after the 12:30 runthrough, just before the cast went into dress rehearsal, was always chaotic—especially in the makeup stalls, where many of the women got a last-minute touch-up and had their hair done before they proceeded to wardrobe for the afternoon's costumes. It was here that Nina followed Valerie, taking a vacant seat a few feet from Valerie's makeup chair, supposedly waiting her turn with Bonita Collins, her favorite "beauty mechanic."

Observing the weary expression on Bonita's face as she regarded Valerie, Nina knew she was in for a long wait. Which was just fine by her; she'd planned it that way. Nina pretended to study her script as Valerie sank back into the chair and closed her eyes and Bonita began her ministrations. When Bonita put chilled witch hazel pads on Valerie's closed lids, Nina was ready. The script "accidentally" slid off her lap, and as she leaned over to retrieve it, she stealthily reached for Valerie's bag, where it rested beside her chair. Neither woman, busy with cosmetology witchcraft, saw her bring it up, place it in her lap.

Pretending that it was her own bag and that she was rummaging around for something inside, Nina sifted its contents feverishly. When Valerie's wallet, a bedraggled lavender kidskin, was in her hands, Nina began flipping through the dozens of small pockets, scanning the glassine inserts containing driver's license, social security card, and credit cards. Keeping a watchful eye on Bonita and Valerie, Nina felt her heart race madly; her fingers felt as though they were made of wood.

And then, in a section containing three credit cards, tucked between American Express and Visa, she found the photograph in a plastic sleeve. Momentarily she felt giddy. Her fingers trembled as the images came into focus. The photo must have been taken a few years ago and showed a very young, very innocent version of Valerie Vincent in an awkward, frozen embrace with an older, dark-skinned man—the same man Nina had seen in the restaurant the other night, the man who'd been watching her and Dino and had tried to run her down.

Nina turned the plastic sleeve over—and stiffened, barely suppressing a gasp at the photograph on the other side.

It was a more recent photo, of a more poised, more mature Valerie in yet another embrace, apparently taken by a roving photographer at an Atlantic City casino. Only this time, the man was none other than Byron Meyer, and both Valerie and Byron looked positively ecstatic, like a couple who were very much in love.

Carefully she reinserted the sleeve into its place

behind the credit cards, slid the wallet back into Valerie's purse, then returned the purse to its original place.

She picked up her script and rose unsteadily. "I'll be right back, Bonita," she said brightly. "Remember, I'm your next victim!" Then she was hurrying out of the makeup booth, fighting to appear casual when all the while her head was spinning like a top. And just how, she thought, confusion rampant, do I begin to make any sense out of all this?

There was only one solution that Nina could come up with, and it was so harebrained—and possibly dangerous—that she knew with absolute certainty she couldn't suggest it to Dino. But to accomplish her objective, she would definitely need help. If not Dino, then who?

# Chapter Fourteen

In the end Nina decided to reveal everything to Robin Tally—everything, that is, except the fact that she'd been to bed with Lieutenant Dino Rossi.

"You *what*?" Robin exploded when Nina finished filling her in, and proposed her scheme. "You want to go to Leatherwing *tonight*? You want to *break in*? Are you completely out of your *tree*?"

"Robin, you're the only person I can trust. Why do you think I told you all this? Just to brighten your day? You used to work out there. Certainly you must know how to get in without alerting the palace guard."

"Well, sure, I know. But that doesn't mean I'm going to do it, even for you!"

"Listen, Robin, you *have* to do it. I'm convinced there's something strange going on out there, something everyone's overlooked that will shed light on the murders. I just want to nose around in Byron's rooms a little bit, see what might turn up. Don't you want to help me? I thought I could count on you."

"Oh, Lord, don't lay a guilt trip on me," Robin groaned. "Sure, I want to help, but—"

"Look, I already told you that I heard Sprague

say that Helen and Byron were going to Philadelphia tonight to attend an independent television producer's convention or something, and they'll be gone until Monday. Once the writers are finished, they take off for the night, don't they, and there's nobody out there? All you have to do is call one of your writer buddies, verify that the house will be empty. Once we're sure, we'll go to Leatherwing tonight, get it over with. You don't even have to come in with me. Just fix it so I can get inside without setting off any burglar alarms.''

Robin frowned, still unconvinced. ''Isn't that kind of weird, Nina? Helen going off on a jaunt so soon after Morty's death, I mean.''

''Knowing Helen, I can't imagine sentiment standing in the way of possible business advantage. She probably wants to show the world that she's taking charge, and Byron's the tail on her kite.''

Robin shook her head wonderingly. ''You . . . you're really serious about this, aren't you, Nina?''

''Of course I am! Do you think I would have told you everything if I wasn't? Now, you tell *me*—how are we going to get into Leatherwing?''

Bowing to the inevitable, Robin explained that there were no security alarms on the six-foot-high stone wall ringing the Meyers' ninety-acre estate. To be on the safe side, they'd have to park the car outside. Getting over the wall was easy enough; no guard dogs roamed the property. Once they reached the house, it was only a matter of finding the special cache under one of the stepping-stones in the garden adjoining the writers' studio where the writers kept what they called an ''idiot key.''

Once inside the studio (the key wouldn't trip the alarm system) there was yet another key. This one— unbeknownst to the Meyers—opened the door connecting the studio to the mansion proper. Some of the writers, desperate for alcoholic inspiration, invaded the premises when the Meyers were away, helping themselves to Morty's liquor; no one ever missed it.

"And then we'll go upstairs, search Byron's rooms," Nina said eagerly. "Helen and Morty's suite, too, if necessary. I tell you, there *has* to be a clue of some sort out there, or I miss my bet. That thing with Valerie, for one. You still don't believe that Byron is the father of her baby?"

"Baby?" Robin echoed incredulously. "We don't even know there *is* a baby! Just because you caught her tossing her cookies this morning and then found that lovey-dovey photo of Val and Byron doesn't mean that baby makes three. Drop it, Nina. What if they catch you out there? Are you willing to jeopardize your job just to play some idiotic hunch? Please, Nina, leave this kind of stuff to Lieutenant Rossi. If he thinks there are clues out there, he can get search warrants, he can—"

Nina dredged up her most disarming smile. "What's the harm, Robin? Where's the risk if nobody's home, if we've got a key, if we don't leave any traces that we've been there? We'll be in and out in an hour or so. I'm absolutely positive that Byron has something incriminating stashed out there. And besides, as I told you, I'm acting in a semi-official capacity as Lieutenant Rossi's silent partner."

Robin changed tack. "I don't quite get it, hon. How come you and this dishy cop are so thick all of a sudden? You don't expect me to believe he actually chose you for his inside man because you're a Miss Marple clone, do you?" Her eyes narrowed, and she looked hard at Nina. "You two wouldn't have a little thing going, would you?"

Robin was getting a little too close to paydirt now, and Nina was determined to keep the personal aspects of her relationship with Dino totally secret, at least until that relationship was on more solid ground. So she bantered, "I told you, baby. He loves me for my mordant wit, my cool intelligence. No, there's no hanky-panky going there. It's strictly a business arrangement."

"I'll bet. I smell a rat, Nina."

Nina looked around the studio quickly, saw the production crews making final setup for the day's last take. "We're written out of the script tomorrow, both of us," she reminded Robin. "We've got the day off. So a little wild nightlife won't hurt, will it? Or do you want me to go out there by myself? Because I will; I'm just that determined. Now, we've just got ten minutes. Are you going to call your friend out at Leatherwing and find out when Byron and Helen are leaving, or not?"

Robin rolled her eyes, sighed exasperatedly. "The things you get me into!" she said. "Okay, I'll call."

She was back five minutes later, a wry grin on her face. "The Meyers left at noon," she announced. "They won't be back until Sunday night. It looks like we've got ourselves a date, honey. What time does this magical mystery tour of yours commence?"

It was 9:00 P.M., and darkness was settling in as Nina and Robin in Nina's car hit Route 9 just beyond the Bronx and began following the Hudson River due north. With any luck, they would reach their destination well before ten.

Both women were subdued, staring straight ahead

into the encroaching night. Each entertained serious second thoughts about what they were letting themselves in for. Even to Nina, their mission, a seeming lark by light of day, was becoming less so by the minute.

It was a moderately chill evening, and both wore jeans, windbreakers, sweaters, and dark, soft-soled shoes. Each had wrapped their hair in a dark bandana. Once they were within the Leatherwing grounds, they would, they hoped, blend easily into the background.

Nina held the speedometer at a steady 55 mph—it was no night to get picked up for speeding. Staring into the darkness ahead, she let her mind drift. Dino Rossi had called her shortly after seven. There had been no earthshaking discoveries in the day's investigation. But, Rossi assured her, the police were on the right track; the last piece of the puzzle was sure to fall into place within the next twenty-four hours, make no mistake. His cocksure prediction only served to make Nina more stubbornly determined to proceed on her own. She'd show him she wasn't just going to sit demurely by, twiddling her thumbs. And he'd be impressed when she laid in his lap last night's attempt on her life, the news of Valerie's involvement with Byron Meyer, and whatever she and Robin might discover tonight.

Even if they didn't find anything that would incriminate Valerie and Byron in his father's murder, she was sure they'd come up with some new piece of evidence the police had overlooked, maybe something connecting Byron with the unsavory character who had followed her and Dino, had tried to run her down, and was snuggling with Valerie in that photograph. Though she was strongly tempted to tell him of her plan, she decided against it, knowing that he'd either forbid her to go at all, or insist on providing a police escort complete with siren, flashing red lights, and search warrant, none of which, to Nina's way of thinking, were at all necessary. No, she was going to do it *her* way, without a lot of bureaucratic red tape to trip her up.

Still, as she headed for Leatherwing, Nina had to admit she had nothing concrete to go on, certainly no evidence strong enough to send her out on as foolhardy a mission as tonight's might prove to be. There were just her gut-level premonitions, and those two photos she'd found in Valerie's wallet. There *had* to be a connection, no doubt about it, and whatever it was, with Robin's help she was going to find it.

Nina checked the odometer. Roughly ten miles to go before they reached the turnoff for Leatherwing. Fools rush in, she thought fatalistically.

Once they left the highway, heading toward the Hudson, Nina put herself in Robin's hands; she knew a secret back way into Meyer country. Now they threaded their way down narrow country roads, the faint, blurred outlines of other estates and country homes emerging out of the blackness, then being swallowed by the night as they glided past. They began to get glimpses of the river through openings in the trees and dense brush.

"Slow down!" Robin hissed. "There's a turnoff along here somewhere—yeah, here—this is it. Hang a right. I remember a cul-de-sac along here someplace. . . . There! See that driveway?"

"Where?" Nina snapped. "I don't see a thing."

"Right there! Stop!" She pointed to a stand of tall grain, already tasseling. "There's a driveway leading back in there that nobody ever got around to finishing. Here—I'll get out, guide you in.''

It was as Robin had said. Nina drove her car behind Robin another fifty feet along a level stretch, down into a little hollow. Then she backed up, turning the car so it was headed out in case a quick getaway was necessary. The sporty blue Mazda was completely hidden from view.

Nina picked up a flashlight and joined Robin. ''How far?''

''About a quarter of a mile. We'll cut through this field. We used to have picnics out here sometimes. Leatherwing's right over there. We'll come in from behind.''

The tall grass made a sibilant swishing sound as they walked through it. The shrill, incessant shriek of the crickets was unnerving. Nina was glad for the thin cloud cover; it dulled the brilliance of the full moon.

When they reached the craggy fieldstone wall surrounding the Meyer mansion, Nina dug the toes of her sneakers into the cracks and climbed to the top within seconds. She eased herself over and landed on the other side with a soft thump. While she waited for Robin to climb over, she looked across a wooded lot to where Leatherwing crouched, mantled in eerie gloom, like some watching animal. No lights shone anywhere. Far to the right, she made out the shadowy silhouette of the bat silo and shuddered involuntarily. Spooky, no doubt about it.

''There's a little creek down there,'' Robin said, leading the way. ''I'll show you a narrow place where we can cross.''

Nina felt increasingly nervous as they got closer to Leatherwing. Would any of the bats be making nocturnal forays? Bats were not exactly Nina's favorite creatures. She had the most creepy feeling that someone was inside that pile of stone, looking out the windows at her and Robin as they advanced—waiting, preparing to pounce. Then the quaint thatched cottage Gladys Parr had once occupied loomed up to the left. More shivers.

A wild, whirring sound exploded, almost at their feet. They had flushed a pheasant. Nina and Robin both gasped, clutching each other. "My God!" Nina said. "That gave me a scare!"

Now they approached the writers' studio, stealthily working their way toward the bank of windows to the north through the extensive maze of gardens. "This way," Robin whispered. "That door over there. That's the writers' entrance."

Then, at the base of a brick retaining wall that flanked a set of low steps, Robin crouched. "The flashlight, Nina," she ordered. "Turn it on and aim it this way." She lifted an octagonally shaped tile, slid her hand beneath. A moment later a silvery key dangled in the rays of the light. Nina clicked the light off.

They climbed the shallow stairs and furtively crossed a large, tiled veranda, where tables, ornamental iron chairs, and large umbrellas were randomly scattered. And all the while, hearts in their throats, they expected someone to jump out and challenge them at any moment. Nina glanced at her watch. It was only 10:20. Weird, she thought. Seems like we've been away from the city for hours.

Robin leaned forward and inserted the key in the lock. The door swung open noiselessly. They stepped inside, locking it behind them. Nina turned on the flashlight again, sweeping the beam about the rambling studio. Desks, banks of files, computers, typewriters, long tables, a copier—all the comforts of home. "Old Morty really took care of you folks, didn't he?" Nina said, impressed.

Quickly she extinguished the flashlight, just in case someone passing by outside might see a suspicious light in the Meyer house. One couldn't be too cautious.

Robin Tally advanced to a desk near the center of the room and paused beside it. "God, when I think of the hours I spent here," she muttered, "grinding out episode after episode . . ."

"At least you didn't have to try breathing life into it," Nina said dryly. "How do we get out of here? Upstairs?"

Robin went to the largest desk of the lot, digging her fingers into a small canister of paper clips. Again a key glinted. "This way, hon."

Nina got a fresh case of the shakes when they invaded the Meyer house, going through that same great room where, less than a week ago, Morty had died. Her eyes quickly adjusting to the interior gloom, she saw Robin gliding up a flight of creaking stairs that led to the second floor. As they came to the top, pausing to get their bearings, Robin announced, "Lingerie, loungewear, women's footwear . . ." Then she wheeled and fled down a long, carpeted hallway. "The son-and-heir's cage is down here."

Byron Meyer's large, lavishly appointed suite had a western exposure, and Nina was glad to see that the drapes had been pulled earlier against the afternoon sun. They could use the flashlight freely without fear that its beam might be seen from the road leading to the house proper. If someone should, by some freak stroke of fate, return to the mansion, it wouldn't be a dead giveaway.

Nina played the light over the high-tech, state-of-the-art stereo center that occupied one entire wall, then picked up the outsize TV and its matching, super-elaborate VCR setup. A rich boy's toys, she thought sarcastically. Too bad he can't get that cute little Porsche of his up here, too. The room's big enough for him to drive around in. The circular bed was set on a dais, with a preposterous little canopy over it. Nina bet the sheets were satin, and that there was a mirror set into the canopy, but she didn't bother to check.

"Well," Robin said with a sigh, "here we are. And just where do we start?" She pulled out her own flashlight, an oblong-shaped miniature, from a pocket in her sweatshirt, and shone it about helter-skelter.

"I only wish I knew what we were looking for," Nina said dubiously. "I'll start on this desk—you begin on his dresser drawers. And remember, replace everything exactly as it was. He mustn't suspect that anyone's been here."

Nina slid open each desk drawer and riffled through sheafs of papers, notebooks, sales catalogs, personal memorabilia, her frustration mounting. Since she didn't know exactly what to look for, whatever it was would have to jump out and bite her before it would register, she grumbled inwardly. Maybe there were more photos of Byron and Valerie, some love letters, something of that sort. She lifted the desk blotter, peered beneath it, then felt between the layers for any hidden scraps of paper. She ran her fingers underneath the bottom of each drawer (she'd seen that gimmick in a detective movie once) but with the same result—nothing.

"Oh, my God!" Robin giggled suddenly. "Come take a look at this!"

Nina joined her friend and peered beneath some

sweaters which Robin had pulled aside. There—a secret treasure—were three or four copies of girly magazines. ''C'mon, Byron,'' Nina said scornfully. ''Who're you hiding this stuff from? Afraid Helen might scold?''

Just the same, she gingerly lifted out the magazines, flipping through the pages and shook them to see if there might be something incriminating tucked inside. But nothing fell out. She carefully put them back in the exact order they'd found them.

While Robin finished with the dresser, Nina went to a bedside bookcase and began taking out each book, shaking it and thumbing pages for any hidden materials. There were dog-eared paperback mysteries, a couple of erotic novels, but most of them were action-adventure—Mack Bolan, The Destroyer, The Death Merchant. Gals and Guns, she mused. It certainly makes an interesting statement about dear Byron, but it's hardly incriminating evidence.

The Meyers had turned off the central air conditioning, and the bedroom was becoming stuffy. Nina was beginning to get uncomfortably warm, so she removed her charcoal gray windbreaker and threw it over a chair in the corner. Then she dropped to her knees, playing her flashlight under the chairs and bookcases. Finding nothing but a pair of badly scuffed black loafers, she stood up and went to search Byron's wardrobe closet.

As she stepped inside among a seemingly endless array of suits, shirts and ties, she heard Robin's harsh whisper: ''Nina, listen! I think someone's downstairs!''

Nina killed the flash, darted from the closet. She froze in the center of the bedroom, straining to hear, but her heart was hammering so loudly she couldn't be sure that she heard anything else. But finally,

"That's the front door," she hissed. "Someone's down there, all right. Didn't you hear a car, see lights or anything?"

"Nothing," Robin hissed back. "How could I, with the drapes closed? What if it's the police? Maybe we tripped an alarm somehow. What'll we do?"

Nina shushed her, listening intently. She heard the unmistakable creak of approaching footsteps ascending the stairs. "Whoever it is is headed this way. Hide! Quick—get that drawer closed, get under the bed!"

They had barely crawled into the tight space beneath Byron Meyer's bed, when someone entered the room. The lights flashed on, and both terrified women sucked in raspy breaths. It seemed that the intruder must certainly hear the thunderous booming of their hearts.

The person strode purposefully into the room and went directly toward the wall where the stereo/TV setup was located. Curiosity overcoming caution, Nina squirmed on her belly, her face flat to the floor, angling her head so that she could squint through a slight gap between the bedspread and the carpeting.

Byron Meyer! But how come? He was supposed to be 150 miles away, in Philadelphia.

She watched as Byron, dressed in jeans and a dark jacket, placed a large manila envelope on a convenient shelf. He dropped to his knees and began tugging at the stand that housed the huge TV set. Then her blood seemed to freeze in her veins as she caught sight of her windbreaker on the chair, not more than four feet from where Byron was working.

Oh, my God, she groaned inwardly, what if he sees it? What if he looks it over, wonders where it came from? Idiot! she lashed herself. You blundering idiot!

But Byron was apparently too preoccupied with his own errand to notice the jacket. Now he reached behind the TV, lifted a corner of the rust-colored carpeting. Next he took the bulky envelope from the shelf and tucked it beneath the carpeting, then dropped the loose flap back into place. A moment later he manhandled the heavy TV back into place. After a final shove to bring it even with the other cabinetry on that wall, he rose to his feet.

In that instant, as he paused and looked around the room, Nina was convinced that he must have seen her eye peering at him from beneath the bed, for it seemed as though he had looked right at her. She eased her head back an inch or so.

Another thought hit her. Her perfume—Robin's perfume. What if he recognized an alien scent, became suspicious? Was that why he was double-checking things? Oh, Lord, why didn't I think of that before we came out tonight?

Her tension grew as she saw him turning slowly around, seeming to reconnoiter his room with extra care. She virtually writhed in her hiding place. That damned jacket! If he sees that . . .

Then, to Nina's horror, she realized that the accumulated dust under the bed was getting to her. She was going to sneeze! The tickling became unbearable. She sucked in a deep breath, clapped her hands over her nose and mouth, pressed hard. Her sinuses itched and burned; her eyes watered. Her head felt as if it would explode from the building pressure. No, don't sneeze, she pleaded. Not now!

Then the room suddenly went dark, and, to her overwhelming relief, she heard soft footsteps padding away down the hall. Another few minutes passed before the distant bang of the front door carried to her ears. Only then did Nina finally let loose, with a muffled *ah-choo*! that brought a startled lurch and squeak from Robin.

"Who was it?" she demanded. "I couldn't see a blasted thing!"

"Byron."

"*Byron*? What was he doing here?"

"Your guess is as good as mine. Shhh—listen!" Nina squirmed from beneath the bed, hurried to the window, peered out cautiously between the drapes. "Thank God! His car's going down the drive."

She was suddenly trembling uncontrollably. "Oh, that was terrible," she gasped. "That was too close for comfort. I was so sure he'd see my jacket lying on that chair."

"Your jacket? What are you talking about?" Robin asked as she scrambled out of her hiding place.

"I got warm, took it off, threw it there . . ." Nina played her flash on the chair. "Why he didn't notice it . . ."

"Great move, honey," Robin grumbled. "A super sleuth you're not." Then, looking about the room, "What did he want? What did he do?"

"He hid something," Nina said excitedly. "Over there, underneath the TV."

Robin aimed her flashlight toward the corner. "What was it?" she asked. "Let's dig it out."

"An envelope . . ." Nina clutched her head. "Give me a minute to catch my breath, will you?"

"I don't understand. He was supposed to be in Philly with Helen. But he comes home for five minutes and then he's off and running again. Holy Aunt Nelly, I was *sure* he'd find us under that damned bed!"

"Me, too. Whatever his reasons for coming here,

they had to be good ones. Maybe he gave Helen the slip in order to sneak off and stash whatever it is.''

''Okay, okay,'' Robin said impatiently. ''The TV. Let's get this show on the road.''

Nina fled to the window and peered out a second time. Assured that Byron was really gone, she turned back and contemplated the massive TV stand. Would they be strong enough to move it? And having moved it, could they get it back in place so Byron wouldn't know it had been disturbed?

She leaned down and gripped the back edge of the stand on the right side, pulling with all her strength. The stand moved two inches at best. ''More muscle,'' she grunted. ''See if you can get a grip too, Robin.''

Three minutes later, amidst much huffing and puffing, the TV rig was moved far enough away from the wall. ''Well?'' Robin said. ''Where's the envelope? I don't see anything.''

''Here,'' Nina said, falling to her knees and peeling back the carpeting. Her eyes widened as she saw not one, but two large manila envelopes secreted there. ''Wow!'' she exclaimed. ''I think we've hit the jackpot. Quick, let's have that light down here!''

In the beam from Robin's flashlight, Nina undid the clasp on the top envelope and slid its contents out. A stack of eight-by-ten glossies slipped from her fingers, fanning out on the carpet. As Robin slanted the light to eliminate the blinding glare, she grimaced in disgust. ''Oh, yuch!'' she said. ''Looks like Byron is really into porn!''

But it was not just a batch of raunchy photos like those in the magazines they'd previously discovered. Two women and a naked man were involved in a series of obscene tangles. The women, one a blonde, the other a brunette, wore only garter belts, black, silky hose, and spike-heeled shoes. In one set of photos the two women serviced the man in ways Nina was sure even the Kama Sutra hadn't thought of. In another set the man used the blonde, then the brunette in equally astonishing ways.

In addition to the revulsion she felt, Nina knew a more chilling sensation—one of failure. Was this Byron Meyer's secret obsession? What bearing, if any, did it have on the murders? But then, as she concentrated more closely on the performers themselves, she let out a little gasp.

"Good God!" Nina said. "Look, Robin! Look at that blonde. Does she look familiar to you? Or am I having a hallucination?"

"That's no hallucination," Robin replied grimly. "That's Valerie. Valerie Vincent."

Then, both trying to disregard the repulsive acts Valerie was involved in, they concentrated on the frightened young face, rapidly flipping through the rest of the photos to further confirm their finding. There could be no mistake. It was Valerie, all right.

"How old?" Robin asked. "What do you think?"

"Just a kid, fresh from the boonies, I'll bet," Nina responded grimly. "She couldn't have been more than eighteen, nineteen when these were taken. Look at that long hair, how skinny she was. And those eyes—so empty, so haunted." Compassion welled up within her. "That poor thing! How did she let herself get involved in something like this?"

Robin made no reply. For a moment, both women stared silently at the photographs, torn between pity and disgust.

Finally they pulled themselves together, remembering their precarious status. Much as Nina hated to do it, she retrieved the second envelope from its hiding place and opened it with trembling fingers. Again a flood of glossy photographs slid out.

"This is weird," Nina said amazedly. "They're all the same. What's going on here?" She forced herself to count each batch of photographs. "That's right—thirty in each envelope. Identical, shot for shot."

Robin frowned. "I don't figure it, Nina."

"Why," Nina mused out loud, "does Byron need *two* sets of these photos? And what is so all-fired important about them that he came all the way from Philadelphia to hide this second set with the others?" She frowned. "Unless there's something different here that we're not seeing."

On impulse, Nina held the second envelope upside down and shook it. With a soft hiss, a smaller envelope fell out. Even before she opened it, she knew. "The negatives," she said. "*That's* what's different. *That's* why Byron came back tonight. To hide them in a safe place."

"But why tonight?" Robin asked. "Couldn't it have waited? Was this worth a trip all the way from Philadelphia in the dead of night? What's the man up to, anyway?"

Nina shook her head. "You got me." She thought a minute, then theorized aloud. "Could Byron have been blackmailing Valerie? Not for money—he's got more than she'll ever have—but maybe to force her to go to bed with him?"

Robin made a face. "That's a possibility, I guess. Byron's manly charms certainly aren't enough to sweep a girl off her feet!"

"Suppose he found out about Valerie's sordid past, managed to get these pictures and the negatives," Nina continued. "Valerie gives in, gets pregnant, pressures Byron to support herself and the child. He refuses, holding the photos over her head so she won't tell anybody he's the father. . . ."

"Nina, *you* ought to have been a writer, not me," Robin said, exasperated. "You can dream up the most outrageous plots I ever heard of! And you'll excuse me for saying so, but even if there's a single grain of truth in your kinky scenario, what does it have to do with the murders of Morty and dear old Gladys? Seems to me it would be more logical if Valerie had bumped off Byron, but she didn't."

"I know." Nina sighed and began sorting through the photos, separating three from the rest—those with the clearest images of Valerie's face. She then took the corresponding negatives and, after taking a fresh envelope from Byron's desk, dropped her selections inside.

"I'm taking these along, anyway," she said. "I'm going to show them to Lieutenant Rossi, see what he has to say."

Suddenly it felt as though a huge hydraulic press were closing on Nina's head. The confusion, the fear, the boiling welter of conjecture threatened to explode her brain.

"Dear Lord," she muttered as she and Robin wrestled the TV console back into place over the two original envelopes, "let's get out of this place, and fast, before I lose touch with reality altogether!"

Snatching up her jacket, she fled from the room, Robin close on her heels.

# Chapter Fifteen

Tired though she was, and drained by the tension of the Leatherwing break-in, Nina slept only fitfully that night. Whereas on a normal day off, she'd have indulged herself in the luxury of sleeping until noon, she was up, sleepy eyed and groggy, shortly before 8:00. Black coffee, some juice, and a piece of buttered toast she was barely able to force down, constituted breakfast. Too weary to do so last night, she showered, then took special pains with her toilette. There was some consolation, she told herself—considering the mishmash her life had become of late—in the fact that she'd be seeing Dino Rossi this morning. The thought had the power to make her heart lift.

There was no point, she'd decided, in talking to him on the phone. She'd check on his availability, then drop in at the precinct house. There would be no big buildup. She'd merely drop the photographs on his desk, and let them speak for themselves. She couldn't help smiling a little smugly as she envisioned Dino's reaction. What would he make of her detective work? Would he be impressed, take her seriously? And what theories would *he* come up with to explain Byron's stealthy behavior and his possession of the photographs in the first place? How would he handle it?

Certainly Dino couldn't come down hard on Byron at the outset, flash the glossies at him. There was, after all, the little matter of illegal entry. Nina knew that stronger cases had been thrown out of the court over little technicalities like that. But the photographs would surely convince Dino that Byron Meyer was deeply into something most unsavory and possibly illegal. He'd have to bear down on Byron—and Valerie. One way or another he'd convince them to talk. Then all the ugly details would come tumbling out.

What these details might be Nina couldn't even begin to imagine, unless her conjecture of last night might prove to be correct. The mere existence of evidence that Valerie had once posed for pornographic pictures, possibly was still doing so for all Nina knew, was a staggering enough revelation. She was content to leave the rest to Dino and his squad.

At 9:30, exquisitely coiffed and made up and dressed in a cream-colored linen skirt, apricot silk blouse, and custom-made Italian pumps, Nina dialed the first number on Dino's business card.

"Sergeant Lopez," a man's laconic voice answered on the third ring. "May I help you?"

"Yes. Lieutenant Dino Rossi, please."

"Sorry, ma'am, but he just stepped out."

"When do you expect him back?" Nina asked.

"In a half hour or so. He went into the inspector's office. Shouldn't take very long."

Nina thought a moment, then made her decision. "Well then, I'll just come on over. He should be back by the time I arrive. Will he be in all morning, do you think?"

"I think so, ma'am, but I can't tell for sure."

"Then I'll just have to take my chances, won't I? Thank you so much, Sergeant."

"May I tell the lieutenant who's calling, please?"

Nina hesitated, then said, "It's not important." She laughed lightly. "He'll know who it is soon enough."

She hung up the receiver, turned on the answering machine, and went to gather up her bag and the vital envelope, which she tucked inside. It would be fun to surprise Dino. She could hardly wait to see the expression on his face when she walked into his office.

As Nina emerged from the elevator into the ornate lobby and headed for the entrance, she noticed idly that the doorman was absorbed in reading the *Daily News*. She was about to give her customary greeting, when the banner headline on the front page leaped out at her: PORNO KING MURDERED. But it was the grainy photograph beneath the words that gave her a shattering jolt. She froze, staring at the face. It was her man! The man from the restaurant, the man who'd tried to run her down in the shopping center, the man whose picture she'd found in Valerie Vincent's wallet.

Collecting her wits, Nina said, "Harry, could I borrow your paper for a minute? Forgot to check my horoscope today."

Harry beamed. "For you, Ms. McFall, anything at all. Here—take the whole thing. I'm through with it."

"Thanks—you're a sweetheart," Nina murmured, depositing her bag on a French Provincial bench near the huge baronial fireplace. With trembling fingers she opened the paper to the article she sought.

"Alexis Kyros, 48, publisher and distributor of pornographic magazines and books and producer of X-rated films, was found dead in his East 52nd Street apartment shortly after twelve o'clock last night," the account read. He had been stabbed, a single thrust to the heart having caused instantaneous death.

The article went on to list Kyros' various convictions and jail terms. The police were following several leads. Kyros was known to have a number of enemies who were being sought and questioned. An arrest was imminent. Murder weapon not found . . . no sign of a break-in . . . Kyros had apparently known his assailant . . . apartment in disarray . . . murderer evidently seeking something specific . . .

Nina's knees buckled, and she sank abruptly onto the bench. Porn king murdered sometime before midnight—murderer seeking something unknown—porn photos hidden by Byron Meyer some time before midnight at Leatherwing. . . .

"Oh, my God," Nina whispered.

"That bad, huh?" said Harry sympathetically. "Listen, Ms. McFall, don't take that astrology stuff so seriously. A big star like you, you ought to write you own horoscope . . . hey, that's funny! Get it? A big *star* like you? Funny, right?"

"Yes, Harry, very funny," Nina replied. But she didn't feel like laughing. "Thanks for the paper— I've got to run."

Oh, yes, she had to run all right, straight to Dino Rossi!

"Harry, I need another favor," she said breathlessly. "You're an absolute genius at conjuring up a taxi when I need one, and I really need one now. I'm late for a very important appointment. See what you can do, okay?"

210

"You bet, Ms. McFall. Sit tight—I'll fix you up right away."

Heart pounding furiously, Nina followed him out of the building, pacing back and forth as Harry searched for a cab. But today his magic wasn't working—every taxi that passed was either full or off duty.

As Nina peered frantically up and down the street, her heart plummeted into her imported kid-skin pumps. "Oh, Harry, what am I going to do?" she wailed. "I've absolutely *got* to get across town, the sooner the better!"

"Ms. McFall, you know I'd do anything for you," Harry called over his shoulder as he nimbly jumped out of the way of a loaded gypsy cab, "but one thing I *can't* do is find an empty cab when there ain't no empty cabs." He stepped back onto the curb, almost knocking down a burly man in a windbreaker who was strolling past the building. "Hey, sorry, Mac—listen, Ms. McFall, maybe you better take your car. Traffic's terrible this time of day, it being rush hour and all, but it don't look like there's any other way unless you go up to Broadway and catch the subway."

Nina rejected the suggestion out of hand. Her subway days were far in the past, and she intended to keep it that way. "Right. I'll take the car. And thanks for trying, Harry. I really appreciate it." She fumbled in her bag for her wallet, pulled out a bill and thrust it at him. "For your trouble. Bye!"

As Harry stared at the twenty in his hand, she turned around and dashed back into the building, punching the elevator button viciously. "Come on, come *on*!" she urged the elevator, her eyes glued to the indicator making its downward progress from the sixth floor. "Dino—I have to get to Dino!"

What seemed like hours later, though it was really only a few minutes, Nina was hurrying down the incline to her parking space. The security guard who usually patrolled the area was nowhere in sight. Keys in hand, she ran to the Mazda, unlocked the door, slid inside. It was only then that she realized there was someone in the passenger seat. Before she had a chance to cry out, someone clapped a hand over her mouth while another hand dug painfully into her throat. She fought for breath, lights whirling before her eyes.

"Not a sound, Nina," the familiar voice rasped close to her ear, "or you buy it right here. This is where they'll find you, with your pretty throat slit from ear to ear!"

Then, the pressure lifting from her neck, she saw the six-inch switchblade before her eyes.

Instantly all the strength drained from her body. Her bones seemed to dissolve.

"Byron!" she groaned.

"That's right," he said, sliding a hand around to click the lock on the back door. "Good old Byron, your old buddy. Poor, dumb old Byron. But I'm no dummy, Nina, no matter what you think."

The point of the knife was now pressed just beneath her right breast.

"Put on your seat belt, Nina. We don't want to take any chances, do we? And no heroics, understand? No trying to jump out of the car. We're going for a nice long drive, out to Leatherwing." He snickered. "Only this time, you won't be coming back. You've poked your nose into my business once too often."

As Nina strapped herself in with hands that shook uncontrollably, Byron deftly invaded her purse, removing the envelope containing the photographs and negatives she'd been bringing to Dino.

"Nina, Nina," he said sadly. "You took something that belongs to me. That was naughty, Nina, breaking into my house like that, going through my things. Very, very naughty. And Valerie's been telling me about all the questions you've been asking her. Snooping's not nice, Nina."

"How . . . how did you know I'd be here?" Nina asked, stalling for time as she tried to start the engine. "That was . . . very clever of you, Byron. I didn't know myself until a few minutes ago."

"Oh, I've been watching you, Nina. I figured you'd scamper off to your *good friend*, Detective Rossi, first thing this morning. So I hung out. I must have walked past your building a dozen times before you came out, trying to get your doorman to find a taxi. He almost knocked me down when he was flagging down that gypsy cab. I heard every word you said. Great voice projection, Nina. You should've been a stage actress. Your talents are wasted on TTS."

The man in the windbreaker! Nina closed her eyes briefly, recapturing the scene. So that was Byron! Oh, God!

"How . . . how did you know I was there? At Leatherwing last night?" she blurted. "I thought . . ."

"You thought wrong, bitch! I didn't catch on at first. But later, as I was driving away, I remembered something—a jacket on the chair that wasn't mine. I was forty miles on my way to Philly before it registered." He snickered again. "But of course, when I got back, that jacket was gone, wasn't it? And so were three photographs and a strip of film. There's only one person I know who'd pull a stupid trick like that. Someone with a long, long nose. So I came looking for you, sugar. I knew it had to be you.''

''What . . . what are you going to do with me?''

''I think you already know the answer to that one. You know too much, McFall. Altogether too much.'' The knife sawed lightly; she felt it snag in the silk of her blouse, touch her tender flesh.

''But everything in good time. Now, lady, drive. Give the world one of those beautiful smiles. Go along like nothing's wrong. Take it easy, work your way out of the morning rush hour. Pretend you and your boyfriend are heading out for a lovely day in the country. One funny move, and it's mastectomy city. Blood all over this pretty car of yours. Got it?''

It was then that Nina noticed the large Band-Aid on Byron's right hand, slipshod first aid for the shot she'd given him with the heel of her pump at the shopping center the other night. The identity of the other man who had attacked her was now established.

Nina shook herself to alertness, willed strength into her hands and arms. She stole a look around the garage in desperate hope that the security guard would appear, that she could somehow risk a scream for help, but it was a futile thought; no one was around.

She started the car, backed slowly out of her slot. Now she drove down the aisle leading to the garage exit on West Seventy-fourth Street. She would be brave, she told herself, she wouldn't let herself fall apart in front of this slob. You haven't reached the end of the line yet, she told herself, pumping up counterfeit courage. You're coming out of this alive, understand?

She aimed her electronic eye control box as they approached the gate. The steel guard doors rumbled up. Oh, God, if only someone would walk by just now, if I could just let someone know I'm in trouble! But there was no one anywhere near. Then she was driving out onto the busy street, heading to Riverside Drive. In her rearview mirror she saw the garage doors slide down behind her.

The knife nudged anew. There goes $120 worth of Leo Fabricci blouse, she thought dourly. Now she concentrated on the traffic, her mind buzzing with all sorts of last-ditch stunts she might pull to draw attention to herself. Deliberately ram the car ahead? Run a red light? Graze a police cruiser? Each ploy was discarded as quickly as it presented itself. Byron Meyer was a desperate man. It was true, he had little to lose. He would kill her on the spot if she tried anything; she would be dead before anyone reached her car. As the realization hit home, she drove even more carefully.

If Nina nursed any last lingering hope that some member of the TTS writing staff would look up from his or her desk as she drove onto the Leatherwing grounds, she was in for vast disappointment. Once through the main gate, Byron guided her down an alternate drive—narrow, overgrown, and winding— that brought them to the opposite end of the house. Nobody in the studio would ever suspect that anyone else was on the grounds. The doors of the four-car garage were open; Byron ordered her to park in the space normally occupied by his Porsche. Holding the knife menacingly, Byron slid out of the Mazda, touched the control button on the wall. Prison walls came crashing down.

"Your car?" Nina asked as he stood at her side, waiting for her to unbuckle, and get out. "Where is it?"

His mustache rose and fell as his mouth settled on a sly smile. "You mean you didn't know about my place in the city? How's a guy expected to score if he's got to bring his broads way out here? Don't fret. My wheels are safe and sound. I took a cab over to your place. Nobody's gonna trace me."

He gave Nina a hard shove forward, nearly knocking her off her feet. "Move it, sweetheart," he grunted. Nina knew she'd be bruised tomorrow. If their *was* a tomorrow, she reevaluated grimly, the thought triggering fresh fear. "In the house. I've got a snug little place all ready for you. You'll keep just fine. Until later on." He chuckled evilly. "Ever go swimming in the Hudson at midnight?"

As they entered the hushed, rambling interior of the Meyer manse, Nina felt that same sense of awe as last night, a feeling almost of otherworldliness. The deepest parts of the house were dark, gloomy, and still gave off an aura of medieval castle. Just stumbling through the vast living room sent cold shudders down her back.

"Up those stairs," Byron said. "I've got a place nobody knows about—not that anyone's going to come snooping around. They've got no way of connecting me with you. . . with anything at all. They'll never know where to look. Even if they did, you'll be long gone before they get around to it."

He was right, Nina thought, her stomach constricting. With the exception of Robin Tally, there was no one else who could connect her disappearance to Byron Meyer. And if Dino didn't wonder what had happened to her, if Robin attached no particular importance to the fact that she wasn't answering her phone messages, who would sound the alert? And should Robin get panicky, call Dino and spill everything to him, who was to say she wouldn't put it off until late in the day? Long before an all-points manhunt could be launched, she'd be dead. At the bottom of the Hudson.

Damnation! she raged, as still another chilling realization homed in. When I spoke to Dino last night, I never mentioned that I wouldn't be at the studio today, that I had the day off. In all likelihood he'll wait until after five before he even tries contacting me, and by then it will be too late.

Oh, Robin, she pleaded desperately, do be concerned! Do worry about me. Call Dino! Tell him everything you know. Please, honey, don't wait, don't put it off another minute!

She climbed the stairs blindly, unquestioningly, lapsing into almost a zombie state. What was the use? It was all cut and dried now, the conclusion preordained. This was the end; she'd never come down these stairs again alive.

When they reached the top of the first flight, they proceeded down the hall past Byron's door and entered the master suite. A door to the north opened on stairs leading into an enormous attic.

Someone would find the attic eventually. But this secret corner, reached by the removal of a wide piece of planking (who would even suspect there was another opening behind it?) would throw the most experienced wall-tapper off.

"I found this when I was just a teenager," Byron boasted proudly as he shoved her into the dark hole, playing his flashlight among the rafters and tie beams, revealing a stifling, dank cubbyhole. "I used to hide my special"—he giggled inanely—"*things* in here so my dad, and Helen, couldn't find them."

A sheet of plywood lay across the exposed, insulation-stuffed beams, a mangy, torn blanket spread upon it. Nina couldn't help wondering if Byron had brought high-school tarts here, used that selfsame blanket for his adolescent sexual conquests. Would he force her to submit to him here as well? After all, it was only noon now: the whole afternoon lay before them. Her stomach rolled. Oh, no. Not that. Not with a slug like Byron. I'd rather die! I probably *will* die!

The interval of self-pity was cut short as Byron produced a roll of silver-backed duct tape. "Sit down, darling," he commanded. "Stick out your pretty little feet. I'm going to have to tie you up. I've got a lot of errands to take care of, and we can't have you wandering off while I'm gone, can we? You might get ideas about calling that cop buddy of yours, and that would never do."

Nina knew an even more demoralizing sense of despair as she helplessly submitted, allowing him to cross her ankles, wrap them with the wide strips of adhesive. Her stomach curdled as he paused in his labors to slide his hands along her thighs, hissing with delight as he did so. "Pretty," he crooned, "so pretty! I do love female silkies. Maybe later, when I get back, honey, I'll show you my soft side. Hell, what's the harm? Nobody's ever going to bother you that way again."

"Don't touch me!" She recoiled, twisted, kicked out at him. "I'll . . ."

"You'll what?" he mocked, placing a fist at the base of her sternum, flinging her back like a sack of rags. "Don't play Miss Aristocrat with me, or I'll take firsts right now. Who do you think you are— the virgin queen? I bet you and that Rossi creep have already got it on. So why not me? There's no harm in sharing the wealth, is there?"

"Filthy swine," Nina spat, writhing viciously,

trying to reach his face with her nails. "You'll be sorry, I swear!"

It was so much wasted venom. For Byron, surprisingly strong, captured her wrists and twisted them, smiling at the pain that contorted her face. Then he turned her onto her stomach, drew her arms behind her back. Crossing her wrists, he methodically began tightly whipping tape around them. He laughed thickly, seemingly deriving great pleasure out of making her cry out in pain.

He dropped her back on the rumpled blanket, stared down at her. "Any last words, Nina?" he said smirking. "Before I tape that big mouth of yours shut?"

"Where?" she said dazedly, desperately fighting the urge to burst into tears. "Where are you going?"

"As I said, I've got things to do—like ditching that flashy little car of yours. There's an old abandoned quarry about ten miles from here—no bottom. Once your car goes in, there's no way in the world anybody will ever find it again."

"Oh, no," Nina pleaded, not thinking, "not my beautiful car!"

He laughed delightedly. "Oh, McFall, you're a real cut-up! Can't you get anything through that thick head of yours? *You aren't ever going to drive it again, understand*?" She heard a sharp, rasping sound as Byron Meyer tore off another length of duct tape. She thrashed wildly, flinging her head back and forth, but her exertions were futile; the tape was slapped across her mouth, drawn tight, smoothed into smothering contour.

"Catch you later, sweetheart," Byron said. She saw the flashlight flick on again and watched helplessly as he picked his way from the cramped hiding place. Then everything fell out of focus, dissolving into blackness as he entered the finished part of the attic and carefully fitted the plank back into place.

But the darkness was no match for the midnight in her soul. For the first time, Nina capitulated to bitter hopelessness. Hot tears welled up in her eyes, overflowing with terror-sick abandon. And then she fainted.

# Chapter Sixteen

How long she lay there on the floor semi-comatose, Nina had no way of knowing. What time is it? she asked herself groggily, twisting her body, trying to find a more comfortable position. Then the full impact of her predicament rushed back. She froze, listening. Had she heard something? Was Byron returning? No—it was only her imagination. She turned her head and focused on one small square of light—a ventilating screen in the eaves—some distance from where she lay. Funny, she hadn't noticed that before. She stared at it fixedly, sinking into what was almost a trance. There was a world out there, if only she could get to it.

Was the light dimmer now? How late was it getting to be? Perhaps the sun was going down. How could she tell? Fresh despair closed in. What did it matter, anyway? This decoy was about to become a dead duck.

Where was Byron? Had he completed his destructive errand? If the quarry was ten miles away, how long would it take him to walk back? Two, maybe three hours? If I could just get at my watch, see the time!

Nina took several long, deep breaths, trying to bring her racing heart back to normal tempo. But every time she thought of how her life was slipping away, minute by irretrievable minute, it began racing again. Take it easy—try to gather your wits!

Once more her brain returned to the apparently hopeless task of coming up with an escape plan. There must be some way to get out of this. There *had* to be! But Nina's mind wouldn't focus. Instead, she kept thinking about things that had already happened and reliving moment by moment that morning's terrifying drive to Leatherwing, when she had learned beyond a shadow of a doubt that Byron Meyer was not only a murderer, but very possibly insane as well.

Byron didn't know that Robin had accompanied Nina to Leatherwing last night, and Nina had been determined to keep it that way. As they'd driven out, the switchblade constantly digging into her flesh, he had repeatedly asked her how she'd gotten into the house by herself. Again and again Nina had insisted that she'd done it alone. "David Gelber," she'd lied, "told me about a hidden key the writers use. He and I had a brief fling once—we shared a lot of inside information. When I decided to go to Leatherwing, it all came back."

Would he believe that? Apparently he did.

"And if I hadn't shown up when I did," Byron said, "you would have come up empty. Tough luck, Nina."

Oh, yes, tough luck indeed!

Then Byron's eyes narrowed. "How did you move that TV set all by yourself? That thing's heavy."

"I'm a lot stronger than I look. I may have knocked my back out, but I did it. *All alone*." She had to convince him that she'd done the whole thing on her own, for Robin's sake. Otherwise Nina was sure her friend would be the next victim on Byron's hit list.

"So nobody but you has seen those pictures?"

"Nobody," Nina assured him vehemently. "I was on my way to show them to Lieutenant Rossi when you found me."

A self-satisfied grin spread over Byron's face. "Then you're the only one who could connect me with that blackmailing scumbag, Alex Kyros."

"You *did* kill him, didn't you?" Nina's sweaty hands clenched more tightly on the steering wheel. "When you came out to the house, to Leatherwing, you must have just left his apartment."

"Yes, that's right," he replied. The smug grin broadened. "You might as well hear the whole story—you won't live long enough to pass it along! It was the first time I ever stabbed anybody. One quick shove in the chest, and it was all over. He just wheezed, coughed once, and went down, just like that. I was kind of surprised how easy it was. I got even with the bastard, in spades!"

In spite of her terror, Nina's curiosity impelled her to find out more. There were still a lot of missing pieces to the puzzle, and it was obvious that Byron was more than eager to talk, to display his cleverness to his captive audience. For once, Byron had the leading role, and he was enjoying every minute of it.

"I—I thought you were supposed to be in Philadelphia with Helen," Nina managed to say.

"That's what you were supposed to think—what *everybody* was supposed to think. But I worked it out with Helen that I'd join her there some time later today. I told her I was spending the night with Valerie.''

Nina blinked. ''Helen knows about you and Valerie?''

Byron nodded. ''She knows—but she doesn't know everything. She thinks Valerie's just another girlfriend. But she doesn't know that I'm in love with Valerie, that I want to marry her.''

At that piece of information, Nina almost went off the road, earning a sharp nudge from Byron's switchblade. Had she ever been barking up the wrong tree!

''W-wouldn't Helen—disapprove of your marrying Valerie?'' she said, when she could speak again.

''Disapprove?'' Byron gave a short bark of ugly laughter. ''You bet she would! She's almost as bad as dear old Dad was. God forbid I should dishonor the family name! As if Morty hadn't dragged it through the mud ever since I was a little kid. They think Val's a tramp, not good enough for a Meyer. Can you beat that? But I don't have to worry about Dad anymore, and I can handle Helen.''

''What about the baby?'' Nina blurted out.

Byron actually did a double take. ''How did you find out about that? Did Val tell you?''

''No, she didn't. She hasn't been looking well lately, she's been putting on weight, and yesterday I found her throwing up in the bathroom. I just put two and two together, and for once I came up with four, it seems.'' After a pause, Nina repeated her question. ''*Does* Helen know about the baby?''

''No. And she's not going to until after Val and I are married.'' The smug smile was back. Nina wasn't sure which was worse—Byron threatening, or Byron filled with psychotic pride. ''When that happens, she'll just have to lump it. She thinks Val's trash, but she's not. I know. I love her. I really do.'' There was actually a catch in his voice, and out of the corner of her eye, Nina saw him brush away a tear. She felt sick with sympathy for poor Valerie Vincent, carrying a murderer's child.

''Did Morty—does Helen know about those pictures?'' Nina asked.

''*She* doesn't. *He* did, the bastard!'' Now Byron was quivering with rage. ''She was just a poor, green kid—no money, nothing. Those parasites took advantage of her. She was up against it. She had nowhere to turn. And once Kyros got her started''— he almost choked on the words—''he wouldn't let her go.'' He gasped, battling for control. ''My dad could have bailed her out, but he wouldn't. Not big shot Mortimer Meyer, no, sir! It's all Dad's fault!''

''Is that why you killed your father?'' Nina asked quietly.

Byron broke off in the middle of a sob, his face twisted in an ugly snarl. Bringing the knife blade up and pressing it to her cheek, he hissed, ''Not another word. I don't want to talk about it. I don't want to talk about anything anymore. Just shut up and drive!''

Which she had done. And soon Byron would be returning to carry out his threat. Lying in her attic prison, Nina shuddered. Byron had probably killed Kyros with the very same knife that he'd been digging into her ribs. She stared at the small vent above her, developing a scenario in which she'd manage to crawl across to that wall, somehow dislodge the strip of screening, begin feeding bits of puffy pink insulation through the opening. Somebody would be passing by down below, see the stuff floating down, wonder what was happening, come up to investigate . . .

Right. Sure. Dream on! How are you going to get over there with your feet bound like this and your hands taped behind your back? You probably have only a few hours to live, and you're wasting them on fantasies!

But she couldn't just lie there like a trussed chicken, waiting for the chef to come and carve her up. Should she lie on her back and drum her heels on the floor? Forget it—the studio was two floors down, and even if the writers hadn't all gone home, there was virtually no chance of their hearing her.

Nina's desperation grew. There had to be *something* she could do! For the hundredth time she twisted her wrists, trying to create enough slack in the tape to get her hands free. But Byron had done his work well; there was no give whatsoever. In maddened frustration Nina wanted to scream, but even this release was denied her by the tape across her mouth.

Nina rolled and stretched, trying to get the kinks out of her legs. She ground her knees together, flexed her ankles to regain circulation in her feet. Suddenly she became aware that her pantyhose were creating a small amount of slippage beneath the tape. If she kept working her ankles, might she be able to slide at least one foot out?

Her right ankle was moving more freely now. She flexed it rapidly, grateful that her stumble two nights before had caused no real damage. If she could just walk, maybe she'd be able to escape before Byron got back. Or if not, she might be able to take him by surprise somehow. She could cover her feet with the blanket so he wouldn't know she'd gotten free.

Several minutes later, her heart pounding murderously, her entire body bathed in sweat, she kicked off her right shoe. If she could only work her foot through that cuff of tape . . . She felt her panty-hose snag repeatedly in the splintery plywood as she worked. Then, with one last effort, her foot slithered out of its shackle. But even though she could now move her right leg independently from her left, her mutilated panty hose still bound her. If she was going to be able to stand up, she had to rip that gossamer, yet amazingly strong, fabric to shreds. Damn Christian Dior! Nina wailed inwardly. Why didn't I wear a cheap pair today, the kind that fall apart if you look at them cross-eyed? If I could just get my hands on it, she raged, my teeth, anything!

A splinter in her rear suddenly reminded her of the rough-edged board she lay on. Carefully Nina positioned her ankle against the ragged edge. Twisting her leg this way and that, wincing as the slivers tore at her flesh, she laboriously sawed back and forth. She could do it! She had to! And once that happened, at least she'd have a fighting chance.

Nina glanced up at the distant vent, noting that the light was definitely getting dimmer. Time was running out.

Please, Byron, her mind screamed, take your time! Just a little longer . . .

# Chapter Seventeen

Robin Tally's voice on the phone was thin, panicky. "You mean to tell me she's not with you?" she demanded. "You haven't seen her, had word from her all day? God, Lieutenant Rossi, I've been calling her apartment since ten o'clock this morning, but all I get is her recorded message! So I just naturally assumed she'd gone directly to you with the evidence we uncovered last night."

"Evidence?" Dino Rossi barked into the receiver. "Last night? What in hell are you talking about, woman?"

Verging on hysterical tears, Robin told the detective about last night's adventure. "She told me not to tell a soul," she said, beginning to sob. "She was going to take care of wrapping up the details by herself. I assumed that meant taking those awful pictures to you, telling you everything."

For a long moment Dino Rossi remained silent, staring bleakly into space. He felt as though he'd been hit in the gut with a baseball bat. The pain left him feeling hollow, desperate. Christ, he groaned, if anything's happened to Nina—You fool! he raged, you blundering idiot! And you call yourself a cop?

Why didn't you call her? And now, at 7:45 on Friday night, you discover that she's been missing all day! I need her. I've only just found her. I love—He faltered, backed off momentarily.

Yes, you pigheaded stupe, he railed inwardly, admit it. You *do* love her. If anything's happened to Nina, you're dead in the water, and you know it. Oh, Nina, darling, why couldn't I tell you—I mean *really* tell you? Make you believe it?

Sergeant Lopez had mentioned an unidentified female caller when Dino had returned from his meeting that morning, but he'd shrugged it off. Probably Marisa Manelli, the opera star, about her stolen jewels. The call had sounded like just the kind of coy horseshit she'd pull. There were no new leads on the burglary; there'd been no point in calling back. And when nobody had appeared at his office by noon, he'd simply forgotten the whole thing, preoccupied with the details of various cases, including the Meyer/Parr murders.

"It's okay, Miss Tally," he assured the sobbing woman. "We'll find her, don't worry. You just stay by your phone in case I need to ask some additional questions. Give me your address—I may have to send someone to pick you up. . . . You say you know how to get into the Meyer place? . . . Okay, sit tight. I'll be in touch."

Immediately upon hanging up, Rossi began punching numbers furiously, gathering his squad.

"Charley, get that info on Byron Meyer's Manhattan pad. Get a radio car over there right away, see what you can find. If he's there, drag him in by his goddamned balls!"

"Nick, find out where Valerie Vincent lives. Bring her in—like ten minutes ago."

"Bruno, get on the horn to the Philadelphia PD.

Have them corral Helen Meyer. . . . Some god-damned TV convention—check it out. Tell them to lean on her hard. Tell her we need to speak to Byron Meyer immediately—new evidence has come up in the Meyer murder case.''

Finally, he reached Ben Logan, the primary investigator at Leatherwing. ''Sure I can run out there,'' Logan grumbled. ''But that's just about all I *can* do. I can't go breaking in. I've got no search warrant. Can *you* get one at this hour on a Friday night? If you can, bring it along. The Meyers are important mucky-mucks out here. We don't go ruffling feathers of birds like that.''

''Yeah, I'm on my way. I'll do a radio relay in a half hour or so, tell you what I found. . . . You'll be rolling? Okay, we'll patch in as best we can.''

But Dino Rossi wasn't on his way, not until he received preliminary reports from his subordinates. If Byron Meyer was in Philadelphia or holed up in Manhattan, there was no sense in chasing out to Leatherwing. Valerie Vincent? What account would she give of herself? His blood felt as though it had turned to ice.

And in the meantime, God alone knew where Nina was, what someone might be doing to her at this very moment. His terror deepened. For all he knew, she was already dead. Dear God, he renewed fervent prayers, don't let it happen!

Byron Meyer smiled idiotically, swaying slightly. ''Party, party,'' he said, two glasses clutched in one beefy hand, a liter of Bombay gin in the other. ''We celebrate, baby. Ring out the old, ring in the new.'' He snickered thickly, his slurred words indicating that he'd already had a few. ''Or maybe we don't

231

ring in the new after all, huh? If you know what I mean, doll.''

Byron had brought a small lamp into Nina's prison, and now he set it near the attic partition where it glowed softly, giving the hellhole hideaway a deceptively cozy glow. Nina hoped fervently that he wouldn't think to check her ankles. In the increased light, it would be impossible to conceal the fact that she'd freed them. She'd also wriggled her right foot back into her shoe, and managed to cover her lower body with the scruffy blanket once more.

But Byron didn't seem to be interested in her feet at the moment. As he ripped the tape from her mouth, leaving a raw red mark across her face, he said, ''I'll untie you later, when it's time for fun and games. We don't want you getting any funny ideas now, do we?'' He put the glasses down on the plywood, filled them halfway with chilled gin, then tipped one to Nina's lips.

''No, please!'' she protested. ''I don't want any. I haven't eaten all day. Besides, gin makes me sick.''

''Sick, my ass!'' Byron growled. ''You'll do as you're told, Nina. I want you in the right mood, understand? Broads are a lot more fun when they're sloshed.''

Again Nina felt a pang of sympathy for Valerie Vincent, Byron's ''one true love.'' Did she have the slightest idea what kind of man Byron really was? That the father of her unborn child was not only a murderer, but was looking forward with great glee to becoming a rapist as well?

Reluctantly Nina parted her lips, letting Byron feed her a small swallow of gin. It was cold, it was wet, and it burned all the way down, giving her a touch of Dutch courage. Nina was glad to see Byron take a hefty swig from his own glass. The drunker he got, the better her chance of getting out of this mess alive. She would have to pick her moment very judiciously; there would be no retakes on this scene. Just thinking about what she must do when the time came tied her stomach into knots.

"What did you do with my car?" she asked, knowing that she had to keep Byron talking as long as possible. If by some incredible chance help was on the way, she needed to stall for time. If not, it would at least delay the next scene in Byron's little script.

"What I told you I was going to do," Byron replied. "I drove it to the edge of the quarry, then jumped out at the last minute. Made quite a splash. Pity. It was a cute little car. Not many miles on it, either."

There aren't many miles on me, either, Nina thought miserably. Voicing her thoughts, she said, "And you're planning something similar for me, right?"

"More or less," he said with a groggy leer. "But not right away. As I said before, a midnight swim. Only you won't be coming back."

"Right here, near Leatherwing? What if my body washes up on the rocks? Won't the police be suspicious?"

"You still think I'm stupid, don't you?" Byron scowled. "No, I'm going to dump you closer to the city. The cops will never make the connection."

"You seem to have thought of everything." Nina made a face as Byron forced more gin between her lips.

"Better believe it!" Pleased with himself, Byron sat down next to Nina.

Uh-oh! Talk! Keep him talking!

"It was you in that car behind the shopping center the other night, wasn't it?'' she babbled. ''You were the one who was chasing me. That bandage on your hand—that's where I hit you with my shoe.''

''Right again. And I'd have taken care of you, too, if that guy hadn't come out when he did. Kyros should have run you both down, but he screwed up, as usual.''

''And at the studio? Which one of you dropped that piece of steel?''

Byron grinned. ''That was me. I know the studio like the palm of my hand. All I had to do was sneak in when everybody was busy elsewhere and climb up to the catwalk. The second that steel started down, so did I. I never even saw it land.'' He sighed ruefully. ''How it missed you, I'll never know. Kyros was really pissed.''

''What *about* Kyros?'' Nina asked. ''If he was blackmailing Valerie and you hated him so much, how come you two were in cahoots?''

''Money, what else? He wanted big bucks, and there was no way in hell I was going to get my share of dear old Dad's estate if someone—guess who, Nina—was out there making waves, trying to pin Morty's murder on me. Oh, Kyros was helping with both hands toward the end there, but then he got greedy. And when he upped the ante of those negatives, I had to kill him.''

Byron leaned back on his elbows, gazing reflectively at the beams overhead. The gin had loosened his tongue, and he needed no urging to tell the rest of his story. ''Yes, Kyros thought he had it made in the beginning. When he found out I was seeing Valerie on the sly, he went to old Morty. He figured Dad would pay through his nose to prevent him from letting the cat out of the bag about the one and only Meyer heir being involved with a former porn starlet. And he was right—the first time. Dad paid and got the photos. But Kyros still had the negatives. When he came back, he wanted a quarter of a mill. Dad laughed in his face and kicked him out.''

Byron didn't find out about that until the day he got up his courage to tell Morty that he was going to marry Valerie. No son of Mortimer Meyer was going to marry some guttersnipe porn queen. No way! Morty showed Byron the photos, exulting in his shocked reaction. But if he expected Byron to slink away with his tail between his legs and obediently give Valerie up, Morty was very much mistaken. Instead, Byron decided to pay Kyros himself for the negatives. Since he couldn't lay his hands on such a large sum, Byron started gambling.

''Pretty soon I was in hock up to my eyeballs,'' he said. ''I thought I was some kind of blackjack hotshot—went to Atlantic City every other weekend. I got them to raise the limits on a private table one night. I even brought Val along, for luck.'' He laughed bitterly. ''Some luck! I lost my shirt. They were holding my markers for over three hundred grand. Hell, I couldn't even pay the *interest* on that! But they could afford to wait. They thought Morty'd cover it sooner or later, and I didn't exactly disillusion them.'' He turned to Nina now, and she saw tears in his eyes. ''You can laugh if you like, but I *do* love Valerie. I don't care about her past. I just want to marry her. I want to see our little baby get born, grow up . . . I want for us to be happy, just like other people, you know what I mean?''

''I guess so, Byron,'' she said weakly.

''So everything was going wrong at the same time. I was determined to marry Valerie, no matter what, but I had to buy those negs, or what kind of a life could we have? Only I didn't have the money, and those sharks in Atlantic City weren't going to cool their heels much longer. And then Morty told me flat out, either I ditched Valerie, or he was going to write me out of his will. That was last Thursday. He gave me the weekend to kiss her off. He was going to see his lawyer on Monday morning.''

''That's when you decided to kill him at the party?'' Nina asked.

''No, I had it planned for Sunday. We were scheduled to go out on the ocean in the cruiser that afternoon. He was going to have a little accident, go over the side while Helen was taking one of her damn naps.''

Nina was fascinated in spite of herself, almost forgetting her own jeopardy. ''What changed your mind?'' she asked.

''That goddamned Parr busybody! She knew about Valerie, of course, and about the pictures, and that Morty was planning on changing his will. She got on my case, told me she'd go straight to the police if anything happened to him.'' Byron shook his head wonderingly. ''She was like a sorceress—she could read my mind like a book.'' Then he shrugged. ''She had to go, too, and fast. So I decided to do it at the party. There'd be lots of people around, plenty of confusion to keep the cops occupied.''

That was when Byron and Alexis Kyros became accomplices. In desperation, Byron went to Kyros, promising him the money for the negatives the minute Morty died and Byron came into what was sure to be a vast inheritance. But the deed had to be done quickly, or they'd both be up the creek. Recognizing a goose that might very possibly be an endless source of golden eggs, Kyros agreed. It was he who provided the poison, he who ransacked Gladys

Parr's cottage for the set of photos Morty had given her for safekeeping, he who spirited her away while the party was in full swing and dropped her over the cliff.

"The poison. . ." Nina mused aloud. "I still can't figure out how you got it into Morty's glass without him being aware of it."

Byron positively beamed. "That was my bright idea. I knew all Dad's idiosyncracies, like the fact that he always had to have ice in his drink, even when it was vintage brandy."

Realization dawned in Nina's mind like a light-ning bolt, illuminating the memory of that moment after the gala dinner when she'd noticed with dis-taste the ice in Morty's brandy snifter. "The ice cubes! The poison was in the ice cubes!" she gasped.

Nodding and smiling eagerly, Byron said, "Dad was also an ice *cruncher*. Drove Helen and me crazy. He chewed up ice cubes like they were candy. So all I had to do was freeze a special one before the party. Five hundred milligrams of cyanide—rapidly soluble in water, doesn't have the characteristic almond smell or bitter taste. When they started passing out the after-dinner drinks, he shoved his glass at me like I was one of the servants, and I just dropped in a couple of regular cubes, and one Meyer Special." He actually laughed. "The old fart never knew what hit him!"

Byron's gleeful pride in the cleverness with which he'd murdered his father made Nina feel sick.

"With Kyros dead, nobody will ever be able to pin Morty's death on me. Hell, it could have been anyone at the party. Dear old Dad had enemies he hadn't even met yet," Byron continued cheerfully. "And when you're out of the picture, I've got it made. I'm home free. And I do mean *free*!"

All Nina's terror returned in a rush. "Please, Byron," she begged, "don't start that again! You don't want to kill a third time. You'll never get away with it. Listen to me, Byron! I told you nobody but me knows about those pictures of Valerie, but I lied. I called Lieutenant Rossi this morning before I left and told him about coming out here last night, and finding the photos. And I told him what I suspected about you and Kyros. He knew I was on my way to police headquarters. When I didn't show up, he must have put out an all-points bulletin. The cops probably have this house surrounded by now. You'll never get out of here alive!"

Nina was babbling, and she knew it. How she wished there was one word of truth in what she'd just said! Was it possible that *he* believed it?

For a moment Byron looked uncertain, and her hopes rose. Then he smirked and shook his head. "Nina, Nina, Nina." He sighed. "You don't really expect me to swallow that old chestnut, do you? Let's see—what episode of TTS was it when Robin was kidnapped by that hood who was holding her for ransom? She pulled the same thing, and *he* fell for it. But, honey, that was soap time. This is *real* time. Fun time!"

Dear God, he was right! Now Nina remembered the episode, and that at the time they were taping it, she'd thought it was a pretty unlikely ploy. Nina closed her eyes, fighting back tears of rage, frustration, and fear. When she opened them, Byron was holding her refilled glass to her lips.

"Come on, Nina—gotta make up for lost time. Too much talking, too' little drinking. Chugalug, sweetheart."

"No, Byron," Nina whispered, twisting her head away. "Please—no more."

238

"Just one little drink. C'mon, be a good girl," he mumbled into her ear. "Drink up—warm up—loosen up!"

Nina choked as some of the gin went down the wrong way. She tried to evade his mouth, but she wasn't quick enough. Before she could duck again, his lips were clamped to hers, his arms trapping her. Her stomach lurched as she felt his tongue invade her mouth.

"Byron, don't," she gasped, pulling away. "Not yet, not like this. Please, give me a little time."

"I want you to feel good," he persisted, a growing frenzy registering in his voice. "Believe me, you're going to enjoy it. Your last time, baby. And with a goddamned expert!" He finished the gin in the glass and tossed it aside.

"Oh, Byron, how can you?" Nina cried desperately. "After all the things you just told me about Valerie, about how much you love her, how you want to marry her, bring up your kids. . ."

He hesitated momentarily, but then the crafty smirk came back. "Nice try, Nina," he said. "But what I do with you has nothing to do with Valerie. She'll never know. I've wanted to jump on your bones since the very first day I set eyes on you. What's the big deal? You're gonna die anyway. And if the man wants to be nice, see to it that you go out with a big smile on your face, is that so bad?"

Again his mouth swooped down. She felt his lips on hers, the stink of the gin on his breath making her queasy. Let him, one part of her brain advised. Make him think he's got you going. He'll let down his guard and you'll have a clearer shot at him. But revulsion was stronger than common sense, and she twisted away. He pushed her down onto her back. Her hands, still bound behind her, dug into her spine, sending waves of pain through her torso. Now he was lying on top of her, making it difficult for her breathe.

"You want it, baby," he mumbled. "Old Byron can tell. Let it happen, Nina. Enjoy yourself." Now his fingers slithered over her body, mauling her breasts.

"All right," she said in a flat, cold voice. "If you insist, let's do it right. Unfasten my hands and let me get my clothes off. Neither of us is going to enjoy it this way."

Byron's grin became victorious. "That's my girl," he exulted. "I knew you'd see it my way. But let me undress first, so you can see what you're getting!"

With that he lifted his weight off her body and started to lift his pullover shirt over his head.

It's now or never, Nina decided grimly. Momentarily blinded, arms temporarily immobilized, he'd never be more vulnerable.

In one lightning motion, Nina kicked the blanket off and swung up her legs, bent at the knees. Her feet tightly together, she aimed them precisely at Byron's prominent midsection and thrust forward with all her might. Her feet hit him squarely in the belly, the heels of her shoes stabbing into the soft flesh.

Byron bellowed with rage, astonishment, and pain. Fighting the constricting tangle of his shirt, he fell backward, as Nina's feet continued to hammer at him, one heel striking his right shoulder, the other gouging his face through the fabric of the tee shirt, barely missing his eye.

He screamed again, clutching at his face with one hand while he struggled to pull the shirt down with the other.

Nina sprang up, teetering for balance in the tangle of blanket at her feet. She lurched awkwardly toward the plank barrier and bumped it with her bent knees. It fell outward, sending up a cloud of choking dust. Behind her, she heard Byron scrambling to his feet, starting after her, roaring like a wounded bull.

"Now you're gonna get it!" he shouted. "No more Mister Nice Guy! You're dead, Nina, and I mean *dead*!"

In the murky darkness of the outer attic, Nina strained to find her way, relying on instinct and vague impressions of its layout. Stumbling, gasping, she reached the stairway at the end. There was a door at the bottom, she remembered, leading into the large sitting room of the master suite. If Byron had locked that door . . .

She reached the stairs, started clumsily down. Close behind her, she heard the heavy clump of Byron's boots. He'd paused for a moment to recover his flashlight, and now it shot erratic beams on the walls and ceiling as he approached.

She was at the bottom of the steps. The door was ajar, and Nina flung it open with her shoulder as Byron thundered down the stairs. Once in the sitting room, she hurtled through the darkness, her terrified eyes trying to pierce the gloom. Byron was closer now, his curses ringing in her ears, the flashlight's beam briefly illuminating the room—and incidentally showing her the location of the door to the hall. Nina raced through the doorway, heading for the stairway to the first floor.

And then, barely a foot away from the head of the stairs, she tripped.

As she fell, unable to catch herself with her bound hands, her body landed on the carpeted floor of the hall. Nina knew this was the end. Melanie Prescott was about to be written out of the script permanently. Byron was right behind her, flashlight in one hand, switchblade in the other. But in his headlong rush, he couldn't stop. He stumbled over Nina's outstretched legs, and she heard a thin, terrified scream as he fell down the stairs. The flashlight sailed through the air in a long arc, landing on the tile floor far below, and shattered. Seconds later, Byron followed. He was still clutching the knife when his body struck the floor with a dull, sickening thud.

Nina lay at the top of the stairs, too limp to move. Was it over? Was it really over? When there was no further sound from below, she began inching her bruised, aching body down the stairs step by step. At the bottom, she huddled there, her head resting on her knees, unable to think, unable even to exult in her miraculous escape.

Suddenly the huge chandelier above her burst into blinding light. Nina raised her head, unable to believe her eyes. She saw Dino Rossi and Ben Logan, flanked by two policemen, running through a door at the far end of the hall. Robin Tally, her face paper-white, was right behind them. One of the cops fell to his knees beside Byron's inert form and turned the crumpled body over.

I'm dreaming, she thought. This isn't really happening. Or I'm dead, and this is an out-of-body experience. And then, idiotically, I must look a fright! My hair's a mess. And my clothes . . .

Dino knelt beside her, his eyes filled with unmistakable joy and relief. Laughing hysterically, Nina fell into his arms. It seemed to Nina that he was crying—but macho detective lieutenants never cry, so she must be dreaming after all.

"I don't suppose," she croaked weakly, "anybody here has a spare pair of pantyhose?"

# Chapter Eighteen

An ambulance was summoned by Ben Logan, the detective under whose jurisdiction the Leatherwing murders would ordinarily have fallen, and a comatose Byron Meyer was rushed to the nearest hospital, where it was learned that he'd suffered contusions, a concussion, a broken arm and leg, and broken ribs, not to mention several strange puncture wounds to his abdomen and shoulder, and a disfiguring gouge in his face.

The good news was that he would recover to stand trial, and eventually to become a star guest in one of New York State's finest penal institutions. His stay would undoubtedly be most lengthy. It was considered unlikely that he would be released until some time in the year 2096, if he lived that long.

When Nina had recovered sufficiently to show Dino and his men the attic hideaway where Byron had imprisoned her, and when Rossi's squad had dug out the rest of the incriminating photographs from Byron's room, the convoy of police vehicles broke up, wending their separate ways to their respective headquarters. Nina herself was bundled into a car between Dino and Robin for the journey back to Manhattan, and after they had dropped Robin at her apartment where Rafe was anxiously awaiting her, Dino and Nina proceeded to police headquarters. There, Nina's superficial injuries were tended to by several overawed medical technicians to whom she graciously gave her autograph. After several cups of atrocious coffee, she spent the next hour and a half tape recording her formal statement, witnessed by Dino and Charley Harper. As the account went on and on and Nina's highly unorthodox exploits came to light, both men exchanged stunned glances and shook their heads wonderingly. If ever a woman had been born under a lucky star . . .

When finally the complicated yarn had run its course and Dino was preparing to drive Nina home, he said, "That poison gimmick was pretty damned clever, Nina. Meyer was right—nobody could ever have pinned it on him. If he hadn't blabbed to you . . ." His eyes became molten. "And if you hadn't managed to wriggle your way out of that attic . . ." Deep respect showed on his face. "We . . . I owe you one. You are some piece of work, darling! A one-man . . . one-woman . . . detective force."

Nina smiled modestly, and for once was at a loss for words. His accolade and its implied message of acceptance meant more to her than she could ever begin to express.

The next evening, Dino stopped for Nina shortly after 8:00 P.M., and they went to dinner at Ernie's Steakhouse, a favorite hangout for cops working the downtown precincts. His choice of restaurants, though not commented on by either of them, had been symbolic of Dino's acceptance of Nina as a bona fide partner, not just an amateur meddler. Nina thought that overdone steak had never tasted so good.

Later, back in Nina's apartment, they began to wind down over some very mellow Sambuca. The lights were turned low, and a compact disc was playing Gershwin. Seated next to Dino on the sofa, Nina found it very reassuring to snuggle in the safety of his strong arms. They kissed often—gentle pecks, nothing too passionate, since Dino was very much aware of the tenderness of Nina's mouth and lower face due to the duct tape gag. Nina had never felt so content, so peaceful, so cherished.

But instead of whispering endearments, both were still so wrapped up in the Leatherwing murders that they could speak of nothing else.

"I had a call from Helen Meyer today, Nina," Dino said. "She's hiring the best lawyers in New York to defend Byron—or rather, to defend the Meyer name. She's also managed to pull enough strings and grease enough palms to keep the whole thing out of the papers."

"Thank goodness." Nina sighed. "I wasn't exactly looking forward to seeing myself splashed all over the front page of the *Star* or the *Enquirer* the next time I go to the supermarket!" She grimaced. "Although I'm sure she'd be delighted to tell the world that it's all my fault."

"You're not exactly Helen Meyer's favorite person just now," Dino agreed.

Nina shrugged. "I never was. But I can't help feeling sorry for her, in spite of all Morty's millions. She's a lonely, bitter woman."

"I wouldn't waste my sympathy," Dino said dryly. "That lady is one tough cookie, and it'll take more than a couple of murders and a jailbird stepson to make her crumble."

"I suppose you're right." Nina sipped her liqueur, moving closer to him. "Am I allowed to feel sorry for Valerie Vincent? She's the big loser, it seems to me. What's going to happen to her? What *has* happened to her?"

"Your guess is as good as mine," Dino said. "She seems to have flown the coop. We're trying to track her down, as an accessory after the fact, but somehow I doubt we'll find her."

"Maybe she'll be able to make a new life somewhere for herself and her baby," Nina mused aloud. "She's not a bad kid—she just got in with the wrong crowd."

Now Dino sat up. "I have a great idea. Let's change the subject, okay?" He reached for his suit jacket, which he'd tossed over the arm of a chair, and after fumbling in the pocket, took out a small package wrapped in silver paper. "Here—a little token of my esteem."

"What in the world? . . ." Nina took the package from his outstretched hand and began untying the ribbon. "I guess I'm supposed to say, 'You shouldn't have.' And you shouldn't, Dino, really."

"Yes, I should." He watched intently as she opened the box, glancing almost shyly at her face to see her reaction.

"Oh, Dino!" Nina whispered, her eyes widening. Inside the box she found a gold pendant suspended from a fine gold chain, and a pair of earrings. The pendant and earrings were miniature replicas of Dino's detective badge. She put on the necklace immediately. "They're beautiful, Dino! I love them! Where on earth did you find them?"

Dino actually blushed. "Well, there's a jeweler I know who keeps them on hand. Whenever a cop wants to give his wife—his lady—something really special, Manny delivers the goods."

Nina's voice caught in her throat. "And am I your lady, Dino?"

"Would you consider it? Being my lady?"

She looked at him archly. "I'll have to think about that." And after a pause of about three seconds, "Okay, I've thought about it. I would."

"You fruitcake!" He hugged her so hard she thought her ribs might crack, then gently released her. "That's not the only reason I bought these for you. I also wanted to reward you for being such a good cop. After the job you did on this case, I figured you needed a badge of your own."

"I like your original reason better," she said, nibbling at his ear.

"Nina . . ." he said hesitantly, "what about next time?"

"Next time? What do you mean?"

"The next time I have a show-biz case, something that maybe you could help me with . . . I know it's asking a lot after what you've just been through, but would you—could you—be available?"

Nina's eyes lit up. "You mean it? We're still partners?"

"Something like that." He grinned at her. "You know, as a lady snoop, you're not half-bad."

"*Half-bad*?" she repeated with mock annoyance. "If it wasn't for me, this case might have gone on for years!" Then she sighed, subsiding back into his embrace. "In answer to your question, yes, I definitely could be available. Any time, any time at all—just so long as it doesn't conflict with my TTS schedule."

Dino's arms tightened around her. "There's just one thing you're going to have to understand if we're going to keep on working together, darling, and that's this: Under no circumstances, *none*, are you to go off half-cocked the way you kept doing this time. *No* hiding information from me. *No* playing decoy. *No* taking unnecessary risks. *No* trying to be a one-man band. Damn it, Nina, I love you! I couldn't stand it if anything happened to you.''

Nina had stiffened at Dino's list of ''no's,'' but now she drew him closer to her. Her lips brushing his, she whispered, ''I love you, too. And I promise to be very, very careful . . . *partner*.''

There was nothing tentative about the kiss that followed, and Nina's lips didn't hurt a bit.

''Dino,'' she whispered, running her fingers through his dark, curly hair, ''now that we've got all that settled, I think it's time we got down to the really *important* business of the evening.'' She looked deeply into his eyes and saw desire that mirrored her own.

''You angel!'' Dino murmured into her hair. ''You adorable little angel!''

As he lifted her effortlessly in his arms and began carrying her to the bedroom, Nina purred into his ear, ''I'm no angel, darling. Far from it!''

As it turned out, he wasn't much of an angel either.

*In Book Two of Eileen Fulton's Take One for Murder . . .*

Nina McFall is delighted to learn that her friend, middle-aged actress May Minton, has been cast in a cameo role in a special segment of *The Turning Seasons.* She'll be featured with two other vintage actresses, but May's is the juiciest part, one she hopes will revitalize her flagging career. But when Nina arrives at May's posh apartment to celebrate the good news, she finds her friend murdered.

Dino Rossi is called in to investigate, and enlists Nina's aid in discovering the murderer. Though all clues seem to point to a member of *The Turning Seasons'* regular cast whose professional jealousy of May is well known, Nina as usual distrusts the obvious and does some sleuthing on her own. And when she picks up a really hot lead, she finds herself in deadly danger from a killer who won't hesitate to strike again.